THE BURNING MEN

An absolutely gripping killer thriller with a huge twist

STEVE PARKER

JOFFE
BOOKS

Published 2018 by Joffe Books, London.

www.joffebooks.com

© Steve Parker

ISBN-13: 978-1-78931-060-3

For John White.

CHAPTER ONE

Detective Inspector Johnny Clocks pressed his handkerchief to his mouth and nose to try and block out the smell, which was strongly reminiscent of burnt pork. He licked his lips. He could even taste it.

'My old Aunt Barbara used to cook everything like that,' he said, his voice muffled. 'Said it gave it more of a taste, but I always reckoned she was full of it. Me cousin Gary said she was just shit at cooking. He loved coming round our house for Sunday dinner. I mean, how the fuck can you eat food that's as black as Newgate's knocker day after day? Fat as a barrel now, he is. Found a woman who can cook properly so he's making up for lost time.' Beneath his feet, the little metal platform started to sink slightly into the mud. 'Sod this, Ray. Bloody thing's sinking. Now me shoes'll get covered in crap.'

Detective Superintendent Ray Paterson tore his eyes away from what they'd been looking at and glanced sideways at his colleague, who was gingerly lifting his feet one at a time while casting anxious glances downward. 'I doubt it, John. You're wearing slipovers and it's not like we're standing in a quagmire, is it?'

Having no idea what a quagmire was, Clocks shrugged.

In front of them, two CSIs, covered from head to toe in paper suits, were just finishing up. A few more minutes and they'd be done, and then they could all get out of the tent. Paterson glanced at his watch. Nine thirty in the morning. Another great start to the working day.

Clocks shifted his feet on the plate, steadying himself. 'Where's the crime scene manager, mate?'

One of the white-suited men briefly stopped what he was doing. 'No idea, sir. Must be milling about somewhere outside.'

'Yeah, I figured that when I couldn't find him in this little ten-by-ten tent. But thanks for stating the obvious, mate. Very helpful.'

The CSI, fresh-faced and young, probably about twenty-five, looked mortified. It was difficult to tell behind the mask, but it was pretty safe to assume he'd gone a deep shade of red. 'Sir, I'm sorry. I . . . I didn't mean . . .'

Clocks grinned at the man's discomfort. 'Only joking, mate.'

'Take no notice of my DI, fella,' Paterson interjected. 'He always wanted to be a comedian but no one ever seemed to laugh. Came as a bit of a shock to him. In fact, he's never gotten over it.'

Paterson turned his attention back to the reason they were all there. The blackened corpse, the still-smouldering source of the smell, was handcuffed to a post. Judging by the look of agony on his blackened face, he'd still been alive when somebody had set fire to him. 'What can you tell me so far?' he said to the CSI.

'Only that this was deliberate . . .' He shot a look at Clocks. *What a dumb thing to say*. Clocks rolled his eyes to the tent roof. The CSI turned to Paterson, but he was doing the same.

'What I meant was . . .'

'We know what you meant, son. But, to be fair, a bloke cuffed to a pole is hardly likely to have set himself on fire, is he? How'd he get hold of the matches for a starter?'

The CSI shook his head. 'Fair point.'

'Are you new?' Clocks asked.

The CSI nodded. 'To fieldwork, sir, yes. Not been here too long. One of my first live ones, so to speak.' His colleague, on his knees and packing up his bag, kept his head down. The young 'un had to learn.

'Back up a bit then, son, take a breath and think. Tell me what you see. Tell me what you believe at this point.'

Grateful that he wasn't about to get a mauling, the CSI took a few seconds to get it together. 'From what I can see — and this is only speculation at this point, sir — is that he was doused in some form of accelerant, most likely petrol, but we won't know for definite until tests have been done. We think he was about thirty-odd years old, Caucasian and judging from the look on his face, or what's left of it, he was alive when the perpetrator set him alight.' He closed the lid of his case. 'And he was in agony.'

'How long would it have taken him to die?' Paterson said.

'Difficult to say for sure, sir, but I would guess no more than a few minutes. Usually, when people are tied to a stake and burned to death, the fire starts from the feet.'

'Have you seen this sort of thing before, then?' Paterson asked.

'No, sir. Never. But we covered it in class. Think of what they used to do with witches. The flames would then work their way up the body but along with that there would be smoke. The smoke would have done them in, but they would have still been in agony until they passed out. With this guy, whoever did this, they went from the top.' He pointed to the legs. 'See? Less burning there. Black up top. I'd say he died of shock from the pain and fear of what was happening.'

'Jesus H. That's harsh,' Clocks said.

'Any thoughts, John?' Paterson asked.

'Yeah. Bloody glad it ain't me.' He smiled at Paterson. It wasn't reciprocated. 'Dunno. Barbecue gone wrong? One of the guests got the 'ump 'cause his sausage got a bit burnt?'

Paterson sighed. Less than a minute on scene, and Clocks had started with the black humour.

'Where are we today? November the first? Second? Maybe someone was practising for Guy Fawkes night.'

A couple of years ago, this attempt at humour would have bothered Paterson and he'd have voiced his disapproval, but Johnny Clocks, the eternal child, had gradually worn him down. By now, he'd grown used to the quips. He'd even taken to seeing the funny side of death himself. Paterson moved a couple of steps closer to the corpse.

'Might even be me old Auntie Barbara's handiwork. Haven't seen her for a few years now,' Clocks said.

'As ever, thank you for your valuable insight, Mr Clocks.'

'No worries, guv, 's what I'm here for.' He gave Paterson a grin.

Paterson frowned. 'Why would you do this and leave the body in full view? This sort of thing is usually done in the woods, in underground garages or secluded garden properties, surely to God. Not smack-bang in the middle of a park in Bermondsey. Serious answer, John.'

Johnny Clocks pulled himself up straight and looked at the body again. 'Seriously? This is a statement, Ray. Obviously. Someone's sending a big fuck-off message to someone else. We need to find out who's saying what to who a bit quick.'

'To whom,' Paterson corrected. Clocks gave him a look.

Paterson turned to the CSI again. 'Any ID?' he said.

'None that's readable, sir,' he said. 'But take a look at this.' They all stepped in closer, and the smell of burnt meat and petrol grew overpowering. Paterson and Clocks grimaced. The CSI gently lifted the man's top lip and showed them a row of cosmetically enhanced gold teeth, one of which was inlaid with a small, slightly blackened diamond.

Paterson looked perplexed. 'Do you know anyone with teeth like that, John?'

'I know people with gold fillings but not a whole top set of 'em. Not like that.'

'No one springs to mind?'

'Well, there was a rapper a few years ago, name of Goldie. He had a set of gold gnashers — hence the name. He wasn't as black as Mister Crispy here, but it might be him, you never know.'

Paterson gave a deep sigh. Nodding to the CSIs, who were leaving, he said, 'I doubt it, John. Really I do.'

Alone in the tent and free to speak, Paterson said, 'This isn't good, is it?'

Clocks looked him dead in the eye. 'No. It's not. As you said, most people burn bodies to stop them being identified, at least in the short term. If whoever did this didn't want him recognised, they'd have smashed his teeth out with a lump hammer or something. They knew they were making it easy for us. They want him identified, and they want it done quick. Whoever did it is throwing down a challenge, not only to the person the message is intended for, but to us, the police, as well. They're saying that they're not scared of Old Bill, that they don't give a shit. "Look at me! I'm Billy Big Bollocks. See what I can do? I don't give a crap about anyone!"' He scratched his head. 'I've got a bad feeling in me water, Ray.'

Paterson rubbed the back of his neck. 'Off the top of your head, John, who do we know that's really not scared of the police?' He opened the tent flap and beckoned to Clocks. They were finished for now.

Clocks nipped through the opening, took in a deep lungful of London air and said, 'Honestly? These days, I'd say we're looking at everybody in Britain under the age of seventy-five. Nobody gives a monkey's anymore.'

'You have a point as usual, but we'll have to try and narrow it down a bit better than fifty-odd million people.' Paterson shook his head at his colleague.

* * *

A couple of hours later, having assembled the team of detectives, briefed them according to what they knew so far and sent them out onto the streets, Paterson and Clocks made their way along a dimly lit corridor that smelled of formaldehyde and death. It led to the workplace of Jock Hudson, the senior forensic pathologist for Southwark. Buried deep inside one of the older buildings within the complex of Guy's Hospital, the morgue was a weird mix of eighteenth-century architecture and twenty-first-century technology. They entered the room through large, heavy, wooden doors with well-worn brass handles and inlaid with small squares of a greenish frosted glass. The walls and ceiling had long ago been painted an insipid mix of beige and green, which the passage of time had dulled even further. The decor contrasted starkly with the sleek, shiny metal of the cutting tables where the dead were laid out for inspection.

Unusually for Hudson, he hadn't attended the scene, as would be expected for a crime of this gravity, but had decided instead to leave it to his team to deal with. Paterson had heard rumours that Hudson's drinking was fast approaching epic proportions and wondered if perhaps he was slipping professionally. He hoped not. Although they were never going to be best buds, he had a genuine respect for the man.

As the two detectives walked into the room, Hudson was engrossed in his work, hunched over the charred corpse and carefully peeling back what could have been either skin or clothing. It was difficult to tell from where they stood.

'Alright, Scotty? Good to see ya.' Clocks's voice was a bit too bright and breezy for the setting, but it didn't faze Hudson. He was probably glad of the lift.

He put down his scalpel and turned to look at the two men, who were busy donning green wraparound gowns 'Timex!' he said, using one of Johnny Clocks's more repeatable nicknames. 'I thought I recognised your voice, you cockney bastard.'

'What's that, Scotty? I can't understand you. Speak English, man.'

Clocks pulled out two Vicks nasal sticks and shoved them up his nostrils. Paterson gave him an odd look. So did Hudson. They glanced at each other and shook their heads.

'Mr Paterson, can you no' have a word wi' your gobshite of a bag carrier here and tell him to stop calling me "Scotty."' He went back to his corpse. 'It's fucking racist.'

'John,' said Paterson, stifling a laugh as Clocks bowled over to the table, green wraparound undone and vapour sticks dangling from his nose, 'don't call Jock "Scotty." He said it's racist, I think. I couldn't really understand him.'

'You two are like the poor man's Morecambe and Wise,' Hudson said, now hunched back over his work. He peeled off another bit of what they now saw was definitely skin. It made a slight crackling sound. 'And they weren't funny at all.'

Clocks, sounding as if he had a bad cold thanks to the Vicks sticks, said, 'What? Eric and Ern? Not funny? Comedy gold, mate, and a sight funnier than anything your lot have ever pushed out. Apart from Billy Connolly, that is. He's a hoot an' a half. Oh, and that Nicola Sturgeon. She amuses the life out of me.'

The two policemen joined Hudson at the table. Struggling with the smell, Paterson was forced to pull out his handkerchief. He pressed it firmly over his nose and mouth and breathed in the scent of cotton. It wouldn't last but, for now, it took the edge off the stink.

'I like you two,' Hudson said. 'You always bring me interesting stuff to work on.'

'Glad you appreciate us,' said Paterson. 'We're all about the interesting, Jock, you know that. So, what have we got?'

'Male, white and about twenty-five, maybe thirty at a push, but no more than that. He appears to have been of average weight and height, nothing overtly abnormal about his skeletal physique. No gammy legs, club feet, that sort of stuff.'

'What killed him, Jock?'

Hudson stopped what he was doing for just long enough to give a Paterson a look that said, *are you serious?*

'You know what I mean. Does he have any other obvious injuries to his body, other than the fact that he's been burnt to a crisp — stab wounds? Head wounds?'

'None that I can see, sir. But I still haven't managed to get off all of his clothing. Some of it's fused with his skin, see?' He pulled up a piece of the dead man's coat and they both watched a bit of his chest come up with it. Clocks pulled a face. 'But, if I'm honest, I don't think we'll get a full, clean separation. If he does have an injury, I suspect it'll be to the face or head, something that would have incapacitated him, but at the moment, I can't be definite. And the smell? Apart from pork, I'm getting a faint aroma of . . .' he waved his hand around like a French *parfumier*, 'nothing too fancy. Common or garden petrol, I'd say.'

'How can you be sure?' Clocks asked.

Hudson sighed. 'Well, John. What first gave it away is simple. It's what I put in my car. I know what it smells like.'

Clocks grinned. *Fair play.* He'd have said the same. Hudson went back to his examination.

'I know it's a dumb question, Jock, but I've got to ask it. Was he alive when this was done?' Paterson said.

'No such thing as a silly question, sir,' Hudson nodded toward Clocks, 'except when he asks it. Then you know it will be dumb.' Clocks gave him the finger. 'Yes, sir, he was most definitely alive. I've not done a full autopsy as yet, as you can see. I'm just trying to remove him from his clothing as carefully as possible, to preserve evidence. But the look on his face,' he jutted his chin, 'his mouth wide open in a scream, and the fact that his fingers are so clawed up would indicate that, yes, he was most definitely alive and in intense pain for a while.'

'How long for him to die? Your man on scene said a few minutes, maybe.'

Hudson looked at the corpse again, and Paterson seemed to see compassion in his eyes. He shook it off immediately. No room for sentiment in his game. 'Possibly. I'd need to look at his lungs to be certain, but given what I can see here, I'd say no more than two minutes.' He pointed to the head. 'Head and shoulders are the most badly burnt bits of him. Once he'd been set on fire, he would have screamed in agony. His mouth would have been wide open, he'd have sucked in heat and flames, burned his lungs and hopefully, the shock would have killed him. I say hopefully because I can't tell you how painful this would have been for him. A horrible way to die, Mr Paterson. Horrible. Whoever did this to the fella is a nasty bastard.'

'Is that your professional opinion, Scotty?' Clocks said.

'It's my professional fact, Clocks.'

'Okay, then,' said Clocks. 'We'll get double busy looking for a nasty bastard. Plenty to choose from.'

'Anything else?' Paterson asked, ignoring Clocks. He'd given up on the handkerchief and was now busy writing notes in his little book.

'From what I can see, he still has some fingerprints but one or two of them have burned away. Most of the flesh above the shoulders and head is about ready to fall off, so at this stage it's impossible to say if he had any facial deformities, marks or scars or tattoos. I'll do more extensive tests of course and let you know if and when I find anything, but I'm going to need some specialist equipment to check for that which, I'm afraid, will take time.'

'What about the teeth, Jock? Can you get an impression of them?' Paterson asked.

'Of course I can,' he said, sounding a little indignant. 'I take it you'll want them expedited over to the Bureau?' Paterson thought about it for a second. Standard procedure involved first checking the daily missing persons' reports and, if the body was unidentified after forty-eight hours, the case details would be reported to the Missing Persons Bureau, who held the central index for missing persons and unidentified bodies. They would require the deceased's dental charts for comparison purposes, but Paterson wasn't going to hang around on the off-chance the victim was a reported missing person.

'Yep,' said Paterson. He stopped writing. 'We've got nothing else to go on at this time, so we need to get it up to them quick. To be honest, I doubt that we're looking at a misper in the usual sense of the word. Just doesn't feel like it. Once you send them over to me, I'll get the boys and girls out to the local dentists, see if we can find out who this is.'

'Aye,' said Jock. 'The sooner the better I would say. It's about time you lot got yourself a central database together for teeth. Got one for everything else.'

'You're right,' said Clocks. He did actually agree with Jock, which was a first. 'I'll bring that up at the next bigwig meeting. Give me something to get me teeth into,' he said, big grin at the ready. 'We'll see ourselves out.'

CHAPTER TWO

The murder room was in full swing — everywhere detectives were busy typing, making calls and drinking coffee. Up on the board were the customary pictures of the deceased, but against the central head and shoulders shot was a big question mark in green ink. Same for the close-up of the teeth. Paterson, surprised that no one in the team had any idea who the victim was, chatted to a few uniform constables — locals — in the hope that they might have come across the victim before, on their travels around the streets and estates.

'No, sir. Sorry,' said a young WPC. 'You might want to speak to Pete Best, though, he's the neighbourhood guy. He's been on the manor for donkey's years. If this guy is local, or even a visitor, Pete will likely know him.'

A male uniform nodded. 'Yeah, sir. Nothing gets past Pete.'

'Is he on today?' Paterson asked.

'Should be. I'll give him a call, tell him to bell you. You in your office for the next half hour, sir?' Paterson said he was, and thanked them both.

He spent the next ten minutes speaking to individual officers and picking up the little bits of information they'd managed to glean, before heading back to his office. Leaving the door open, he made his way quickly to his desk and grabbed the bottle of whisky he kept in the bottom drawer. Pouring himself a` bigger glass than was necessary, he settled back into his chair and closed his eyes. He was out of luck. His phone began ringing, denying him his few moments of luxury. With a sigh, he picked up the call. He grabbed a piece of paper, scribbled a name down, thanked PC Best and hung up.

He picked up the desk phone, made a swift call and then dialled Clocks's extension. 'John! Office!'

Clocks looked up from his desk, gave Paterson the thumbs-up and shot out of his chair. That two-fingered typing always frustrated the life out of him.

Clocks came in and shut the door behind him. Paterson pointed to the bottle on his desk. 'Help yourself. I think we might have an ident on our vic.'

'Bloody hell, that was quick. Didn't think they'd come though until tomorrow at the earliest,' Clocks said.

'No. This is from a local beat bobby. Bloke called Pete Best. Obviously, we won't know for certain till the proper results come back, but this Pete seems to think our vic is known to us. Sounded quite certain of it.'

'Go on then,' said Clocks necking a good half of his glass of whisky.

Paterson handed him the piece of paper. 'Have a look for yourself. According to Best, our vic is a certain David Caine. White, twenty-eight.' He began typing into the PNC. 'Name mean anything to you?'

Clocks gave it some thought. 'Maybe. Rings a bell anyway. Can't think from where, though.' He leaned forward to hand the note back but stopped himself. 'Caine? It couldn't be . . .'

'There's a marker on the PNC. We're to call a DCI Martin Alliston at SCO7, the Serious and Organised Crime

Command. Doesn't matter what time of day. Any kind of interaction, they must be informed. I've already done it and he's on his way over now.' Paterson looked away from the screen. 'This Caine's a big boy, by the sounds of it.'

Clocks held his glass up. 'If it's who I think it is, then yes, he is a big boy. Very big. Well, not so much him as his dad. If this is Billy Caine's son, then we've got grief coming. Billy's one nasty arsed bastard, who runs the whole of the south-east.'

'Do you know him?' Paterson took another mouthful of whisky.

'Of him. Never crossed paths with him. Well outside of my league, Ray. This is a proper old-school villain. Makes the Richardsons look like a bunch of sweethearts.'

'The Richardsons?'

'Fuck me, Ray. Didn't they give you lot any history lessons at fast-track school?' He didn't wait for an answer. 'They were big-time back in the sixties. The torture gang, they were known as. Apparently, Charlie, the guv'nor, used to hook people's bollocks up to a car battery if they gave him the 'ump.' Paterson winced. 'That's when he wasn't nailing their legs to the floor. Ran south London from a scrap metal yard in Camberwell. It's gone now. Had a few run-ins with the Kray twins too.'

'I've heard of them,' said Paterson.

'Well, at least your education wasn't a total waste of the Met's money then.'

'So, our . . . Billy Caine,' he checked the name again, 'is worse than them?'

'So it's said.'

'Okay. We'll hang on for this DCI Alliston to show up and fill us in, then we better go see Mr Caine senior. Tell him what's happened to his little soldier.' He reached for the phone.

Clocks stood up to leave. 'The guy's been dead — what?' he glanced at the wall clock. 'Nearly eleven hours that we know of. You think Billy Caine doesn't already know? He's gonna be way ahead of us, Ray. Way ahead. And we best not go anywhere until DCI Alliston gives us the nod. Don't want to screw up any operation they may have running on him.'

* * *

'Here's what you need to know about the Caines.' Martin Alliston, a detective chief inspector with SCO7 was a sharply dressed, impeccably groomed man of about fifty with an evident taste for the finer things in life. The second he walked into the office, Paterson smelt money. It was the Rolex, the Aspinal of London attaché case and the two-grand Montegrappa fountain pen. The Dolce & Gabbana suit topped it off nicely — Paterson reckoned that must have cost him three grand if it cost him a penny. He wondered briefly how Alliston could afford it on a chief inspector's salary, but then remembered his own circumstances. Perhaps this bloke also came from family money.

Paterson was seated, feet up, tie undone, behind his desk. It had been a long day so far and it wasn't anywhere near over yet. Johnny Clocks took a sip of coffee and stuck out his burnt tongue, all the while weighing Alliston up.

DCI Alliston was obviously weighing his words with great care, and Paterson sighed inwardly. He would tell them as much as he wanted them to know and no more. He'd probably read through their files on the drive over, and would be aware that he and Clocks were not the whitest of whites. If so, he'd probably calculated that the less they really knew the better.

Alliston passed them some photographs. 'The older one is William "Billy" Caine, sixty-four years old. Billy is the head of one of the biggest crime empires in London. He's been under twenty-four-hour surveillance for the last five years.'

'Christ!' said Paterson. 'That must be costing a fortune.'

14

Alliston picked up his coffee, took a quick sniff and put it back down. 'That it does but, as I said, this one is big and very active. He has an army of men at his disposal, all one hundred percent loyal. He's suspected of at least fifteen murders attributable to him directly and at least three dozen he's ordered. David, or Davey, was his only family that we know of. His wife died about ten years ago. Breast cancer. It devastated him, and although he's had more than his fair share of women since, he's never settled. Very much the loner, family-wise.'

'How'd he get on with his boy?' said Clocks.

'Alright. Don't think their relationship was anything special and I'm betting that if we looked inside the Caine photo album, we wouldn't see too many family picnics. We know that Dad was grooming him to take over at some point.'

Paterson was making notes. 'Would the boy have been capable of running Dad's little schemes?'

Alliston studied Paterson for a moment. 'Mr Paterson, I'm sorry, perhaps I wasn't making myself clear. Billy Caine is not running "little schemes." He has risen from nowhere to take control of the whole of south-east London, and he has done it by sheer force of will and a propensity for extreme violence. Nothing happens out on those streets, crime-wise, that he doesn't know about and if anybody crosses him, he'll destroy them.' He snapped his fingers. 'Literally. He has no fear, no conscience and cannot be intimidated. When you face someone like that, you can only lose.'

'Apologies,' said Paterson. 'I wasn't trying to belittle what you said. I spoke without thinking.' The two men eyed each other, and Alliston nodded. 'Tell me about the son.'

'He has a bit of form for minor things — theft from motor vehicles, criminal damage, mostly when he was a pissed up teenager, odd bit of shoplifting here and there.

Nothing to get excited about, y'know?' Both men nodded. 'But we know that he has killed at least two people.'

Clocks shifted in his seat. 'Sorry? You *know* he's killed at least two?'

Alliston turned to face Clocks, who was sitting with one leg over the other knee and his arms folded. He looked pensive.

'Uh huh,' was all Alliston offered in response. It wasn't enough for Clocks.

'Explain to me, sir, why wasn't he banged up inside, then?'

Alliston eyed Johnny Clocks with dislike. No doubt the file he'd read had already coloured his view of him, and now they were face to face, that view had concretised.

'Old story, I'm afraid,' said Alliston. 'No direct evidence. No witnesses — at least none that would come forward — and without that, we have nothing. You understand, of course.' The statement wasn't designed to evoke a response, and Clocks let it go.

Paterson looked at a head-and-shoulders shot of Davey. Not a bad-looking kid.

'He was a flash little bastard though,' Alliston said. 'Liked to show off. Davey was a bit of a wild one, liked the parties, the girls, the drugs and the kudos of being who he was.'

Clocks took out his mobile phone, took a photo of the picture and tossed the phone onto the desk. 'So, was he up for taking over the business?'

'We believe so, yes. Caine has been in and out of the country with the boy several times of late, and we think he was trying to put together deals or, and this seems more likely, introduce him to some overseas faces. Helps to put a name to a face.'

'You don't know for sure?' Paterson said.

'Can't be a hundred percent, no. It's difficult to perform the same level of surveillance overseas as we can here. No point trying to put boots on the ground to follow him, they'd stick out like a sore thumb. We have a few expats in various countries that pick up a bit of work from us from time to time — tops up their pensions — but this time we haven't had much luck.'

Paterson sat back and eyed Alliston. 'So, big question time. Who would do this? Who'd have the balls to torch Billy Caine's pride and joy?'

Alliston grimaced. 'This is where it gets difficult. Gang-wise, and I'm talking professional criminals, not the snotty little kids running around with knives, London is divided up into north, east, south and west. Caine has the south, and a guy called Tanner has the east. The north and the west are run by Albanians.'

Clocks raised an eyebrow. 'What? Albanians? They're just painters and decorators, ain't they?' He glanced at Paterson who shook his head at him. 'No,' said Clocks, 'that's the Polish. They're the decorators.'

Alliston looked at Clocks with undisguised contempt. 'Yes, DI Clocks. Bloody Albanians or, as they're now known, the Albanian Mafia. These boys are a problem. A big problem. They've established good relationships with cocaine suppliers in Latin America and this is their primary trade, although human trafficking is another lucrative source of income. London is their principal hub, but they operate across the whole of the UK. They started taking over back in the nineties, muscled in and when confronted, hit back, hard. Vicious bastards to a man. They used well-planned, extreme violence and took the north quite quickly. The west fell soon after. Word is they're looking to expand and, make no mistake, the threat we face from them is substantial. For the most part, these different gangs keep themselves to themselves. They stay out of one another's businesses and, for want of a better word, respect the boundaries as they stand but now . . .'

'So, you reckon the Albanians are puffing up a bit?' Clocks asked. 'Trying to take over Caine's patch, perhaps?' He shot another glance at the photos of Davey Caine —

the charred corpse's head and shoulders, the face seared in agony. 'And they sent him a little housewarming gift gone wrong.'

If Alliston didn't like Clocks, it was a racing certainty Clocks didn't like him. Paterson knew what Clocks thought of men like Alliston. He'd have pegged him as too smarmy within the first thirty seconds of meeting him. And it was true. There was an arrogance about the man that hid under the surface but bobbed up when he had the floor.

'It's possible. As I said, we've heard rumours that the Albanians are looking to strengthen their position in London. A successful grab for the south would give them three quarters of the city, and that tips the balance right over.'

DCI Alliston took a sip of his coffee and screwed his nose up. His look said it all. *Far too cheap.*

'Tell me about the guy in the east — whassis name? Tanner?' said Clocks. 'What's his deal?'

DCI Alliston settled back into his chair. He wasn't about to give too much away but it was obvious that Clocks was going to be a pushy pain in the arse unless he got something more than just a superficial impression.

'He's at the same level as Caine. Under twenty-four-hour surveillance. A few years back, he tried it on with Caine. Saw the Albanians had the north and west and realised it was just a matter of time before they came for him. He didn't want that to happen, so he made a grab for the south. It was a, er, tactical error, shall we say? Caine smacked him down big-time and there's been tension ever since. They despise each other. Always have, always will. They tolerate each other's presence because they have to, but that's it.'

'Why didn't they just band together like the Albanians? Seems the sensible thing to do,' said Paterson. He stood and stretched his legs and his back, then plonked himself back down in his chair a little too heavily. It sent his back twinging in pain again.

Clocks chimed in before Alliston could answer. 'London boys don't think like that, guv. They're not big on playing sharesies. What's theirs is theirs and that's it, plain and simple.'

'That's about the strength of it, Mr Paterson,' Alliston said.

Paterson frowned. 'I'm not suggesting they share anything, just stand together against a common enemy.'

'They're villains, guv. They're vicious bastards, but not known for their thinking abilities. Besides, if they went full-on for the Albies, fifty-fifty, good chance they'd get their arses handed to them in a carrier bag.'

Paterson shrugged. He couldn't have cared less what they did, either way. 'So, you were telling us about this Tanner,' he said to Alliston.

Johnny Clocks stood up and stretched, then opened the office door. 'Pete, get us three more coffees, would yer, mate? Make one of them with the good stuff, Gold Blend or somethin'. The DCI's a bit of a connoisseur. Good lad.' He shut the door.

'Thank you, Mr Clocks. I appreciate the sentiment, if not your taste.' He lifted his briefcase onto the table, avoiding eye contact with Clocks.

Paterson sat forward in his chair and steepled his fingers. 'Try again then, Mr Alliston. Tell us about Tanner.'

Both sets of eyes bored into Alliston, and he looked uncomfortable. 'Sorry. Tanner. Albert Joseph Tanner. Sixty years of age. A tall, thin *fuck* of a man that you wouldn't want to meet in your worst nightmares.' Clocks frowned. He had more than his share of monsters running loose in his nightmares and was always willing to find space for one more. 'He is an out-and-out psychopath with a proclivity for killing.' Alliston stopped, mulled something over and then came out with it. 'His preferred method of execution is . . . burning. He likes to have people burned alive.'

'Jesus! What? Did you just say . . .?' said Clocks. 'You know, the police know that Tanner has people burned alive?'

'We do, yes. But note that I said "likes to have" them burned. I didn't say he actually partook.'

'And he's still free to wander about? A geezer like that? You're gonna have to enlighten me, because I don't understand this.' Clocks looked over at Paterson with a *back-me-up-here* expression on his face. Paterson frowned. He didn't understand either.

'And, again, no evidence to link him directly. Y'see, Caine and Tanner are what we call "cleanskins." You heard the term before? Either of you?' Clocks had and he wasn't happy about it. He said nothing. 'Officially, a "cleanskin" is someone who has no criminal record or has never come to the attention of the police or security services. We use it to describe villains who are crafty enough to stay under the radar. Billy Caine has a small record but for all intents and purposes is living his life as a good citizen. Same for Tanner. Both have legitimate businesses, and both keep themselves out of the dirty work. Neither one gets himself directly involved — and they both stay well out of harm's way. They order the killing and pay those lower down the food chain to do it for them. If that poor sod gets caught, he shuts his mouth and takes his time in prison. His family are well looked after while he's inside and he'll have a nice lump sum when he comes out. If he opens his mouth, then he'll die in prison somehow but not before he hears about the death of his family.'

Clocks shook his head in disbelief.

'I can see you're upset, Mr Clocks.'

'Well spotted, man.'

'You just have to trust that matters are in hand. We have deep undercover operations in place in both camps, and when the time is right, we'll take them both down at the same time.' He pursed his lips. Paterson wondered if he'd given too much away. 'Huge PR bonus for the Met,' added Alliston.

'PR? Fuckin' PR? Jesus. If you lot had done your job, David Caine would be alive now. Nasty little bastard or not, he didn't deserve to die that way. Christ almighty! And you know that Caine and his boy 'ave killed or 'ad people killed and you couldn't nick 'em either.' Clocks stomped over to the window and stood looking out for a minute. He rounded back on Alliston. 'What the fuck is wrong with you lot? You scared of 'em or something? Jesus wept!'

Paterson saw DCI Alliston stiffen. 'Take a step back, Inspector,' he said, with just enough tone to get Clocks even more riled. 'You don't get to question me about the methods we employ or accuse me of incompetence. These people are not the run-of-the-mill low levels you occasionally run across in your squad. These are professional, organised criminals and they're vicious. We have been slowly amassing shedloads of intel on both these men—'

A quick tap on the door was followed by DC Peter Lord backing in with a tray holding three coffees which were sloshing around alarmingly. 'Shit!' he said. 'Sorry, sorry.' He set the tray down on Paterson's desk and, recognising the look on Clocks's face, made a swift exit.

'Well, if you've been watching them for years and can't put either of 'em inside, then you obviously need to step yer game up a little bit and watch 'em a bit fuckin' harder. Surely you must have something to show for it, aside from soddin' big houses on the overtime you've all made.'

Paterson picked up a coffee. He couldn't tell which was the one good cup that Clocks had asked for and he didn't much care, figuring that DCI Alliston wouldn't be staying too much longer.

Alliston, though, wasn't one to back off. If Clocks was going to make it personal, so would he. 'I've heard of you,

Inspector. There are rumours that you have a few . . . mental problems apparently.'

Paterson rolled his eyes.

'Fuck me!' said Clocks. 'That's a bit non-PC, isn't it? If I was a sensitive bunny, I'd have you for that, but you know what? I'm not. So, let's 'ave it then. You're right, *sir*. I grew up on a council estate, sir. Didn't have much. I'm just a poor boy, from a poor family, but I'm easy come, easy go, y'know? My moods used to swing. I used to be a little high, then a little low, y'know?' Alliston stared at him, not sure what was going on. 'Anyway, the wind was blowin', doesn't matter which way, and I got into trouble. Bit of a breakdown. The police were called and found me eating me own elbows and I got sectioned.' Paterson grinned. Total bullshit. Clocks was taking the piss out of Alliston big-time. The man looked bemused, allowing Clocks to set him up for a fall. 'So, I did me time in the cuddle coat but, here's the mad bit, the officers that nicked me took pity on me and came ter see me when I got kicked outa the Maudsley. They told me that if I was a good boy and turned a blind eye to all the naughty people out there, then I could be a DCI one day, and then I'd get to pretend I knew what I was fuckin' doing. And look at me now.' He splayed his arms wide. 'I'm just one rank away from being a total waste of space like you, sir, and then I can stop taking my medicine.'

This was too much for Alliston. Face red and fists bunched, he swung around to face Paterson. 'Are you going to let him speak to me like that?'

Taking a swig of his coffee, Paterson screwed his face up. Tasted like bitter chocolate. The cheap stuff. 'I'm gonna have to say, yes. To be fair, you did poke the bear, didn't you?'

Alliston's mouth fell open slightly. He'd obviously expected the chain of command to kick in and for Paterson to support him. That was how it was done — always had been. If he'd had the time to read their files

22

more closely, he'd have discovered that inviolable convention was something that sat quite low on Paterson and Clocks's radar.

'And why the fuck,' Clocks continued, 'didn't you think to mention Tanner's little hobby earlier?'

Alliston harrumphed. 'I mentioned it soon enough.'

'Not in my book.'

'That's enough. Pack it up, the pair of you.' Paterson really didn't feel like sitting here any longer listening to these two kick chunks out of each other. It was obvious that neither one was going to give up first, and he knew that at some point, Clocks would probably just lamp him one. 'Are we clear to inform and interview Caine?' he said to Alliston.

'By all means you can inform him of his son's death, and you can ask questions as part of your normal enquiries, but he is not to be formally questioned or interrogated. Understood?'

Paterson's eyes flashed, and his jaw tensed. 'Perfectly. But . . . why?'

Alliston rolled his eyes. 'I've just explained it you, *sir*. This is a deep and sensitive enquiry involving two of the—'

Paterson held his hand up. 'Got it. Now do yourself a big favour and knock off the fucking attitude when you talk to a senior officer, and don't go giving me orders, *Chief Inspector*. Is that understood?'

Alliston choked back his rage. 'Yes, sir. Sorry, sir.'

'And, just for the record, I don't give a rat's arse about your operation. I'm investigating a murder and that puts you firmly in position two of the pecking order. Do you understand that too, *Chief Inspector*?'

Alliston sat still for a moment or two, taking in a few deep breaths. He gave a curt nod. 'Okay then,' he said, 'by all means go and see him, but let me give you some advice. This operation is huge. People upstairs are expecting results. They won't like it if you two go screwing up years of careful work.' He sat back in his chair. 'As for Caine, don't expect anything from him. He'll be sorting out this little problem as we speak and,' he turned to face Clocks, 'do not, under any circumstances, do anything to wind this man up. It will not be good for your health, and we can't protect you.'

'Well, thanks for coming, sir,' said Clocks. 'Appreciate your input but be aware that we don't need no protection and certainly not from a pencil pusher like you.' He waved his hand in dismissal. 'You can show yourself out, *sir.*'

Paterson rose from his chair and walked Alliston to the door. Whatever Clocks thought of the man — and that clearly wasn't much — it didn't do to go pissing off people you might need to call on later. He considered giving Alliston a call a bit later, when things had calmed down, to smooth things over and keep him onside. Paterson opened the door and stood aside for him.

Alliston gave him a faint smile. 'Sir, be careful. Seriously. You're stepping into a world you know nothing about.'

Paterson gave a nod. 'Thank you. I appreciate the warning, but we're kind of getting used to stepping into worlds we know nothing about. Have a look at our last case if you like. Still, duly noted. We'll be careful.'

He closed the door behind Alliston and his phone immediately beeped. 'John,' he said, 'message here from the MIT over at Dulwich. They're asking if we can pop over and see them. They have a dead girl and think we might be able to help them.'

Clocks raised an eyebrow. 'With what?'

'No idea. That was the whole message, apart from we need to meet with a . . .' he glanced back at his phone, 'Detective Chief Inspector Chris Lambert.'

CHAPTER THREE

By the time Paterson and Clocks arrived at the police station in Dulwich, most of the officers on the murder investigation team were either out on enquiries or stuck in front of computer screens, sifting through the statements and what little evidence they had so far managed to glean. They were met at the front counter by the office manager, Detective Sergeant Mickey White, an overweight man in his mid-forties who was clearly better suited to life driving a desk than being out at the sharp end.

He was pleasant enough though and greeted them with a firm handshake and the offer of coffee before they went up to meet DCI Lambert and his second in charge, DI Michael Butler. Looking pointedly at their watches, they declined the coffee. DS White took the hint and showed them upstairs and into the main office. A few interested heads briefly lifted from the computer screens.

Standing in the doorway of his office, DCI Lambert gave a quick wave and a smile and held his hand out. 'Detective Superintendent Paterson, thank you for coming so promptly.'

They shook hands and got the pleasantries out of the way. Lambert turned to the board behind them. Pinned to it were pictures of two corpses. Both were female and both had letters carved into their chest. The close-ups showed the words, "Please" and "I'm."

Clocks closed his eyes for a second. 'Oh, bloody hell!'

'Indeed,' Lambert said. 'You see why we thought it best to call you in? Get some insight if possible.'

Paterson stared at the images while the memories flooded up. *Lisa. Jordan.* He shook them off. 'Is this it?' he said, tearing himself away from the board. Both Lambert and Butler looked at him, curious.

'Er, what do you mean?' Lambert said.

'Is this all you have?' His expression said he thought Lambert a bit of a moron. He sighed. 'These photographs don't show us much. Did he do anything else to them? When Adam Walker killed, he was savage. One victim was disembowelled, a few had their throats cut, all of the women had their vaginas cut out — well, their vulvas, to be more accurate.' Paterson spoke coldly, brisk and efficient, blocking out his memories the best way he could.

'No,' DI Butler said. 'Just this.'

'Are they dead before he starts the cutting?' Paterson asked.

'We believe so,' said Lambert.

Paterson stared him down. 'You believe so? I bloody well hope so. How were they killed?'

'Blunt force trauma to the throat. That brought them down but they also had small bruises around the heart which we think point to the cause of death. Pathologist thinks they're consistent with blows from a hammer.'

'A hammer?' Clocks said. 'That's different. Was the hammer used on the throats as well?'

'Can't be a hundred percent on it, sadly. In both victims, the larynx was crushed and the airways closed up, but the bruising is different to that of the chest. Again, the pathologist says that's all to do with the makeup of the body in that area but, if he was pushed then yes, he'd go with a hammer to the throat,' Butler said.

'Bit of advice, don't push him in that direction. Closes off the possibility of something else.' Paterson had done a quick check into DCI Lambert on the way over and had found that the man was highly competent, well thought of and very thorough in his work, so he knew he was teaching him to suck eggs here. Still, it never hurt to point things out. Mistakes happen.

'So, why exactly did you call us in?' Clocks said.

'We think it's a copycat,' Lambert answered.

'Why?' said Paterson.

'With respect,' said Lambert, 'I'd have thought that much was obvious. Dead girls and words carved into their chests. Exactly like the Walker case.'

'With all due respect to you, this is not "exactly" like the Walker case for the reasons I've just given,' said Paterson, shaking his head. 'If he's trying to be a copycat, then he's not a good one. Too many dissimilarities. I'll concede that someone is maybe trying to give the impression of emulating Walker's handiwork, but this isn't even close. The method of killing is completely different and the rest of the work is, well . . . basic. Walker was quite methodical and thorough in his mutilations.'

Clocks was watching Paterson, unhappy at the way this was going. He was answering too confidently, it wasn't right. Paterson's wife had been butchered, and here he was, standing talking coolly about the man who'd killed her and his methods. He decided a bail-out was necessary. 'How far apart are these killings?'

'Couple of months,' said Butler.

'There you go then. Walker was operating over a very short period. Mr Paterson's right. This is probably just some fucked-up knicker sniffer who's read about Walker on the internet and decided it's his time to put in an appearance. Sometimes it's easier to pick a style you like and start off with that.'

28

Lambert looked like he'd been slapped with a wet fish. 'What? Knicker sniffer? Pick a style and start off? Seriously?'

Paterson grinned.

'Sure,' Clocks said. ''Appens all the time. Everybody has to start somewhere, and copying their heroes is how they start. You know this shit. Builds up the confidence. This guy's probably been chewing the heads off bats and wanking off in his mum's knicker drawer for a few years while he built up the balls to start climbing the crazy ladder. He's been looking on the internet, found Walker and thought it sounded like fun to write on women with a Stanley knife.'

'Jesus Christ!' Butler was as appalled as Lambert. 'You've got to be joking, surely? That's got to be the mother and father of oversimplification.'

Clocks tapped his temple a few times. 'Thank you very much. I don't like to overcomplicate things if I don't have to and here,' he gestured back at the photos, 'I don't have to.'

Paterson gave Clocks a slight grin and turned his attention back to Lambert. 'What else are you thinking?'

'Okay,' Lambert said, gathering his thoughts. 'If it's not a true copycat, and I take your point, we've also considered the possibility that this is aimed at you, Mr Paterson. Or perhaps that it's been done for your benefit.'

Paterson frowned. 'My benefit? Go on.'

'It just seems odd,' said Lambert, 'that the bodies were found here in Dulwich, not far from where you live. Do you think the message could be for you? I understand the last one was.' He fixed his gaze on Paterson, who took the slight in his stride, ignoring it. It was no secret that Paterson had been in a sexual relationship with their serial killer's wife, and that the husband finding out had sparked off the spate of killings that culminated in the message, "Don't touch what isn't yours, Ray" being inscribed one word at a time into six victims. That was all in the public domain — the juicy details that people wanted to remember. Clearly, DCI Lambert did.

'It's possible, I suppose, but I have no idea why,' he said. 'As far as I know, I haven't shagged anyone I shouldn't have this time around. I tend to ask if there's a marriage certificate that I could have a look at first. Find it helps me make better decisions all round.'

Clocks grinned at him.

'Good to know,' said Lambert.

'So, I would think that the fact that the killings were here in Dulwich may just be coincidental — perhaps because the killer lives in or around these parts. Have you taken it up with the geographical profilers?'

Lambert nodded. 'Yes. We have one with us but the sad fact is, two bodies are not statistically significant enough to be meaningful, and the kill sites were at least three miles apart. We can't get any kind of fix as yet.'

Paterson scratched his head. 'Yeah, that's shit. Well,' he said, taking another look at the photos, 'given that the two words make no sense on their own, there's clearly more to come. I just hope that it's a short message and you catch the person responsible sooner rather than later. Other than that, there's nothing else we can add. Right, John?'

Clocks shrugged. 'Can't think of anything, guv.'

'Look, I'm sorry, but we have to be somewhere else I'm afraid. Problems of our own.' Paterson held his hand out.

Lambert instinctively reached out and shook it. 'Yeah, I read about that. Burning man. That's all kinds of sick. Good luck with that.'

'Cheers,' said Paterson. 'I've a feeling we're going to be kept quite busy.'

At the door, Paterson said, 'If there's anything else, anything we can help you with, don't hesitate.'

DCI Lambert smiled. 'Appreciate it, Mr Paterson. I've no doubt we'll be back in touch. Soon.' He stood in the doorway and watched the two men descend the stairs.

CHAPTER FOUR

Gravel crunched underneath the Aston's tyres as the wrought-iron gates slowly swung shut behind them. Paterson estimated the distance from the gates to the front of the house to be about six hundred yards. Dotted around were Ferraris, Bentleys and the odd Roller. Clearly, Billy Caine and the people around him had serious money.

As they pulled up in a parking space, they were met by a mountain of a man dressed from head to foot in black. Paterson wondered if this was how he always dressed, or whether the mourning was already underway. He guessed it was the former. The mountain man looked the type who enjoyed putting the fear of God into people and in his line of work, perception was everything. Complete with broken nose, hands like hams and a couple of rolls of fat sitting between his neck and his skull, he certainly looked the part. Paterson and Clocks introduced themselves and were shown in.

The entrance to Billy Caine's house was big and so were the men standing around in the hallway. They regarded the two policemen who had walked onto their turf with a mixture of contempt and hatred, a feeling that was wholeheartedly reciprocated. The men knew why

Paterson and Clocks were there. It was the sole reason why their presence in William Caine's home was being tolerated. It wouldn't happen a second time.

'This way, please,' said mountain man. His voice was a surprise. Cultured and soft, it didn't fit his image at all. He escorted Paterson and Clocks upstairs into one of the biggest home libraries either of them had ever seen. The whole length of the room, from floor to ceiling, was stacked with leather-bound books, setting off the beautiful mahogany writing desk perfectly. It all seemed a bit out of whack with what they had heard about this man.

Caine, the master of the house, a powerfully built man with a bald head, had his back to them. He stood looking out of a large window, apparently deep in thought. A young girl in her early twenties stared up at them from a chaise longue. She was attractive, beautiful even — or she would have been on a good day. Today was evidently not one of those. Instead, she looked like shit. Her eyes were red and puffy, tears streaked her face, which was blotchy. Paterson clocked the solitaire on her left-hand ring finger. *Old habits.* It was a big rock, expensive. He guessed she was the fiancée.

He cleared his throat. 'Mr Caine, I'm Detective Superintendent Ray Paterson and this is Detective Inspector Johnny Clocks. I'm afraid I have some news for you. It's about your son, Davey.' While he spoke, Clocks eyed up the room in a bit more detail. His face gave away his thoughts. No way did someone like Billy Caine read books, and certainly not ones by Proust or Tolstoy. If anything, Clocks would have had him down for a fan of Martina Cole or Lee Child — Cole for the villains and Child for the troubled, lone avenger Jack Reacher.

Caine sighed deeply and turned away from the moonlit view over the lawns. He had a handsome face, in a beaten-up sort of way. Craggy. The sort that showed he'd lived a life and bore the scars of it. He also had a smile that beamed out at a thousand megawatts when he was in a good mood. The detectives didn't see it, though. Tonight, the light had gone out.

'Thank you for coming to tell me, Mr Paterson, but I already know.' His voice was a deep bass that resonated in his chest. He eyed them up and evidently had their number, for he asked, 'Would you boys like a drink?' He reached for the decanter of whisky on his desk. For all his alleged faults, Caine at least had manners.

'No, sir,' said Paterson, 'but thank you for the offer. Appreciated.'

Paterson stood a little awkwardly and shuffled his feet a bit. He seemed to have been dismissed. He cleared his throat. 'I don't know how much you've been told, Mr Caine, but I'm afraid I have to tell you that your son was unlawfully killed. I'm sorry.' The girl let out a high-pitched wail.

'A polite way of saying he was murdered. I know that too. How about you, Mr Clocks. Drink?'

'No thanks. Better not. Appreciate it though.' Clocks's eyes were still roaming everywhere.

Caine shrugged, poured himself a large whisky and went back to his window. 'Suit yourself. This is April,' he said, with a nod to the girl on the chaise. 'She is . . . was my Davey's fiancée. They were getting married next year. Spring wedding.' She wailed again, much to Caine's evident annoyance, although he said nothing. There was an uncomfortable silence while Caine chugged half the glass of whisky. Eventually, he said, 'April, love, I need to talk to the rozzers. Go downstairs for a while. Get Razor to make you a cup of tea. Might 'elp you pull yerself together a bit. He needs something to keep him busy too.' *Razor*. Paterson wondered what had earned him that particular moniker, but now wasn't the time to ask.

April, wobbly and snotty, pulled herself up from the chair, looked sheepishly at Clocks as she passed him and sobbed her way out of the room. Clocks watched her leave the room, his gaze lingering a little bit longer than was necessary. Caine caught him staring, raised an eyebrow, drained his glass and punched his chest. 'Details, Mr Paterson. Tell me exactly what happened.'

'Er, it . . . to be honest . . .'

Caine's look said, *This one's a pussy.* He turned to Clocks. 'Mr Clocks? What happened?'

'He was handcuffed to a wooden stake, someone poured a few litres of unleaded over him and *woof!* Up he went. He was alive at the time whoever did it, did it. I will have that drink please, Mr Caine.' Caine stared at him, hard. This one was no pussy.

Paterson closed his eyes. *Tact, John. We've spoken about this so many times.*

Caine's jaw clamped shut and his eyes flashed with anger. He poured and handed Clocks his drink. 'Thank you. Now, d'you know who did it?'

Clocks took a swig, made the same face Caine had pulled earlier, and shook his head. 'No idea. We were hoping you might know. Point us in the right direction, like.'

'Me? How should I know?'

'Well, we did a bit of 'omework on the way over so we know you're no fairytale princess. You knew about Davey long before we got here, that's obvious, so I'm guessing that through your extensive network of undesirables, you likely already know who did this to your boy. Tell us, then we go over and nick him and put him away for the rest of his natural. Keeps you out of trouble and us in a job. Sorted. Whoever did this is a nasty, nasty bastard and I really don't want him walking the streets.'

Caine nodded slowly. 'I appreciate your being straightforward with me, Mr Clocks, but I have no idea who did it. Given what you think you know about me, why would I be asking you if I did?'

'Well, that's a fair point but I get the impression you're hoping we're thick enough to swallow what you say and go away thinking you really have no idea. Meanwhile the geezer who did it is already tied up with his toes dangling in a bowl of sulphuric, waiting for you to come and say hello.' Clocks emptied his glass. He was pushing it. He knew it, Caine knew it. Paterson was just waiting for the shit to hit the fan. It never did. Instead, Clocks threw his host a big smile and said, 'Mind if I take a squirt in your loo? I shouldn't have had that. Me back teeth were already floating when I got here.'

* * *

Clocks made his way along the hall followed by, not their friend the mountain man, but surely some sort of relative. Just as big, same nose, same neck and probably the same IQ: T-minus ten and counting. It irked him a bit to be escorted to the bathroom. It made him feel as if he wasn't to be trusted, and he couldn't imagine why anyone would feel that way about him.

Leaving the escort at the door, he entered the biggest and most opulent bathroom he had ever seen. It had to be at least as big as his living room. For a moment, he wondered if he had gone back in time and wound up in Harold Odonte's gold bullion bank. There were gold fittings everywhere — taps, towel rails, hand-held shower, toilet roll holders. He wondered why it was that every villain he knew had so much money and such shit taste.

He didn't bother lifting the seat, and his initial squirt went over the front of the upright lid. From there, he splashed the seat and the floor in equal measures. Very little made it into the bowl. Shaking himself off, he amused himself further by making sure he got a few drops on the hand towel. Having zipped himself up, he decided to have a poke around inside the medicine cabinet. He opened the door and the smells of aftershave and Deep Heat vied for his attention. Apart from the usual stuff — razor, face cream, plasters and corn pads — he was surprised at the number of pill bottles, all in Caine's name. He lifted the first one: citalopram. Clocks recognised that one.

Depression. He knew all about it. The others all had names he hadn't heard of before and on that basis, reasoned they were important.

He pulled out his mobile phone and began taking photos of the individual bottles, being careful to ensure that the names of the medicines were legible. Once he'd photographed them all, he put the toilet lid down, sat on it and began to Google search one of them. After a few seconds of looking, he furrowed his brow. There was a sudden thump on the door. It was the escort. 'Oi! Hurry up in there.'

'Fuck off!' returned Clocks. 'I'll come out when I'm done, mate, unless you want to come and hold my dick for me. Up to you, Tinkerbell.' He went back to his Googling. 'But if you do, make sure you bring a friend. This bastard is a bit too big and heavy for you on yer own.' Tinkerbell gave one last thump on the door but said no more.

Once he'd finished, Clocks put all the bottles back in the cabinet, flushed the toilet and turned the tap on. He sluiced his fingers under the tap and left it running slightly before walking out. Tinkerbell was waiting outside, his face like thunder. Clocks awarded him one of his grins. 'Might wanna give that ten minutes, mate.' Then he wandered off down the hall back to Paterson.

* * *

'So what's the story then, Bill? We can't fuck around here all night. D'you fancy Albert Tanner for this then, or what?' Johnny Clocks had breezed back into the room and fired off the questions before anyone even registered his entrance. Caine shot him a look, stunned. Paterson froze. Things had been going quite well up until now. 'Well, do you?'

Caine moved fast. His face had gone from its customary grey to furious red, and in a split-second he had Clocks by the throat. Caine's momentum drove the startled Clocks backwards until he slammed up against the door frame. He managed to react, but it took the form of a pathetic, wildly thrown punch that barely connected with Caine.

'The fuck you talking to, you prick!' Caine drew back his hand to teach Johnny Clocks the importance of respect, but Paterson grabbed it just in time.

'Caine! No!'

Caine shook him off easily, but it was enough to deflect the blow.

Tinkerbell flung the door open and crashed into the room. Paterson, still holding onto Caine's hand, quickly let go and held his hands up. He wasn't one to shy away from a fight, but he knew when he was outnumbered.

'Woah! Woah, fella. It's alright. It's over! It's done. A misunderstanding, that's all.'

Tinkerbell took in the scene — his boss, holding the copper with one hand, both struggling, and decided otherwise. He put his bulk between Caine and Clocks. 'Boss! Boss! Leave it.' Caine was incandescent with rage. It wasn't a good place for him to be in. Tinkerbell pushed his boss in the chest, but not so hard that Caine would turn his rage on him. 'Boss! C'mon. Not now! Not today!'

Caine glared at Tinkerbell. Then, with a final push, he let Clocks go. He turned to Paterson. 'You! Get him the fuck out of my house before I have him carried out.'

'Okay, Billy. I'm sorry. I'll deal with it. Leave him to me.'

Clocks, having scrambled to his feet, started toward Caine. Paterson pushed him hard in the chest. 'John! Just pack it up. Now! Get the fuck out of here. Wait in the car.' Clocks scowled at him. 'Do it!'

Clocks stormed out of the room, shouldering Tinkerbell as he went.

'Billy. Mr Caine. I'm really sorry. I don't know what that was all about, I really don't.'

Caine walked back to his desk and poured himself another drink. His hands were shaking. He slugged the whisky down in one. 'Man's off his fucking nut, coming in here giving it Johnny Big Bollocks. Fuck's he think he is, disrespecting me in my own house? I'll cut his bollocks off, mouthy little twat!'

Paterson was furious with Clocks for the way he'd behaved and for the position he found himself in now but, at the same time, he knew Clocks would have had his reasons. Clocks was always one for a wind up, but he wasn't stupid. He was perfectly aware that this would be an opportunity for Paterson to go to work on Caine. It was simple psychology. Caine would slag off Clocks, Paterson would agree with him and Caine would, without even realising it, feel that he and Paterson had a little something in common. He'd be more inclined to talk, even if only a little. Only a little could be enough.

Paterson nodded understandingly. 'I know. He can be a twat sometimes, this being one of them, but I promise I'll deal with him. Do you want to make a complaint?'

'Fuck off! Complaint? Jesus. Fuckin' complaint. What d'you think I am? A fuckin' little schoolgirl? Jog on, son. I'll deal with him meself if he traps off to me again.'

Paterson was in no doubt about that. 'He won't. Trust me. I'll deal with him.'

'You do that, mate.' He poured himself another large one and again, it went straight down. 'Right. You've come here and done what you had to do. We're done here.' He gestured to Tinkerbell to show Paterson out.

'Okay,' said Paterson as the big man moved toward him. 'Sorry it went this way, I really am but,' Caine glared at him, 'I have to ask. Why would he dig you out about Tanner? I don't want to get caught in the middle of anything here, but if Tanner's involved in your son's death, we do need to know. You understand that?'

Caine stopped, wiped his mouth, reached again for the decanter but he didn't pour another drink. 'What d'you know about Tanner?'

'To be honest, virtually nothing. I understand that he's in the same line of business as you, but over in the East End. That's it.'

Caine looked intently at Paterson and seemed to decide that he believed him. 'Mate, Tanner's a proper psycho. Through and through. We've had some run-ins over the years, course we have, but he wouldn't dare do this. He wouldn't dare. Come into my manor and do this? Nah, no way.'

'Could he be trying it on? Testing you perhaps? I understand he's tried before.'

Caine looked at him again. 'Who told you that? That prick, Alliston?'

Paterson said nothing, impassive. His mind was racing.

'Don't stress yerself trying to figure it out. He's been keeping tabs on us for years. We both know. Whole fuckin' house is bugged from floor to ceiling.'

'And you can live like that?'

'Part of the job, son. You get used to it.'

Paterson, feeling a bit more comfortable now that Caine had calmed down, put his hands in his pockets. He wouldn't be needing to make use of them now and it would unconsciously register to all in the room as less aggressive. He would still need to tread gently though. 'One thing I do know about him,' said Paterson, 'is that burning people is his preferred weapon of choice. I have to admit, that seems a bit coincidental if it's not him.'

Caine cocked his head. *Good point.* 'Yeah, well, normally, I'd reckon him for it but, it's not. If anything, I fancy the Albanians. Nasty vicious bastards. You know about them?'

Paterson shrugged. 'No. Not that much. Bits and pieces really. We're a murder squad. The Albanians would come under organised gangs, I guess.'

'Jesus.' Caine shook his head. 'You lot have a bloody squad for everything. No wonder you can't get fuck all done.'

'Can't disagree with that.'

Caine seemed to decide to pour a drink after all. He took a swig. 'They're not above this sort of thing, and they're stronger than me. A fuckin' lot more of 'em for starters, and they're a bunch of slippery scrotes.'

'Meaning?'

'Meaning it wouldn't surprise me if they killed Davey to make it look like Tanner did him. Maybe they figure I'll go at him and take the mad bastard out of the game for them. They know that if I did top him in anger, then I wouldn't have planned out how to take over the East End. There'd be a vacuum, and the greasy little shits'd move in with no one to give 'em grief. Then they've got seventy-five percent. From there, it's a short step to a 'undred percent.' He shook his head. 'You've got a lot to learn, 'aven't yer, son?'

'Evidently,' said Paterson. 'We'll look into it, naturally, but I'll also be talking to Tanner in due course. It might be he thinks that after what happened to your son, it'll be easier to make a move on you when you're at your weakest.'

'*Weak*? You've gotta be joking, ain'tcha, son? You think that my boy being murdered is gonna make me weak?' Caine snorted. 'You have no fuckin' idea what this is going to do to me, but I promise you this much.' He stared Paterson dead in the eye. 'It will not make me weak.'

* * *

'Right. You want to tell me what the fuck that little charade was all about?' Paterson pulled the door of the Aston shut. 'You nearly got us both a good kicking at the very least, so whatever it was you found, it better be good.'

Clocks was scrolling through his phone. 'Did he open up then, Ray?'

'No, not really. Said that Tanner was a nutter but he doesn't believe he would have the stones to try for a takeover. Just doesn't believe it. He's putting it on the Albies. Reckons they're trying to get him and this Tanner bloke to take each other out of the game.'

Eyes still on his phone, Clocks shrugged. 'Maybe, maybe not. Listen, when I went for a piss, I had a little ferret about in his cupboards. He's got a shit load of medicine bottles, all in his name.'

'So what?' Paterson said, starting the car and pulling away. 'He's getting on a bit. Bound to have something wrong with him, I guess.' The driveway gates swung open long before they got there, as if urging them to leave.

'So, once I'd pissed all over his toilet seat . . .'

Paterson turned sharply toward Clocks. 'Oh, you didn't?'

'Yeah, course I did. I got some on the floor too, just for luck.'

Paterson shook his head in despair. 'John, how many more times do we have to go through this? You've got to stop—'

'Yeah, yeah, I know. Got to have some fun, though. Listen to this. One of the bottles was labelled, "Donepezil."'

Paterson wrinkled his brow. 'What's that then?'

'Thought you'd never ask. He's got something called vascular dementia.'

'Is that . . .?'

'Yep. Our boy's got Alzheimer's.'

* * *

Paterson swung the car into the car park of the nearest McDonald's, surprisingly less than five minutes' drive from Caine's house. Normally he wouldn't touch this stuff with a bargepole, but he hadn't eaten for the best part of the day and there was no chance of finding a sushi bar open this late at night. Clocks would be desperately craving his daily meat allowance by now. Maybe that was why he'd gotten lairy back in the house.

A few minutes later they were ensconced in a side booth and digging into their meals. Paterson had opted for the thing that looked the least likely to kill him and bought himself pancakes and syrup and a cup of black coffee. Clocks had no such qualms. In front of him, spread out all over his half of the table, was the Chicago Stack — two burgers in a bun with bacon, with two types of cheese and mayo. He'd backed that up with two boxes of large fries and a fried apple pie. Half a litre of strawberry milkshake to wash it all down put him a couple of steps closer to Jock Hudson's table.

'So, come on then. Where are we now, John?'

Clocks was busy with a mouthful of burger. He held his hand up, swallowed and said, 'I know Caine came up with that crap about the Albanians, but he's full of shit. If they want him, they'll come for him straight on. They won't play games and make out that Tanner's done it. They're not gonna waste their bleedin' time. The way I see it is this. Billy Caine is on his way out. He knows that so he was grooming the son, Davey, to be his successor. There's no one else he could leave it to. We know Tanner has tried to take over before and failed, and we know Davey Caine was burned to death. Tanner is a burner of men. So far, so good. So, I think that somehow Tanner got wind of Caine's Alzheimer's and, sensing his weakness, decided to go for it.' He stuffed a large handful of fries into his mouth.

'Why not just wait until Caine dies?'

'Poor move, tactically. It could take a good few years for that to happen and by that time, the son would already have taken control. And, meanwhile, the Albies would probably have already made a move. If they went south and took it from Caine, then they'd have seventy-five percent of London. Bad for Tanner. Or, they could have gone straight to the east and taken Tanner out first. Either way, bad for him. The only sensible move is to take out the boy before he gains any traction, and then move in on the old man, Caine.'

'What about Caine's little army? Won't he just divvy it up among them? He's got people in place who can carry on after he's gone. They're not just going to roll over and give up the keys to the kingdom, are they?'

Clocks had his mouth full of burger. 'Probably not. Don't get me wrong, mate, there'll be fisticuffs alright, but I think Tanner's got this all planned out. I reckon once the fighting stops, he'll just absorb Caine's boys into his new organisation and then he can take on the Albanians, fifty-fifty. Don't forget, there's no loyalty amongst villains. These fuckers go where the money is, mate, and it wouldn't surprise me at all if Tanner's already got a few of 'em on the payroll. They'll grease the wheels on the way in.' He shoved in another handful of chips.

Paterson just looked at him and shook his head. 'You'll be dead in a year if you keep that up. You know that, don't you?'

Clocks shrugged, swallowed his food and took a quick slurp of milkshake. 'Yep. Unlikely I'll go out on top of some little eighteen-year-old blonde, 'specially since I'm all luvved up with . . . wassername?' He threw Paterson a wink. 'Oh, yeah, Lyndsey. Death by burgers for me, Ray. I've made me peace with it.' He burped loudly.

Paterson smiled, sipped at his coffee, pulled a face, put the lid back on and picked his tray up. Time to go.

'Hang on, guv,' said Clocks, stuffing the last of his burger into his mouth. Paterson stopped. 'Before we go, what's the questions? What don't we know?'

Paterson eyed him, thinking. He rubbed his face for a second or two. 'OK. A couple of things. We don't know for certain who barbecued Davey Caine. Tanner's the best bet but we've no evidence. We don't know who else knows about Caine's illness but, if we go along with what you're saying, and you think Tanner knows about him being ill, then we don't know how Tanner found about his Alzheimer's.'

'No, we don't, so that suggests to me an inside job. Probably that big bastard who was in the room with us. He knows his way about.'

Paterson stood up, tray in hand. 'So, if Caine also thinks that one of his own has told Tanner about his illness, then he'll have no one to trust, no one to leave his empire to. With his son murdered by another villain looking to move in while he can and him dying of Alzheimer's, he's got nothing to lose. He knows this is down to Tanner and he's trying to chuck us off the scent. He's going to go after Tanner, isn't he?'

Clocks nodded. 'Yup, course he is. Shit's gonna get very wobbly, very quickly, Ray, and I'm going home to bed while it happens.'

CHAPTER FIVE

Ray Paterson had been brought up to believe that whatever he did, whatever he achieved in life would always be down to his own decisions and the actions he took in support of them. His father had drummed into him the importance of making the best choice he could with the information he had at the time. Now, sitting on the floor in his apartment, head bent over a coffee table, tears in his eyes and dragging a line of coke up his nose, he believed, heart and soul, that chemical abuse was the only choice available to him to numb the pain that, night and day, tore his heart apart.

A thin shaft of light pierced through the heavy drapes that he hadn't closed properly the night before. It fell on the photograph of his dead wife Lisa which stood on the table. It was this image he carried in his wallet and in his head. *Vogue* magazine twice voted her one of the world's most beautiful women, and that was the face he struggled to carry with him, not the version he'd seen lying on a mortuary slab, raped and disembowelled.

Snorting the odd line of coke to help him cope with the stresses and strains of the job was par for the course, but after the deaths of his wife and his friend, Dave Jordan, at the hands of serial killer Detective Adam Walker, he'd upped his intake big-time. In the aftermath of the killings and his subsequent suspension he'd found himself alone with too much time on his hands and an inability to cope. He wasn't alone. Johnny Clocks liked a drink, always had, and his way of dealing with what had happened was to hit the bottle, which he did in spectacular fashion. Both of them thought they'd been successful in hiding their demons and, for the most part, they'd been right, but Clocks had been the luckier one — he was still at work and had his mind occupied.

During the Walker case, Clocks had been waiting on the results of his application to become an inspector. He'd passed the exam, but no one believed he'd actually make the rank. However, fate, in the form of Commissioner Young, decided to help his application along. He knew good, loyal officers when he saw them and if Johnny Clocks had a bit of an attitude, so what? He'd had it himself at Clocks's age, still did. He knew he'd had Paterson's back, up on that bridge, and he respected him for it.

So Young, with his ability to understand people better than most, had their number, and threw as much help their way in the form of counselling and therapy as the Met could muster. Clocks was on the mend, Paterson not so much.

The thin razorblade made a tiny scratching noise on the glass table top as Paterson scraped together the last few traces of powder. It formed a pathetically thin line. He took one last snort, rubbed his nose furiously for a second or two, then let out a sharp breath as the drug reached his brain. He pulled himself to his feet and wobbled a bit before standing upright with a ram-rod-straight back, like a sergeant major showing off before drilling his new recruits.

He looked down at his trousers to make sure that there were no traces of powder on them, brushed himself down a couple of times and picked up the photo of Lisa. With the heel of one hand he wiped tears from his cheeks, kissed her photograph and put it back on the mantelpiece along with a dozen others. He stood and looked at it for a moment, then screamed and, crying and cursing, kicked in the screen of his TV. He tore open his jacket, struggled violently to get his arms out, flung it on the floor and jumped up and down on the back of the telly until he was spent. Less than thirty seconds had elapsed but it was enough. It had helped. For now.

His chest heaving, he cautiously stepped off of the broken telly, careful to avoid the shards of glass and plastic. Calm now, he retrieved his jacket, shook it straight, put it back on and walked out the door. He'd have to call his cleaner on the way in and explain.

As he drove through the streets, his mind began to serve up unwanted images, and the anger began to rise once more. Paterson gripped the steering wheel, clenched his jaw and let out a roar. As he did, his mobile phone rang.

CHAPTER SIX

'Well, that didn't take long, did it? What's it been since Davey Caine? Twenty hours?' Standing behind the blue and white tape, Paterson looked across at the dead man. This time they'd arrived on scene as the forensic tent was going up and gotten a rare opportunity to see the victim's body out in the wild. The wild, in this case, was Rose Alley, a five-minute stroll from the Globe Theatre on Southwark's Bankside. The victim was a white male, middle-aged. He'd taken a bullet to the side of the head and, for some reason that would amuse Johnny Clocks for hours to come, his trousers were around his knees and his penis out.

Peter Repps, the crime scene manager, was busy barking his orders in a strong Yorkshire accent. Paterson and Clocks already had theirs. Sign in, await instructions, stay on the plates — don't even think of touching him. Normally they would have been given paper suits and a whole lot more protocol but Repps was under pressure and the two cops knew what they were doing. Repps wanted the tent up as soon as possible and he wanted the press kept away. He knew it wouldn't be long before the pack of hyenas turned up and he wanted the scene locked down before they started taking photographs of everything in sight.

'I'll be with you in a minute,' said Repps. He gave them a thumbs-up and went back to his work.

'Talk to me, John.' Paterson turned away from the dead man. 'Speculate with me.'

'Okay. First and most obvious, why's he got his knob out?'

'Taking a piss, perhaps?'

'Hey!' Clocks shouted to Repps. ''S there a puddle of piss anywhere near him?'

Repps, a tad annoyed at the interruption, shook his head.

'Okay, then,' said Paterson. 'Perhaps he got lucky with someone, so to speak. They brought him here and killed him.'

'And left his knob hanging out?'

'Why would they put it back?'

Clocks nodded. Good point. 'Maybe whoever did it took it out.'

'What? After they killed him?' said Paterson. 'Why would someone do that?'

'Don't have a bloody clue. Maybe it's some sort of message. I'm speculating,' said Clocks. 'There's not much around here, not in this street, not in this area. It's mostly offices. You've got the theatre over the back there,' he pointed with his chin, 'and that's about it.'

'Fair enough. Perhaps he was a burglar then.'

'Who shoots burglars?'

'Mostly old men on farms, I think.'

'Clearly doesn't apply here. Besides, how many burglars do you know make a habit of running around with their dicks out?'

'I've not known any to be honest. Perhaps it's a new craze, stops people getting a look at their faces. Yeah, the dick's the mystery here, innit?'

Clocks took a quick sideways look at the dead man. 'Not a bad-looking fella, so maybe we stick with the theory that he was having a knee-trembler with a girl.'

'Could have been a man, John. Equal opps and all that.' Paterson shrugged.

'Okay, a bloke then. So, he's doin' the nasty dance and whoever he's dancing with shoots him in the head?'

'Possible.'

'Unlikely though,' said Clocks. 'If you're gonna shoot someone one-on-one in the head, it's usually gonna be either in the front or the back, not the side. Front or back requires distance. Arm's length as a minimum. Shooting in the side of the head requires a shot taken up close, which would put the shooter too close to the gun. Things could go wrong. Or, they were standing side on to each other which ain't normally first date behaviour. People havin' sex don't usually stand side by side.'

'So, chances are someone else pulled the trigger. A second person, hiding,' Paterson looked around, 'behind the bins?'

'Yeah, maybe. Seems the most likely. 'Scuse me,' Clocks shouted to Repps. 'Any chance we can have a look now?'

Repps looked slightly put out, but his team were well into the swing of things now. He could spare five minutes. He beckoned Clocks and Paterson forward and they slipped under the tape. 'This is Detective Superintendent Paterson and I'm DI Clocks. Murder squad. What's the story with him?'

Repps barked a few more orders to his team before turning to Clocks. 'Sorry. Don't like things being out in the open too long. Buggers up the evidence, you see. Come on, gents. Stay on the plates.'

'Is this how he was found?' said Clocks.

'Aye,' said Repps, dropping to one knee. He beckoned to Paterson and Clocks. They knelt and leaned in close. 'Face up. Small hole in the temple indicates a small-calibre handgun, nice and easy to conceal. The dark marks around the hole are, I would say, powder burns, so the shooter held the gun very close, or likely pressed it against the skin. Won't know for certain until he's on the slab but I'd bet my pension on it. This, gentlemen, looks like a good old-fashioned gangland execution, and you don't see those very often these days.' He launched into self-parody, ramping up his accent. 'Eee, lad. Looks like there's trouble at t'mill.'

'What about his knob?' said Clocks.

'Yes, it's certainly interesting. Don't see many of them.'

'Well, there's plenty of 'em 'iding behind desks in Scotland Yard,' Clocks quipped.

Repps gave a slight chuckle. 'Plenty in my office too.' He pointed to the dead man's penis. 'There's what looks like traces of sperm on the tip.'

Clocks screwed his face up. 'So, he *was* getting his end away then?'

'Would seem so,' said Repps. He shone his torch at it. 'If he wasn't wearing a condom, then we should have plenty of DNA to work with.'

'Any ID on him?' Clocks said.

'Yes, there was.' He called over to his exhibits officer, who rifled through various plastic bags before pulling out one that contained a driving licence. 'Uniform found it next to his body.'

Paterson took the licence, tilted it to reduce the glare from the plastic bag and matched the face on it with that of the dead man.

He handed it to Clocks.

'Graham Stokes,' Clocks read. 'Don't know the name. East End address though.' They looked at each other. 'Bet you a pound to a pinch of shit this is one of Tanner's boys.' He handed the licence back to Paterson. 'Poor bastard's poked his head on the wrong side of the pond and got himself a nutting for his troubles.'

'He also has a couple of tattoos on his neck and his wrists. All images of Jesus. Obviously, a true believer.' Repps pointed to the visible ones. It was easy to recognise the face of Jesus, and the crown of thorns was a dead give-away.

Paterson shrugged. 'Yeah, whatever. Did him a lot of good, didn't it?'

'Guv,' said Clocks, 'keep your eye on his knob for a while.'

'What? What for?'

'Well, I'm thinking,' he beamed at Paterson and turned to Repps, 'if he's a religious man and he had a rocket on when he died, I'm wondering if it's gonna come back on.'

'What?' said Repps. 'Why would it come back?'

'Dunno. I just thought he might have a res-erection!' Clocks erupted in a huge snort. So did Repps. Even Paterson couldn't help laughing.

'You never stop, do you?' said Paterson, and handed the licence back to the exhibits officer. Repps's laughter had turned into a wheeze, and he stood with his hands on his knees for a moment.

'Okay, fun's over,' said Paterson. 'John, this area is going to be smothered in CCTV. I want every tape covering the length of . . . what's the name of the street?'

'Park Street,' said Clocks.

'That's it. There has to be something.'

'I'll get Mick and Pete on it.'

'Okay,' said Paterson, turning back to Repps. 'Your people have our details. I want a report done, double quick.' He paused. 'There is indeed trouble at t'mill, and I want to stop it before it gets silly.'

'Got it, sir,' said Repps. 'As soon as.'

''Ere, guv,' said Clocks.

Clocks pulled out his phone, bent over the dead man and took a few photos, mostly head and shoulders. 'We've got a name and address, and a face to put it to, so we're quids in. He's gonna be in some database or other, so it shouldn't take us too long to see if there's a connection.'

Paterson pulled his collar up against the wind and checked his watch. 'Over to you, John. I've got my weekly with Eileen.'

Clocks rolled his eyes and waved him away.

CHAPTER SEVEN

Paterson really didn't want to be here. It grated on him that he had no choice in the matter. For the last few months, week after endless week, he'd been obliged to come and sit with Mrs Markham, the Met psychiatrist, and dump all of his problems and "buried" anxieties. Commissioner Young had insisted he attend these sessions in the wake of the Kamwelu case.

He knew Young was doing it because the murders in that case, involving dozens of children, had been particularly harrowing and he'd noticed a change in Paterson's behaviour, one that even Paterson knew was becoming more and more obvious. Young had explained that he'd be failing in his duty, as a boss and as a friend, if he didn't try to help Paterson come to terms with everything he'd lived through, but it still rankled him. Clocks was in exactly the same boat, and had railed against it too, but ultimately, you don't argue with the Commissioner if you want to keep your job.

Paterson settled into his chair, a big winged Chesterfield, and closed his eyes. Expressing emotion did not come easily to him, mostly on account of his father, who'd viewed such things as signifying weakness. His dad dealt with things in the good old ways — a session down the pub and a good shag with the missus — his own or someone else's. That's what got the tension out. The theory was the same anyway.

They went through the usual routine. She told him he was doing well, how these sessions were a safe space for him, that everything was confidential and that she'd be recording the session. That bit always gave Paterson a grin. If she was recording it, it wasn't confidential, was it? Some bod somewhere would be evaluating it.

'So, Ray, here we are at week fifteen. Time flies, doesn't it? Tell me about your week. What's been happening?'

Paterson was lounging back, legs crossed, and looking at his right shoe. He noticed a few scratches on it, courtesy of the TV he'd kicked the crap out of. He licked his thumb and rubbed at the scuff marks. Didn't make a difference. 'Not much. Pretty quiet, to be honest. Oh, hang on. Nearly forgot. We did come across some chap who'd been tied to a pole and burned alive. If it hadn't been for him, it would have been your ordinary bog-standard Monday. When we found him he was still smoking, his skin was dropping off and he stank to high heaven. Ever smelt burning man, Eileen?'

Eileen Markham looked exactly like everybody's idea of a psychiatrist. In her early sixties, no nonsense, smartly dressed, hair pulled back in a bun, minimal makeup and nothing remarkable about her appearance. Her one concession to femininity was her long, perfectly manicured nails. She was of the school of thought that maintained that the therapist should be detached at all times, and she was uncomfortable with the more open attitude of some of her younger, more progressive colleagues. The sloppy, hand-knitted jumper and sitting close weren't for her. Freud had served her well over the years, and she saw no reason to lower her standards or open her mind. However, she had seen her fair share of characters in that time, and Paterson's sarky attitude didn't faze her in the slightest. 'No, Ray, I haven't. I would imagine it to be . . . unpleasant. Tell me, how did it make you feel?'

Paterson sighed. Always this one question. The one psychiatrists always wheeled out, and had made whole careers and shedloads of money out of asking. 'Really, Eileen. Two hundred quid an hour, and that's what we start with. Bit early for that trite little question, isn't it?' He shook his head. 'Alright then. Let me tell you, Eileen. I didn't get a warm, fuzzy feeling in my tummy. To be honest, it made me feel very, very bad.' Now how would she react?

She smiled at him. 'Sorry to hear that, Ray. It must have been awful for you. Why don't we cut the silly little games and you tell me what's really going on inside your head? This is for your benefit, you know, not mine.'

Paterson smiled. *Game on.* For a second, it dawned on him how like Clocks he was becoming these days — bolshie with a little bit of fuck-it about him. 'Exactly how do I benefit, Eileen? I have to waste time sitting here talking about my feelings when I have a job to do, a killer to catch and a gangland war about to erupt. If you want to know, I'm bloody frustrated. Can't you just mark up your little sheet as "making progress," so I can get out of here and back to work?'

Eileen scribbled in her pad while he spoke, and that irked him. 'No. I'm sorry, Ray, not yet. I haven't seen much progress today. In fact, I haven't seen a lot of progress in your last few visits. Tell me how you're coping, Ray. Clearly you're upset, and I don't believe it's just to do with having to come here. Are you angry, Ray?'

Paterson leaned forward. 'Angry? Of course I'm fucking angry.' His voice rose. 'Seems to me I've got a lot to be angry about. My wife and friend being butchered. I've seen children dismembered purely out of greed, and I went to Africa where kids are huddled in a shelter with armed guards because some mad bastards with machetes think they can make them into trinkets to fight off evil spirits. I've seen a man burned to death out of ambition, and just before I came here, I was looking at a man who'd been shot in the head. So, yes, I am angry. Unbelievably angry!'

She noted it all down without once taking her eyes off of him. When his fists balled, his face reddened and his jaw set, she stopped writing. 'I understand—'

'No! No, you don't! You sit there in your little chair, in the safety of your big office, playing your fucking silly little mood music CDs in the background, and asking people stupid questions for a living. You have no idea at all what's going on, or how I feel. You couldn't begin to.' He shook his head, frustrated and disappointed with himself for losing it in front of her. He breathed deeply and sat back in the chair. 'Sorry,' he said, drumming his fingers on the arms of the chair.

'It's okay. I underst . . . I'm sorry.' She put the pad down.

The tension in his shoulders lessened slightly. His eyes darted around the room, avoiding hers. 'I'm sorry too. I just woke up in a bad place this morning, that's all.'

'Nightmares again?'

Now he did look at her. 'Yeah. Nightmares again.'

'Lisa?'

'Among others, but yeah, mostly Lisa.' His eyes began to moisten. She'd already seen the tears well up, so this time he let them stay. But, as is the way of men, he turned his gaze outward. He'd always liked the view from Eileen's office, which looked out across Hampstead Heath. It helped, if only briefly, to see some greenery.

'Ray, I know you hate this. I get it. I know you don't want to talk to me, I get that too, but you have to do something to help yourself. You can't keep it bottled it up like this. It's making you sick.'

'Sick? What do you mean sick? I'm fine. Tired and stressed, but that's the job. I'm not sick. In fact, I'm in good health. I eat well.' The McDonald's meal flashed into his mind.

'Have you had a drink lately?'

He shifted uncomfortably. 'No. No, I haven't.'

She looked doubtful, but kept her eyes on him. 'What about drugs, Ray? Are you using drugs?'

'What? Drugs? No. Fuck no. Where's that come from?' He began to fidget, crossing and uncrossing his feet and rubbing the back of one hand with the other. Eileen noted it.

'So, if I sent you for a blood test, you'd come back clean? Because, I must say, that's the worst bit of acting I've seen in a long while.'

Paterson stopped shifting about. 'That's up to you. I'd like to think that my word was good enough for you, but I understand — you have a job to do.' At university, Paterson had made money on the side by playing poker, a skill his father and uncles had taught him. The money was incidental, but the education was invaluable and had stood him in good stead when reading people and situations. He'd learned long ago how to bluff with a shit hand and he'd also learned when to lead into a weaker opponent with that same shit hand. He decided to bluff her and hope she went for it. If he'd read her right, her hand was weaker. He went with leading in. He lowered his head and managed to do a good impression of a little boy who'd been caught out. 'Okay, I've had a drink, I admit. Not much though, just a drop, I swear. I just needed a little something today. I'm sorry. Not drugs though, Eileen. I wouldn't touch that shit. That's not me.'

Many of Eileen's clients lied to her. But Paterson was damn good at it. Drink, no drugs. Okay. She went with it. 'I'll have to make a note of it, Ray. You understand that, don't you?'

Still playing the schoolboy, he said, 'It's okay. I know you have to.'

She gave him a thin smile. Inside, she felt for him. If it were her life, would she be able to bear that level of pain and suffering? She doubted it.

'Are you still seeing . . . what's her name? Carrie?'

Paterson had begun a sort of on-off relationship with DC Carrie Gedmine. He liked her, even cared for her, but it wasn't a particularly deep connection.

He nodded. 'Yeah, she comes around sometimes. She's okay, a good girl. I like her but she's a bit . . .' he shrugged, 'full on, y'know? And, best will in the world, I'm not looking for a life partner. I just can't do it. Not yet anyway.'

'Hmm. Do you think she could be a life partner, down the line?'

Paterson rubbed his tired eyes. 'Honestly? I don't think so. She's just too full on for me, she can be a bit aggressive.'

Eileen gave a wry smile.

'You know what I mean,' he said.

'You do martial arts, don't you?' she said, changing the subject before it became too uncomfortable.

'Hm, hm.' Paterson relaxed a bit. She'd jumped on a subject he was easy with.

'Does it help? The martial arts? I take it you fight, you don't just stand there doing the moves, like you see in the films?'

'Yes and yes,' he said.

'Do you enjoy it?' she said. Paterson nodded.

'When you fight—'

'Do I see people's faces? Is that what you're going to ask?' He rubbed at his shoe again.

'I wasn't, but since you've brought it up, do you?'

He stopped rubbing the shoe and stared at her. 'All the bloody time, Eileen.'

'Walker?'

He gave her a wry smile. 'Among others.'

'And these people you fight. Do you hurt them?'

The smile widened. 'Sometimes. Depends if they're trying to hurt me.'

'You have to let him go, Ray. You have to let them all go if you expect to heal. You can't bring Lisa back, or Dave, and you took your revenge on Walker—'

'Christ!' he shouted. 'How many more times? I've told you over and over. It wasn't a case of revenge. Fucker was trying to kill me or John. He'd already chucked Billy Kingston off the bridge, right in front of us, and was going to do us too. He was about to throw a knife at us. I had no choice.' He lowered his head and his voice. 'I didn't intend to kill him, I didn't.' It was the same lie he'd been telling everyone, ever since the night he'd shot Walker dead.

'Then why can you not accept that he's gone? That it's over?'

He leaned forward. 'I do accept it, I do, but he's not the only one, is he? There are more like him, always will be. Today's a case in point. Different method, this one, but still a killer.' He stood up and buttoned his jacket. 'If you'll excuse me, I really do have to go.'

'But, we haven't finish—'

He held his hand up. 'Listen, I appreciate what you're trying to do for me, but you have to understand. Their deaths . . . that's what drives me now. It's what gets me up in the mornings. It's why I remained a policeman, why I come to work. Their deaths remind me that there's evil out there, Eileen, in the shape of vicious, screwed-up monsters disguised as men,' he recalled Blessing Kamwelu, '*and* women. And for as long as I'm able, I will do my best to catch them and deal with them any way I can.' He headed for the door and stopped. 'Careful how you write up that last bit, Eileen. I don't want people getting the wrong idea about me. See you next week.' He left, closing the door quietly behind him.

Eileen picked up her pad and started to write.

CHAPTER EIGHT

Behind his desk and up to his eyes in paperwork, Paterson was tired. The day had been much longer than he would have liked and there was still much to do. He glanced at his watch. DCI Alliston was due any minute for an update. He wondered if he had time for a quick gulp from the whisky bottle. A sharp tap on the door told him he didn't.

DCI Alliston hadn't waited to be called. He walked in, closing the door behind him. 'Sir.'

'Martin. Good evening. Come on in, make yourself comfortable. Can I get you anything? Tea? Coffee? Whisky?'

'Tea's fine, sir.'

Paterson cursed inwardly. *Bollocks. I'm gasping for a drink.* He called for someone to bring two teas while Alliston took off his overcoat and pulled up a chair. 'While we're waiting,' Paterson said, 'let me give you an update. As you know, we went to see Caine as agreed. Unfortunately, things got a little bit heated. As you said, he's not a pleasant man.'

'Hmm,' said Alliston. 'Perhaps it might have gone a bit better if DI Clocks wasn't such a prick. Wouldn't you say?' There was a slight edge to his voice.

Paterson frowned. Where was this coming from? 'I don't understand,' he said. Then it dawned on him.

'Yep,' said Alliston. 'Caine was telling the truth. Place is bugged, top to bottom. Has been for years. Because he knows this, he does his business in only one of two places. In the house there's a small room, a bit like a panic room, or he uses the sauna at his private club. Can't get into either of those and in the sauna, it would be a waste of time, the steam just screws up the electronics.'

'Ah,' said Paterson. 'Then you know what happened.'

'Yes, sir, and I'm not very impressed.'

There was a pause while the office manager, John Hardiman, brought in a tray with a pot of tea and an assortment of biscuits.

'Sir, I have to ask this. What the hell is wrong with Inspector Clocks? I specifically said not to wind up Billy Caine and I also said you were to do nothing to jeopardise our ongoing operation. Yet within what, five minutes, Inspector Clocks lays into him and nearly starts World War Three — a war, I might add, you were always going to lose.'

Paterson poured the tea and handed a cup to Alliston. 'I'll admit, I was surprised at his behaviour, but—'

'We were all surprised, sir. You should know that we've pulled his jacket from personnel and, quite frankly, I'm quite shocked that he still has a job, let alone a senior position in a murder team. He is unprofessional to the point of being an embarrassment. You might want to reconsider his suitability for his role, Superintendent. I certainly would.' He took a sip of his tea and settled back into his seat.

Paterson sat up straight and bit his lip. 'Did you know Billy Caine has Alzheimer's? That he's dying from it?'

DCI Alliston had raised his cup to his lips. He put it down. 'What? No. No, I didn't. How did you find out?'

'You didn't know? Bear with me a second then, while I get this straight. How long have you had an undercover officer working Caine? Five years, was it?' Alliston nodded. 'Okay, five years wheedling his way into the organisation, including gaining Caine's trust and working closely with him, I presume. Five years bugging his houses. And yet you never knew he had Alzheimer's. Never noted any changes in his personality. Never had a goddamn bloody clue. Jesus! My man was in the toilet three minutes and found out more than your lot managed in five years, *and* what he found out changes everything. So, if I were you, before you come in here showing off and telling me what to do with my officer, you might want to take a good hard look at your UC and perhaps consider *his* suitability for the role, because clearly, he's fucking useless. Wouldn't you say?'

'My apologies, sir,' said Alliston. 'I was out of line.'

'Yes, you were. DI Clocks has his faults and is a tad old school, but he's a bloody solid copper. And that's all that counts. So, we'll leave it there, then.'

'Sir.' Alliston nodded. 'What did DI Clocks find to confirm this?'

'As I said, Clocks was in the toilet and he decided to have a nosey around in the bathroom cabinet.' Alliston winced. Illegal search. Paterson ignored it. 'He found several bottles of medication that are used to treat early to mid-stage Alzheimer's. The bottles were all in his name, so there's no doubt. DI Clocks and I have bounced it around and we're of the view that somehow, Tanner has found out and has seized the opportunity to grab power. We think it's likely that he had Caine's son murdered because he was next in line to the throne. With him gone, Caine's now isolated and weak. Just a theory. No hard evidence. If we did, Tanner would be in custody.' He fixed his gaze on Alliston.

DCI Alliston rubbed his face. He too looked tired. 'Sounds reasonable, sir. Thank you for that. To update you, Caine went to his private club and met up with his lawyer, Larry Trimble. Trimble is at the top of his game, a clever bastard who looks after Caine exclusively, and he's not cheap. Our man says they had a meet in the sauna, just the two of them. Something is obviously going on. Something big. We don't know what, but it may well have something to do with what you just suggested. That said, it could just be that he's looking to sell up, liquidate his assets. We'll work it all up and see what we can find out and get back to you, unless of course Inspector Clocks can do another recce for us.'

Paterson let the little dig go. His mobile buzzed a message. 'Excuse me a sec . . . fuck. It's Clocks. We've got another murder, another burning. Bermondsey Spa Gardens.'

* * *

Paterson and Alliston walked into the gardens and headed toward the crime scene. Paterson could smell the smoke before he saw the few thin wisps illuminated by the halogen lamps set up around the scene. Johnny Clocks broke away from his discussion with the crime scene manager and greeted Paterson. He barely glanced at Alliston.

'What's the story with this one, John?' Paterson looked over his DI's shoulder and could just make out a blackened, smouldering corpse standing upright between two partially burned trees. Alliston coughed. 'Sorry,' said Paterson. 'Mr Repps. Good to see you again. Was hoping we wouldn't for a while, but there you go. This is DCI Alliston.' The two men nodded to each other while Paterson moved closer to the scene.

'Very similar to the last one, guv,' said Clocks. 'Male, handcuffed to a stake, burned alive. Found by a jogger.

Said he heard the screams and ran over to see what was going on. Bet he wishes he hadn't.'

Paterson craned his neck to see if he could get a better look, but the trees hid the dead man. It wasn't a problem. He'd see the photos in due course.

'He said he was out for his evening jog and came into the park from Alscot Road, behind us.' He pointed to the entrance. 'His normal route takes him straight through the middle of the park and out into Grange Road. As he came in, he noticed a car parked up in the middle of the road ahead of him. He thought it unusual because although it's wide enough for a car, people don't generally drive in, and they certainly don't do it late at night. Anyway, as he got closer to the car he heard a God-awful scream and two people come running out of the trees towards him. Get this. One of them was a girl, apparently.'

'He get a look at her? Either of them?' said Paterson.

'Not a proper look, no. Said the man was carrying a gun, which he pointed straight at him, and then they jumped into the car and screamed off into Grange Road.'

'Which way'd they go?'

'Slung a left. Coulda gone anywhere from there.' Clocks shrugged. 'Anyway, our hero didn't know what to do. He tried to help the victim by beatin' the flames out with his hands. Result? Second-degree burns. Probably be on the local news tonight showin' off his bandages.' Clocks rolled his eyes. 'Who in their right mind tries to beat out flames with their bare hands?'

'I suppose he felt compelled to do something,' Repps said. 'Can't just stand around and watch a man scream his way to death. Got to try and do something. We'd all react the same, wouldn't we?'

'I bleedin' wouldn't,' said Clocks. 'I need my hands.'

'Can he give us *any* kind of description of the suspects?' asked DCI Alliston.

'Nah. We can't get much out of him. Shocked up to his eyeballs. He's in the back of the ambulance with a couple of PCs. They may have something by now, but I doubt it.'

'Jesus!' said Paterson. 'This is crazy.' He glanced at his watch. 'Half eight in the evening. What the hell is the matter with these people?' Nobody answered him.

'Not like they're gonna get seen, is it?' said Clocks. 'It's November, dark and miserable. It's a miracle our jogger was around to witness as much as he did.'

'How about the local yobbery? They see anything?'

Clocks shrugged. 'Maybe. But it's not like they're gonna help us, are they?'

'There was a driving licence found on the ground just in front of him,' said Repps. 'Looks like whoever did this wanted this one identified too. My exhibits officer has it.' He swivelled around. 'Ah. There he is.' He pointed to a man standing over a bundle of brown paper bags, writing in a notebook. The three policemen walked over and asked to see the licence.

'It's Harry Long,' said Alliston, tilting the licence to get a better look. 'Harry the Dog, he's known as. All-round vicious bastard and one of Caine's most feared enforcers. He was one of the top echelon of Caine's boys. Well trusted.'

Johnny Clocks looked at Paterson. *Echelon*? Paterson smiled at him meaning, "I'll tell you what it means later."

Clocks shrugged. Then he grinned. 'Well, he's Harry the Hot Dog now, ain't he?' Even Alliston gave that one a smile. 'Right, Ray, I've had enough of this bollocks. This has got Tanner written all over it. We need to stop fuckin' about and get our arses over to him a bit quick and drag the fucker in on suspicion of murder times two.' He looked across at Alliston, who said nothing.

'Mr Alliston,' said Paterson. 'We are going to introduce ourselves to Tanner. You need to do whatever you have to. Go and tell your supervisors, and figure out how to keep your UC man safe, if that's necessary.'

Alliston took a deep breath. He wasn't going to even try to argue this one. 'He's not at home, Mr Paterson. I had intel earlier that he's gone out. He's not been back home all day.'

'Where is he, then?' said Paterson.

'He's in Birmingham.'

'Birmingham?' said Clocks. 'What's he up to there?'

'Business, I suppose,' said Alliston. 'He's keeping busy, no doubt ensuring he's as far away from this as he can get. Soon as he's back, I'll let you know. Mr Paterson, do yourselves a favour and get a warrant. Do it properly, he's well clued up. And make sure you take a lot of backup with you. Serious backup. You think Caine's a handful? This one's off his bloody head.'

Paterson glanced at his watch again. No point going to an empty house.

'I'm not getting a warrant, Mr Alliston. We both know we won't find anything to tie him to this if he's as clued up as you say. We're just gonna go talk to him. Let him know we know and, if he turns nasty, then that's up to him. We won't need a warrant for that, will we?'

Alliston nodded. He turned to Clocks. 'Inspector,' he said, and hesitated. No point giving him advice, but it was worth a shot. 'Watch out for his old dad. You'll know what I mean when you meet him.'

CHAPTER NINE

Jackie Weston had found her little slice of heaven in the shape of a small farmhouse tucked away in a corner of Galway. She looked out of her kitchen window and watched her husband chase their six-year-old daughter around the large garden. At the age of fifty-three, her husband Patrick, a London city banker, had finally made enough money for both of them to retire early. The job had involved setting up a deal between two of the biggest financial institutes in the world and seeing it through to completion. As a reward, he'd been paid a six-figure bonus. Not a massive amount, considering the stress he'd undergone, but it was enough for him to add to their savings, call it a day at work, sell the house in London and buy a nice place back in his native Ireland.

They'd been in their forties when they met — Jackie forty-two, Patrick forty-six — and, after a few unsuccessful attempts, finally had themselves a beautiful daughter. Emily's dark green eyes and red hair pointed to her father's Irish roots, and were what had given him the idea of retuning to Galway. Occasionally, in idle moments, Jackie would find herself reflecting back on her tough upbringing on a Peckham council estate, but she never allowed herself to dwell on it. She was just glad to see the back of her drunken mother, absent father and wayward brother. Leaving London behind wasn't an issue for her, and she'd settled easily into the little community.

Today was baking day and she was busy cooking a batch of fairy cakes for Emily. They were her favourites, just needing to be filled with buttercream and sprinkled in edible glitter, each one crowned with a butterfly. Jackie moved away from the window and danced across the kitchen floor. "Mambo Number Five" was playing on her little kitchen radio. She never could resist dancing to it. It was one of those songs.

She bent down to the oven, pulled out a tray of hot, delicious-smelling cakes and dumped them on the table, where she set about the task of mixing up the buttercream. At the top of the hour, the news came on and, not paying much attention, she heard something about a man in London being shot in the head and that police thought it was gang-related, and something else about a man being burned alive. She spun the dial on the radio until she found another happy song.

The doorbell rang. 'Who the feck's that?' Her Galway accent was coming along nicely.

On the doorstep was a man of about thirty. He was nicely dressed and well groomed — not a bad-looking fella in a way. Behind him, coming up the path, was a younger woman, maybe mid- to late twenties, slim and very pretty. Jackie noted the car parked in the road.

'I'm so sorry to trouble you but I'm afraid we're lost,' said the man. His accent gave him away as a Londoner, but a well-educated one. 'We're on our way to visit some friends in Roscommon. We were doing alright until the satnav packed up, and now we're lost and without a phone signal.' He held up his phone to show her. 'I was wondering if you might have a landline I could use, just to let them know we're still on our way but will be late.'

Jackie wiped her hands on the tea towel and peered at the phone. She couldn't see the screen properly but wasn't particularly bothered. They seemed like a nice couple and, besides, she and Patrick struggled to get a signal on their mobiles at the best of times.

'Are we far from Roscommon?' said the man.

Jackie stepped back and gestured for them both to come in. 'No. Sure an' it's only thirty miles to the border. But you're facing the wrong way for a start. Come in and make your call and I'll draw you a map. Set you in the right direction.'

'Thank you,' said the girl. 'That's very kind of you.'

'Would you like some tea?'

'No, thank you, not for me,' said the girl, 'but would you mind if I used your loo? We've been driving around for hours and the tea I had at the airport has finally filtered through.'

'Of course you may. The bathroom is upstairs, third on the right. Mind the stairs, there's a few toys scattered about. I haven't had time to pick them up yet.' The girl nodded and headed for the stairs. 'Oh, and be careful with the handle,' Jackie said. 'You need to push it down twice, fast, or it won't flush properly.' The girl nodded again and made her way up, stepping carefully over the toys.

'Thank you,' said the man. 'I'm Adrian and that's my wife, Izzy, short for Isabel.'

'I'm Jackie. She's very beautiful, your wife. You're a lucky man, so.' Her accent was becoming slightly more pronounced. Maybe she wanted him to think she was a born local, and not some relocated Londoner. Didn't matter. She was sure he wouldn't notice anyway. He just wanted the phone.

'I am indeed a lucky man,' said Adrian. 'She's the love of my life. I'm sorry . . . Jackie, was it? But I really need to use the phone. Our friends will be worried.'

'I'm sorry. There's me chatting away. Of course, the phone. It's out here in the hallway.' She showed him where it was, went back into the kitchen and looked out of the window. Patrick and Emily were still chasing each other round the garden. She smiled.

* * *

The step squeaked under her weight. Izzy winced. So did the second one, but the rest stayed silent. At the top of the stairs, she took a quick look down before heading for the bathroom, treading lightly in case any other boards should creak. The wallpaper in the hallway had big flowers — old-fashioned, as you would expect with people in their age bracket. Izzy took her smartphone out of her back pocket, wandered into the bathroom, launched the camera app and began filming.

Swinging the camera about, she recorded every little detail before meandering back out into the hall, camera held at arm's length. Immediately to her left was Jackie and Patrick's bedroom. She noted the floor covering. Carpet. No noise. She stepped inside the door and filmed the whole room before moving to the spare room. She filmed that too. Emily's room was at the other end of the hallway, by the stairs. This was the one she really wanted.

She stopped and listened. Heard Adrian's muffled voice and knew she had about a minute of filming left before he got off the phone. That made three minutes in total. The amount of time they had been allocated to avoid arousing suspicion. Adrian was to make a call, and the person at the other end would keep him engaged in conversation for three minutes, to make it all look real.

The room was a little girl's paradise, all rainbows, glitter and pink. Pink walls, broken up by the unicorn and fairy posters blu-tacked side by side in neat rows. The carpet was patterned with rainbows, matching the one big blind, pulled halfway down, casting a faint half rainbow onto Emily's bed, which was covered in small furry animals. Little tiaras and glitter wands were scattered over the full-sized dresser, and a princess dress had been thrown over the chair. Stuck to the ceiling was a poster of the princess of all princesses — Elsa from *Frozen*. Izzy filmed it all, moving in for a few close-ups of various objects. She peeped carefully out of the window and saw Patrick and Emily heading into the house. She held the phone up and caught a few seconds of shaky footage. She was done.

She stepped back out in the hallway and, still filming, took one last look back. There, on the wall, she spotted a framed photo of Emily and Jackie that she'd missed coming out of the bathroom. She heard Adrian say his goodbyes and finish the call. She quickly took some footage of the photo before turning and heading back down the stairs. She almost bumped into Patrick, who was just starting to climb them. He looked startled.

'Oh! Sorry,' she said.

'Who are you?' he said. 'What's going on?'

Seeing Emily suddenly take fright, Jackie explained what was going on. Nevertheless, Emily decided that it was safer to hide behind her father's legs until these two strangers had left. She clung on tight, resisting all attempts at prising her loose, even when the pretty lady told her she was very beautiful, like a princess.

Jackie handed Adrian a rough, hand-drawn map and explained how he needed to turn the car around, follow the road to the next crossroads where he was to turn left. The map would take them onto Roscommon from there.

Adrian and Izzy said their goodbyes, thanked them again for their hospitality and offered to pay for the call. Patrick and Jackie wouldn't hear of it. Glad to help. They stood at the door and watched as Adrian swung the car around in the drive, and then off on their way to Roscommon.

As they walked back into the house, muttering things like, 'nice couple,' and 'lovely girl,' it suddenly dawned on Jackie that she hadn't heard the toilet flush.

CHAPTER TEN

Nestled in the heart of south-east London, Greenwich Park, even on drab days, is still a beautiful place. Situated on a hill with commanding views across the River Thames and the City of London skyline, it was the birthplace of Henry VIII, and today houses the Royal Observatory. Through its ancient courtyard runs the Prime Meridian Line which divides the earth's western and eastern hemispheres and is used as the reference point that marks Greenwich Mean Time. Back in the 1800s, this seriously narked the French, who decided to stick with the Paris Meridian, ignored by all and giving kudos to the British, who have spent the best part of a thousand years going out of their way to annoy them.

The park is well known for its age-old connections with royalty, but today its guest of honour was Metropolitan Police Commissioner Wallace Young, who sat in a small café opposite the observatory in the company of detectives Paterson and Clocks.

Ensconced in an uncomfortable metal chair, Commissioner Young looked every inch the man of high office. He wore an immaculately tailored, navy blue Savile

Row suit with a crisp, white shirt. His cufflinks bore the Met Police crest, as did his tie. He was looking older these days. His steel grey hair was thinner, which Paterson put down to age and the stress of office. God knew, he and Clocks had provided enough of the latter.

Over the last few years, the three men had formed an unusual bond, after Young had taken it upon himself to support the two policemen. He, but few others, believed them to be men of the right stuff — decent, honest, loyal and more than willing to get their hands dirty. He was well aware that neither of them was whiter than white, likely covering up the circumstances of Adam Walker's death and most certainly having had a hand in the deaths of General Kamwelu and his wife Blessing. Even so, Wallace Young was perfectly comfortable with the brand of justice these two villains had been served. He knew, too, that Paterson and Clocks probably had a hand in the demises of the various high-level government officials who had supported the general and paved the way for him and his wife to ply their evil trade.

'Thank you for coming, sir,' said Paterson. 'I appreciate it.'

'No trouble, Ray. It's on the way in to the Yard. Where's Clocks?'

'At the counter. He's getting the teas in.'

Wallace Young grimaced. He'd had tea here before. 'Oh, before we get started, you two haven't forgotten my retirement party, have you?'

Paterson looked a bit perplexed for a second, then said, 'No. Course not. When is it again?'

'Last day of the month. At the Yard, eighth floor.'

'Wouldn't miss it for the world.'

'Hmm,' said Young, 'I hope not. I've made sure we have jelly and ice-cream for John. I'll look silly if I've ordered it and no one eats it.'

Paterson laughed. 'He'll turn up for that, no worries.'

'So, what can I do for you today? Problems?'

Paterson flashed him a quick smile. 'Possibly, sir. You know us.' He looked over to the counter and hoped Clocks had remembered to get the Commissioner a proper cup. Wallace Young was a rough diamond, but over the years he'd gotten accustomed to drinking decent tea from a decent cup. His heart sank a little when Clocks turned around and he saw the tray loaded with three polystyrene cups complete with lids.

'Sorry, sir.'

'There you go, gents. Three teas. Guv, before you say anything, they're all out of cups.'

'John,' said Young, 'with all due respect, bollocks.' He glanced at his watch. 'It's nine thirty in the morning, the place opened half an hour ago and we're the only three in here. I seriously doubt they've run out.'

Clocks gave him his best Cheshire cat grin. 'Fair cop, guv. I could've got you a cup but, straight up, they're all cracked and shitty. Don't know who's had their dirty little gobs on 'em. This is much more civilised, and you get more tea in them. What's not to love?'

Young pulled the lid off his cup and took a wary sniff at the insipid, steaming hot liquid that masqueraded as tea. He wrinkled his nose. 'This abomination that passes for tea, Inspector. That's what's not to love.' He sat back in his chair.

'Sir,' said Paterson, 'you know we're looking into the death of David Caine, Billy Caine's son.'

Young nodded. 'Yes, of course. That chap who burned at the stake, yes?'

'That's him, sir. We went to see his dad, Billy Caine. You no doubt know that he's a big-time villain this side of the river, right?'

'Go on.' Young took a sip of the tea. It tasted every bit as bad as it looked.

Clocks noticed his expression. 'You're not gonna waste that, are you, guv? That cost me one pound thirty.'

Clocks shook his head. Tea like this grew on you. You had to give it time.

'Let me give you some advice, John. Next time pay no less than one seventy-five for a tea. That way you'll know you're at least getting something reasonable. Ray, please go on.'

'Well, we got a visit from a DCI Alliston from SCO7. You heard of him?'

'Rings a bell but I don't recall meeting him. Why?'

'Well,' Clocks jumped in, 'he reckons he's got a couple of UCs in play this side and north of the water. They're sittin' on Caine and a bloke called Tanner. Both are supposed to be buried deep and he don't want us pissin' in his pond and splashin' about in it. When he was tellin' us this, he made a point of sayin' that we was to tread very carefully and that while we could ask Caine questions we were not, under any circumstances, to formally question him. Said there was an interest from upstairs. We both got the impression he was tryin' to tell us there was a hands-off policy.'

Young closed his eyes and hoped to heaven that DI Johnny Clocks would not be allowed to give press conferences. Ever.

'Obviously, sir,' said Paterson, 'we're not comfortable about that. Given the nature and background of both these men, it may well be that we do, at some point, have to get a bit more formal. Never know what we're going to dig up once we start, so I'd appreciate it if you could have a little look into it for me. Find out if there is a hands-off and, if there is, what we can do about it when things go south.'

'What do you mean "when?" What makes you so sure things are going to go south?'

'Well,' said Clocks, 'we now have another two bodies. Another one burned alive and one shot in the nut. It seems our men are involved in a tit-for-tat, and it's only going to get worse. Caine wants revenge for his boy and I reckon he'll do whatever he needs to get it. Once we get things tightened up a bit, we're gonna go ruffling a few feathers.'

Young wriggled in the metal chair and folded his arms. 'Any hard evidence against either of them? Can you bring them in?'

Paterson shook his head. 'Only on suspicion. There's no hard evidence against either of them and to be honest, what would be the point? These two aren't amateurs. They'll get their fancy lawyers in, clamp up tighter than a duck's arse, we'll all get slapped with a lawsuit or some human rights violation or other and all we'd be doing is wasting everyone's time.'

Commissioner Young stared off into the distance. He didn't like the idea of a hands-off policy, even if it had been put in place for a good reason.

Paterson snapped him out of it. 'I wondered if there was anyone you could approach who would be discreet. I know that if we were to start digging around into unauthorised policies it would only upset people, and obviously there's the UCs to consider. We don't want to put them in harm's way, but this is a murder enquiry and that's got to take precedence. Given that the vic is a villain's son and the suspect is another, equally nasty piece of work, no one's coming out of this smelling of roses.'

'Leave it with me, Ray. I'll make some enquiries and get back to you as soon as.' Johnny Clocks's metal chair scraped across the tiled floor with a loud screech. A couple of the staff raised their heads. 'In the meantime, you do whatever you need to. Just make sure you inform me before you do it.'

Paterson and Young both placed their chairs neatly and quietly under the table. Clocks gave his a shove with his foot, taking his time and loving the looks he got. 'Of course, sir,' said Paterson. 'You know us.'

Commissioner Young rolled his eyes and started toward the door. 'And that, Superintendent Paterson, is no doubt some sort of code for "You won't know a thing until the shit hits the fan.'" He collected his cashmere overcoat from the rack and, slipping it on, gave Paterson a wry smile. 'Don't forget my leaving bash. No excuses. You too, John — I can promise you jelly and ice-cream.' Clocks gave him the thumbs-up.

Wallace Young straightened his collar and strode, straight-backed, out of the café.

CHAPTER ELEVEN

Detective Constable Amelia Hill checked her watch. She'd now spent the best part of five hours going over the CCCTV tapes that had been collected from businesses in and around Park Street. There were six tapes in total that covered the area, including one that monitored the entrance to Rose Alley and along its entire length. That one was hers.

Graham Stokes's time of death had been put at any time between midnight and four a.m. and Paterson had instructed his team of officers to watch the tapes from two hours either side. With forty-eight hours of video to view, Paterson's resources were stretched thin, but he'd managed to gather a team of five to pore over the tapes.

Viewing CCTV tapes was the kind of job that called for numerous cups of strong coffee or energy drinks, sometimes both, and it took a supreme effort not to nod off every so often. Here, in the confines of a dark and stuffy room, and working in complete silence, Amelia was struggling to keep her eyes open. On the desk in front of her was a clipboard containing log sheets on which she was to note anything of significance, some scrap paper on which to make her first, scribbly notes, five empty tins of Red Bull and a cup of lukewarm coffee. Staring dully at the screen, she was reaching for the cup when her heart gave a little jump. It wasn't down to the caffeine.

From the top left corner of her screen, a figure entered Park Street and headed toward the alley. The image quality wasn't good enough to pick out any significant detail but from the gait, she made the assumption that she was looking at a man. She noted the time stamp — one fifteen. Unusual for anybody to be around at that time of the morning in that particular area, unless they were up to no good. She stopped the tape, picked up her pen and scribbled a few notes. The man looked to be wearing all black. He was thin and appeared to be wearing some sort of head covering, perhaps a balaclava, or maybe a hoodie. He was walking quickly, head down and he dipped quickly into Rose Alley. Things were looking up for Amelia.

Her eyes glued to the screen, she watched the man walk toward the back of the alley and a small cluster of industrial-sized wheelie bins. When he dipped down behind one of them, she reached for the phone.

* * *

'Evening, sir,' Amelia said as Paterson walked into the viewing room with Clocks. 'I'm sorry to have troubled you but you need to see this.' The other four detectives had all left their seats and had been watching the tape pending their arrival. They moved out of the way, sharpish.

'What we got, 'Melia? I have to be somewhere,' Paterson said.

'Watch, sir.' She rewound the video and clicked pause. 'We've got him on CCTV in the Globe Theatre, watching a play. It seems he was alone there. After the play, we tracked him through the streets but not all of them. Not every business had CCTV, I'm afraid.' She pressed the play button. 'The next time we pick him up, a few hours later, he's with a girl. But look at this.' She pressed play and pointed to the screen and the figure in black. They all watched intently as the man ducked down behind the bins. 'That's timed at zero one sixteen. Nothing happens now until zero one thirty-seven.' She fast forwarded to one thirty-six and pressed play. Within a few seconds, two people walked into view from the right-hand side of the screen — a man and a woman. All three detectives were riveted to the video. The woman seemed to be guiding the man, who was staggering from side to side, clearly under the influence of something.

'That's our boy Stokes, yes?' said Clocks.

'Yessir,' said Amelia, 'most definitely. Watch.'

'Ties in with toxicology,' said Paterson, absently. 'Said his alcohol level showed him to be pissed as a parrot. Coked up, too.'

The woman walked the unsteady man toward the wheelie bins where she suddenly started to kiss him, passionately. Clocks squinted at the screen. 'Quality is shit! Can't see sod all.'

'You'll see what you need to see, sir. Be patient.' After a few seconds of kissing, the woman pulled something out of her clutch bag, put her hand to her mouth and squatted down.

'Is she . . .?' said Clocks, after a few seconds.

'Yessir,' said Amelia. 'She's actually giving him a blowjob and a pretty good one judging by the way her head is moving.' She flashed her eyebrows at him, then turned her attention back to the screen.

'Can we zoom in?' Clocks said.

'No, sir. It's a recording.'

'Oh, yeah. Good point,' he said, sounding slightly embarrassed. 'Fuckin' 'ell. She's goin' at him like a lunatic.' They could see the man's hand grab the back of her head. 'Well, that explains the sperm.'

'Watch now,' she said. 'Wait for it . . .'

The man in black suddenly stood up from behind the bin and pointed an outstretched arm at the man's head. There was a flash, and Graham Stokes dropped like a sack of stones. The girl stood up and put her hand to her mouth. Amelia froze the tape. One forty-one a.m.

'Oh, Jesus!' said Paterson. 'That was harsh.'

'Yeah,' said Clocks. 'Poor bastard came and went all at the same time.' The other two turned and looked at him. 'What? I'm just sayin'. If you've gotta go, there are worse ways to do it. Poor bastard. At least he went out with a smile on his face.'

They watched as the girl bent down and began fiddling around with the dead man's trousers. 'What's she doing?' said Clocks. The girl stood up and popped something back in her bag while the gunman bent down over the body and rifled through his jacket.

'And what's he doing?' said Paterson. The gunman stood up, looked at something and threw it on the ground.

'I'm betting that was a condom she put in her bag,' said Amelia. 'She put a condom in her mouth, brought him off and did away with any DNA evidence.'

'And I think he's got the vic's driving licence,' said Clocks as they watched the two of them turn and hurry out of the alley.

'Okay,' said Paterson, all business now. 'Anything else on this worth seeing?'

'No, sir. Not this one. Pete's got something though.'

Paterson looked around at the assembled group, waiting for Pete to identify himself.

'Sir,' said a young man. Pete was back at his monitor and Paterson took a couple of steps over. 'They both turn right out of the alleyway and do a left . . . here,' he tapped the screen, 'then get into a white van and drive off.'

'Name of that street?' said Clocks.

'Emerson,' Pete said. 'Brings them out into Sumner Street. Could have gone either way from there. We'll extend the seizure of CCTV tapes, see if we can get anything else, but we also need to get onto traffic management to see if anything got picked up on the number plate recognition cameras. There may be something once they got onto the main roads.'

'Good. I want all images of any vehicles, *any* vehicles, with a male and female in the front seats within a five-minute time frame of them getting into that van. Could have swapped out the van for a car somewhere, so let's look for a van but not get hung up on it. Flexible thinking.' Paterson turned back to Amelia. 'Can we get this enhanced, d'you think?'

She shrugged. 'We'll certainly try, sir, but I wouldn't hold out too much hope. They were what, three hundred metres away and in the dark. If it hadn't been for that office light left on above them, I doubt we'd have seen much of anything. It won't be easy.'

'Soon as you know anything . . .' Paterson made the universal gesture for a phone call.

Amelia nodded and went back to her screen.

'I know. Do your best.' He nodded toward the door. 'John?'

Out in the corridor, Paterson stopped. 'Okay, where are we? What do we think?'

Johnny Clocks liked it when they did this. It was a useful way of organising their thoughts, finding holes, going over information and identifying the weaknesses. He looked up to the ceiling, accessing his memories.

'We think he's one of Tanner's men, killed in retaliation by Billy Caine. Not him specifically — two of his little crew did it. We think that the girl most likely knew who he was, was paid by Caine, and somehow knew that he was going to the theatre. We think that the girl got him pissed up and put him on a promise. We think that she probably gave him the coke to lower any resistance, not that there'd have been any, I suspect.'

'And what do we know about Stokes?' Paterson said.

'We know his name and address. We know he was from the East End, Tanner's stomping ground. His time of death is now officially one forty-one a.m. We know he had a ticket to the Globe Theatre for the night he was murdered. We know he went in and left alone, according to the Globe's CCTV. Toxi said he was drunk but also had a fair old dose of cocaine in his system. We know he met a girl. We know she took him into Rose Alley. We know he got his knob sucked and we know he got shot in the nut when he popped his cork. We also know it's unlikely we'll find any saliva DNA. We know they had transport.'

Paterson frowned. 'What do we know in general?'

'Not too much. We know there was a bloke waiting in the alley. We know he was armed. We know he was a ruthless bastard, probably professional. We know the killer and the girl knew each other and we know they left and got into a vehicle together.'

'What don't we know?'

'We don't know who the killer was or where he came from. We don't know who the girl is. We don't know their relationship. We don't know how she knew where to find the vic. We don't know why he was there. It probably don't matter, seeing as he was on his own all night and left alone. We don't know where he went to get drunk, it's mostly restaurants around there, doubt they'd have stayed open so late or that they'd have kept giving him drink. And we don't know where he got the coke. Don't know the van plates yet, or where the fuck it went to. Plates won't matter anyway. It'll be a ringer.'

'What do we need to do next?' Paterson said.

'Check out the pubs and restaurants nearby. Get their CCTV. Find out what the girl looks like, find out who she is. Once we get her, she'll lead us to our killer, hopefully.'

'Right. Add it all together and what does that give us?'

'A fuckin' good reason to kick in a coupla front doors.'

'John, listen. Go get a warrant for Tanner. Can't see that we'll need it, but I want it in my back pocket just to be sure. We'll turn him over tomorrow. I'm going to swing over to Caine's now. This shit has got to stop.'

'You gonna nick him?' Clocks stared.

'For what? Still nothing concrete here and he's far too slippery to be tied to anything. Not like he's gonna fold under a bit of aggressive interrogation either.'

'Yeah,' said Clocks, his brow furrowed, 'I'm not happy about you going alone, though.'

'I'll be fine. I can't take you, can I? You've dropped right off his Christmas card list. You know where I'm going. I'll check back in. Call me when you've got the warrant.'

* * *

An hour later, Paterson was back inside Caine's living room. Neither was particularly pleased to see the other. 'Why are you here, Mr Paterson? Ray, is it? What brings you back so soon?' He waved his guard away, Paterson wasn't the problem one. He poured two glasses of whisky, handed one to Paterson. 'You caught the bastard who did for my Davey, then?' He didn't wait for an answer. Instead, he lifted the glass to his lips and said, 'Tick-tock, Ray. Tick-tock.'

Paterson knew what he meant. He was in a race with Caine to see who would get to the killer first. Part of him hoped it would be Caine. He'd be able to dish out what this bastard deserved.

'I take it you haven't heard yet?'

Caine wrinkled his forehead. 'Heard what?'

Paterson took a gulp of the whisky and put his glass down on the table. He looked directly at the powerfully built man opposite him, waiting to catch a twitch, a flinch, something that might give him away, something that would let him know that, this time, he was ahead of Billy Caine.

'There's been another murder, another burning.'

Caine stood, drink in hand, listening. 'Victim has been identified as a Harry Long.' A vein bulged in Caine's temple. 'I believe you knew him as Harry the Dog?'

Caine's face clouded with rage, the vein in his temple throbbing, his grip on the glass tightening to the point of shattering. He suddenly threw the glass against the wall, startling Paterson.

A sharp rap on the door and the bodyguard's head appeared inside the room. 'Boss? You alright?'

Caine turned his back on him. 'Fine. Wait outside. No, wait! Make some calls. I want Sean and Terry here within the hour.' After a moment's hesitation, the guard closed the door.

Paterson searched his memory for the names he'd just heard, and remembered they'd been in DCI Alliston's briefing dockets. He assumed Terry would be Terry Richards and Sean would be Sean Blake, both high up within Caine's outfit and both nasty bastards to the core.

'I'm sorry you lost a friend today, Billy, but I've also got a man on the slab with a hole in his head. This bloke was an East-Ender. Don't suppose you know what happened to him, by any chance?' Caine said nothing. 'This stops,' Paterson said. 'Now. D'you understand me?' He kept his eyes locked on Caine.

For a moment, a small half-smile played across Caine's lips. It soon vanished. 'I'm sorry? Who the *fuck* do you think you're giving orders to?'

Paterson's gaze didn't waver. At the same time he moved back a step, casually, readying himself for trouble. 'Don't think of it as an order, Billy. Think of it as good advice. You'll find it keeps you from doing things you'll come to regret.'

Paterson waited for the big man to lose it and come charging at him. Nothing happened.

Instead, Caine nodded at him. 'Harry was a good friend. Known him for years. Kids together, all that shit.'

Paterson said nothing and after a while, Caine seemed to be lost in thought.

Paterson glanced around the room. On a small coffee table sat a plane ticket. 'Are you going somewhere, Billy?'

Looking bewildered for a few seconds, Caine followed Paterson's gaze to the ticket. 'Yeah. I'm going away for a few days. I need to get away from all this shit, grieve for my son, and now my friend as well.'

'Anywhere nice?' As if he cared. Paterson just wanted to know where Caine was if he needed to drag him back.

Caine nodded. 'Yeah, Zurich. I've got a place on Lake Geneva. Thought I'd go there for a while. Keep my head down, sort a few things out.'

Paterson gave him a look.

'Don't worry about it, son. I'm not up to anything. Your boys know all about it. They know where all my homes are and they're as well bugged as this one. Can't take a shit in any of 'em without them recording the splosh. Ask 'em to give you a copy of Billy Caine's greatest dumps. I think it's on Spotify.'

Paterson grinned. 'How you long you going for?'

'Dunno. Not long. A few days, maybe a week tops. Gotta sign off on a few business deals out there. I've bought a few shit 'ole farmhouses that I'm gonna do up and flog on. Nothing special.'

'Fair enough. When you get back, can you give me a call? I need to keep you up to speed on where we are with catching your son's, and now your friend's, killer.'

'Yeah, whatever,' said Caine. He started to walk Paterson to the door, then stopped. 'Mr Paterson — Ray. Have you got a sec? Want to talk to you about something. Private.' Suddenly wary, Paterson nodded.

Billy Caine walked down the hallway, past two bodyguards, toward a brown, mahogany door at the end. On the wall was an electronic keypad. Shielding the keypad with his body, Caine entered five numbers. As he waited, Paterson glanced down the hall hoping that DCI Alliston's boys had hidden pin-head CCTV cameras somewhere, and were watching him now. The door swung open, and Caine showed Paterson into a room about the size of a shipping container. It was longer than it was wide and decorated to a comfortable standard. There was a sixty-inch LED TV hanging on the far wall, a couple of leather armchairs, a well-stocked bar and a sex-swing. On one of the walls was a small collection of whips.

'Er . . . What exactly are we doing here, Billy?' Paterson eyed the whip collection, growing increasingly uneasy.

Caine closed the door behind them. 'Relax. Nothing for you to worry about, sonny. You're really not my type. This is my room. My man-cave, if you like.'

Paterson pointed to the swing. 'And this?'

'Fuck me, son! There's some things I really don't want your boys listening to. Belchin' and fartin' is one thing, but I'm not having 'em listening to me get me end away. Room's clean as a whistle. Swept for bugs twice a day. Can't hear a bloody thing.' He moved over to the bar. 'The bastards don't know what I get up to in here. Drives 'em mad. Wanna drink?'

Paterson declined. He didn't like this. 'Apart from the obvious, what else do you get up to in here?'

'This is where I come to think. Plan my next moves . . . strategise.' Paterson's eyes narrowed slightly. 'And it's a place where I can talk frankly, and you and me, son, we're going to talk.'

Paterson cursed himself. He'd walked into the one room that wasn't under surveillance, with a big, bad-tempered, couldn't-give-a-fuck hard man who'd shut the door behind them. And he had a sex swing, which for some reason, still worried him. Caine moved toward Paterson, far enough away not to be threatening but close enough to make things slightly uncomfortable. Then he opened up. He jabbed his finger at Paterson and stepped in close.

'Let's not sod around anymore, son. This had nothing to do with the Albies. Albert Tanner had my boy killed. You know it, I know it and every other bastard this side of the Thames knows it. Tanner's making his grab. He wants the south and this is his opener. Killing my boy was a mistake, a bad one, and he'll fuckin' pay for it. Dearly. He hits me, I hit him. But a whole hell of a lot 'arder.' His voice became guttural. 'I might be an 'orrible bastard but I loved my son. Tanner's not going to walk away from this, so I'm giving you the heads-up, right now. Things are gonna go real bad from here on in, so my advice to you, son, is stay the fuck out of my way or you and that caveman Clocks are gonna get caught in the crossfire, and that's somewhere you really don't wanna be. You understand?'

This is it, thought Paterson, *no more niceties. Cards on the table time.* Coolly, he said, 'Oh, I understand, Billy. Of course, I do. You're pissed off. I would be too but, and here's the thing you need to bear in mind, it's a mistake, a *bad* mistake, to stand there and tell me, a senior murder squad detective, that you're going to take the law into your own hands, and threaten me into the bargain. There's no way this can end well.'

'No one's threatening you, son. All I'm doing is dishing out some advice. Good advice, mind, designed to keep *you* from doing some things *you* may come to regret.' Caine took a half step forward. Paterson edged sideways. 'An' look at you, Mr goody two-shoes. Don't give me that ol' bollocks about being a good cop. I've been fuckin' payin' your lot off for years.'

'Don't doubt it, but you've not been paying me off. Though I'd be interested to hear who you *have* been paying off. It'll give me something to do when you're in prison.' Paterson pulled away slightly, preparing himself.

Caine stared Paterson up and down. 'If you want payin' off, Ray, I'm sure we can come to some sort of arrangement.'

Paterson snorted. 'Oh, Mr Caine. I very much doubt you have enough money to make it worth my while.'

Caine raised an eyebrow. 'What? You do know who I am, right?'

Paterson stared at him. Nodded.

'You know how much I'm worth? I could fuckin' buy and sell you and not even bat an eyelid.'

'That right?'

Caine couldn't believe what he was hearing. Nobody defied him.

'You a gambling man?' said Paterson.

'Yeah. I like a flutter every now an' then.'

Paterson fumbled in his pocket and pulled out a ten pence piece. 'How much you worth cash-wise, Billy?'

'What? That's a bit personal, ain't it? I dunno. Last count, about an 'undred mill. What sort of question's that?'

'Toss you for it.' Paterson flipped the coin and caught it on the back of his hand. 'Your call. Heads or tails?'

Caine searched Paterson's face. The man wasn't joking. And then the light went on. 'Wait a bleedin' minute. I know you, of course I do. You're the rich copper, the flash one with the Bentley. The one that murdered that other copper on Tower Bridge. An' all them Africans. You had them all killed, didn't yer? By a sniper. Yeah, I do remember now.'

'So the papers say but, whatever. Surprised you didn't recognise me though. Everyone else seems to.'

Caine grinned. 'Memory's not what it used to be. Not much good with faces these days. Or names come to that.'

Paterson tried to hide his smile. *Alzheimer's will do that to you.*

'That, and the fact that you're of no interest to me at all. Well, fuck me bandy with a baseball bat! I'm in the presence of royalty. You two are a right pair of coffin magnets, ain'tcha?'

Paterson chortled. 'Coffin magnets! I'll pass that on to Inspector Clocks. He'll have that printed on a T-shirt like a shot. So, do we have a bet then, Billy?'

'Fair play to yer, son. No bet.'

Paterson slipped the coin back into his pocket. 'Damn. I could've done with a bit of spare change. There's a boat I've got my eye on.'

Caine's brow furrowed. He was not amused.

'Alright, Bill. Pissing contest over. Listen up. One more thing happens out on those streets, one more person hurt or killed, and I'm coming right back here to drag you off to prison and, believe me, it *will* stick. Do you understand?'

Caine smiled. Then lost it. Moving fast, he grabbed Paterson by the jaw and slammed him against the wall, where he banged his head on the wood panelling. 'Listen up, you little pri—'

Most people in this situation would have made a grab for the hand holding them, trying to break its grip — and leading to an ugly ensuing struggle. But Paterson was not most people. He brought both of his hands up and slammed them into Caine's ears, hard. The sudden sharp pain and loud bang inside his head unnerved Caine, causing him to loosen his grip. Paterson's hands then came down and swept away Caine's grip. He stepped forward and slammed his right fist into Caine's chest, flooring him instantly. Caine let out a loud grunt, and his eyes widened in fear as his heart went into spasm.

Paterson stood over him. 'You wanted to talk? Right, let's talk. Listen up. I don't give a toss about you or Tanner or the fucking Albanians, or your tin-pot empires. I'm happy for you pieces of shit to kill one another all day long and back again but not on my streets. And don't you ever, *ever* threaten me or Clocks.' Caine looked up at him, beseeching. 'My job is to put you and your kind away, so if you threaten me or any other police officer, I'll make sure you're sorry you tried.' Paterson grabbed Caine's collar, pulled him forward and drew his fist back, 'If that day comes, then let's be clear, Billy, I *will* kill you. Without hesitation. Understood?'

Paterson let him drop, stood up straight and smoothed his jacket and tie. 'Right about now you're probably wondering if you're going to die. You won't. Stay calm. Control your breathing. You'll be alright in about five minutes.'

He opened the door and looked back, chuckling. 'Coffin magnets.'

CHAPTER TWELVE

It was going to be a busy day for Albert Tanner. He had a morning meeting with Caine, and in the afternoon an unscheduled meeting with Paterson and Clocks. He'd been expecting that one at some point, but the call from Caine caught him by surprise. He knew they'd have to meet eventually, but he hadn't expected it to be quite so soon. It was to take place in an old warehouse on the south side of the water and, at first, Tanner was hesitant. He didn't fancy conducting business in someone else's manor, but was confident that he had enough backup should things go wonky. He checked his watch. Time to go.

With the aid of his walking stick, he pushed himself up from his chair. The stick was for effect more than anything, but it also came in handy for beating people half to death.

As a child, on the rare occasions he had attended school, the other children had avoided him. Albert Tanner was the odd one out. He was stick-thin with a chiselled face and, in south London parlance, a bonk eye — one that is off-centre. In Tanner's case, his left eye was set at an angle of about thirty-five degrees. This deformity made him the target of innumerable jokes, which made his already miserable life even more so. As he grew, so too did his eccentricities. He had an unhealthy fixation with animals and fire, the two interests coming together to produce a spate of cats and dogs seen running along the road engulfed in flames and howling in agony. Those neighbours who made the mistake of banging on his father Reginald's door to complain were subjected to a variety of injuries. For some reason, few people ever took their assaults to the police and those that did heard nothing further about it.

Girls were another fixation. He'd been caught several times masturbating outside the houses of girls who had caught his fancy, and when he was fourteen, the police were called to Tesco's where he had taken a particular shine to one of the older cashiers. Again, because of his father's influence and standing, he was taken home, where Mr Tanner senior laughed loudly and patted his son on the back. At the age of twenty, Tanner took himself a wife, a beautiful petite woman with mental problems equal to his own. Between them, they spawned two children, a boy and a girl, to whom they passed on their love of violence. In years to come, numerous professionals would debate whether the children's flaws were due to nature or nurture.

Tanner walked over to his dresser and picked up a small, solid silver, beautifully detailed filigree box and opened the lid. The music box began to tinkle out the first few bars of "When You Wish upon a Star," while Tanner ruminated over his collection of false eyes. At some point in his teens, he'd lost his bonk eye, though no one quite remembered how. The rumours ran from him losing it in a knife fight with his father to Albert cutting it out himself, and all were believable.

As his criminal enterprises flourished and he started to make money, Albert Tanner threw away his bog-standard glass eye and spent some of his ill-gotten gains on ones made of precious stones. Now, in his music box, ruby, diamond, emerald green, garnet and black onyx stones nestled in a blue velvet holder. The ruby was in honour of his daughter of the same name. The diamond was for his father who he considered to be a "diamond." The emerald for his son who loved the colour, and the onyx was for when he was about to deliver bad news.

Tanner's choice of colour matched that day's mood and so far, today was looking like a good day. He selected the ruby and popped it into the empty socket.

Now, with eye set, top hat balanced comfortably on his head, tailcoat pulled straight, cane in hand and a lightweight Kevlar vest under his shirt, Albert Tanner was ready for business.

* * *

An hour later, Tanner's convoy of cars pulled into an old, abandoned industrial estate in Camberwell. Tanner sat back, low in his seat, as the lead car drew to a stop. Ahead of them, two men, armed with small machine guns, stood guard at the entrance to the warehouse Caine had chosen. Tanner's men would enter first, scope out the inside and see how many more armed men were there. Only then would he leave the safety of his car. Standard practice among villains. And there would always be a few more armed men tucked away around the corner in case things went tits up. Tanner's extra was parked at the end of the road, out of sight, but close enough to move in fast should the unthinkable happen.

After a few minutes, his men came back outside and nodded.

All four doors opened at the same time and with a dramatic flourish, Tanner and his boys stepped out of the car into the damp morning air. Gentle rain fell on Tanner who, flanked by three men, breezed past the guards at the door and walked into the damp smelling, dusty warehouse. He shuddered. Tanner had a thing about dirt.

Taking his time, he strolled toward the end of the warehouse where, in the distance, he could see Caine half-hidden behind a packing crate. His eyes narrowed. Two men stood on either side of Caine, both armed. Tanner walked on until he stood in front of Caine.

'Tanner,' Caine said.

'Caine.' The two men weighed each other up. Tanner broke the silence. 'Let's get on with it. This place is a,' he waved royally around the room, 'shithole and I really don't want to be here any longer than necessary.'

'Guns,' said Caine. Tanner looked at him and shook his head slightly, unsure of his meaning. 'Guns on the crate,' said Caine. He put his hand inside his coat, a move that had everyone present on instant alert. Tanner backed up a step as Caine pulled out a .45 and dropped it onto the top of the packing crate. Tanner understood. He pulled out a Magnum .357 and placed it next to the .45. He removed his top hat and placed that alongside the weapons.

'Fuckin' 'ell, Bert, you're thinnin' out a bit, ain'tcha?'

Tanner raised his hand self-consciously to his head. 'Says the man with a head like a billiard ball.'

Caine laughed. 'Yep, I make you right there, but mine's a choice. A razor and a buff up, but it'll grow back if I want.' He dropped the smile. His face went blank. 'Is that it, then?' He gestured toward the guns.

'It is. And you?'

'Yep,' said Caine. 'All the guards, yours and mine, they can back up, out of earshot.'

Tanner lifted his head slightly. This wasn't making him happy. 'And why would they do that?'

'Because this is between you and me, Tanner. Business. Nothing to do with them. Don't worry yourself. I'm not going to hurt you.'

Tanner narrowed his eyes and considered his position. Caine wasn't armed, at least as far as he could tell, and if it came to it, he figured it was a fifty-fifty grab for the guns.

He waved his men back. Caine did the same. All of the guards backed off but kept them in view.

Caine coughed, and punched himself in the chest a couple of times.

Tanner raised an eyebrow. 'Whatever's the matter?'

Caine winced, breathed hard a couple of times and rubbed at his chest. He hated this skinny little bag of bones and his smug, condescending attitude. 'Had a run-in with someone today. Old Bill. Came over to the house and got a bit cheeky, so I had to educate him about a few things. Caught me a lucky one, 's all. Nothing major.'

'Pleased to hear it, Billy. Wouldn't like to think of you getting hurt.' He gave a thin smile.

Caine straightened himself up. 'Expect a visit from 'em, Bert. They know your trademark.'

'I've been expecting them. It's not something I consider to be a problem.'

Caine shrugged. 'Maybe you should. These are not your normal coppers. Different pair altogether. The one I gave a kicking to, he's the one that's got all the money and shot the other copper. Y'know him? Flash little bastard. Drives a Bentley.'

Tanner nodded, almost imperceptibly. '*Of* him. Them. Why are you bothered about the cops all of a sudden?'

'Just saying. These ones can't be bought like the others. The young 'un don't need the dough and the other one, he's in a mad all of his own. Off his nut.'

'Shall we get on, Billy? I have a busy day ahead of me.'

Caine peered at Tanner. 'I see it's a ruby day. Guess that means you're in a good mood.'

'It has started off well and I have high hopes that it will continue that way,' Tanner said, dropping the smile.

Caine had to muster every ounce of his willpower not to reach over the packing crate, grab that scrawny little neck and choke the blackened, evil soul right out of him.

'I take it you asked me to come here for more than just to admire my eye?' said Tanner.

'Yep. Let's get to it then. You're aware that someone murdered my son the other day, yes?' He kept his gaze fixed on Tanner's face, looking for a reaction. *Nothing*.

'Of course. I'm sorry. A terrible way to die. I do hope they catch the monster responsible for it.'

This was really too much. Caine fought down the rising rage. But he wasn't about to let this go. He shook his head. 'No, I'm pretty sure you don't want them to catch 'im, Bert. 'Cause you wouldn't last five seconds inside. Not with your enemies and no one there to protect you all the time.'

Tanner's eye darted to the guns. So did both Caine's. Neither man moved.

'Yeah, that's right. I know it's down to you. You'd have to be Stevie Wonder not to see that.' Caine took a deep breath, holding his mounting rage in check.

'It was . . . necessary,' said Tanner after a few seconds. 'Business. Nothing personal.'

Now Caine did begin to unravel, just a bit. 'Not personal? Not personal? You killed my fuckin' son, you fucked up, ugly bastard. Not fuckin' personal! How much more personal can it get?' Both sets of guards looked alarmed, uncertain whether to act.

Tanner was glad he'd decided to wear the Kevlar vest.

'Why'd you do it? Why kill him? What did we ever do to you? What did *he* ever do to you?' Caine's voice broke.

'Nothing. As I said, business, that's all. Nothing more. I wanted the south. I have done for years. You know that. I've offered to buy you out several times — reasonable offers I might add — and I grew tired of waiting. I thought about approaching you again but I knew your answer would be the same, so I figured that with Davey gone, you'd realise you couldn't carry on.'

'You thought that if you killed Davey, I'd just roll over and give you the keys?' Caine was genuinely astounded. He couldn't tell if the man was just arrogant, or whether he was dumber than a box of rocks.

'That was the plan,' Tanner said with a shrug.

'Well, you can go screw yourself, you stupid piece of shit!' Tanner frowned. The guards shuffled around, waiting for it to kick off, hoping it wouldn't. 'You want my business, come and fuckin' take it if you think you can, but I'm still breathing, and leaving me alive was a fuckin' bad mistake. You've still gotta come through me and we both know I'll slap you down like the rabid dog you are!' Caine started to move around the crate. The guards twitched, staring one another down. First to raise their weapons would bring on a bloodbath.

Tanner held up his hand. 'Wait!' Caine stopped. Tanner reached into his pocket. Caine's boys had a moment of panic. Caine eyed the gun, thought about it but decided to beat him to death. Tanner pulled out his phone. 'Something I want you to see before you do anything rash.' He tapped the screen and a video began playing. Tanner held it up for him to see.

Curious, Caine cocked his head. Then his stomach knotted up.

He was being taken on a jerky walkthrough of a house. He didn't recognise the house itself, but he did recognise the pictures in the hallway. The camera suddenly swung and filmed the scene from a window. Caine saw a little girl with her father, playing in the garden. His niece. He bowed his head, shook it slowly from side to side. 'You motherfucker.'

Tanner ignored him. 'I'm told they're a lovely family, living a quiet, peaceful life surrounded by some very beautiful countryside. It'd be nice if they could continue to do so. That will depend on you though, Billy.' Tanner stopped the video.

Caine was torn. For the first time in his life, he didn't know what to do. He paced behind the crate, his face contorted in pain and indecision. Albert Tanner had him. Whatever he did, his family was at risk. Billy Caine was beat and he knew it.

Caine had been in prison just twice in his life. He was eighteen the first time. Banged up for a month for a bit of criminal damage. He fought all the way. He fought the police that nicked him, he raged at the magistrate who sentenced him and he lashed out at the prison guards who dragged him out of the courtroom and down to the cells. He kicked at the fixed wooden bench, nutted the metal door until the blood streamed down his face until, finally exhausted, he gave up. There was no one left to fight and nothing to destroy. A quiet calm came over him.

The second time, at the age of twenty-two, he didn't bother creating a scene. Nobody gave a flying fuck if he showed off. His first term inside had taught him that if you did get lairy, the guards would either storm the cell and beat the living shit out of you, or wait until you'd calmed down and then storm the cell and beat the living shit out of you. He served his time quietly.

'How the hell did you find out about her?' he asked, his voice flat. 'Nobody knew about her, or where she was. No one.'

'I keep my ear to the ground, Billy. If you dig deep enough, it's amazing what you turn up. It would seem that every family has their white sheep, Billy. Nothing to be ashamed of.'

'You haven't fuckin' 'urt them, Albert, have you?'

Tanner wrinkled his nose. 'Oh no. I'm hoping it won't be necessary.' He paused. 'It won't be, will it?'

Caine took a deep breath, trying to think of some way he could salvage the situation. He came up with nothing. 'If I give in to you, how do I know you won't hurt them?'

'To be honest, you don't, but, for what it's worth, I give you my word.'

'Your word's not worth shit to me,' Caine said.

Tanner sounded almost kindly, if that were possible. 'I can understand why you would feel that way, Billy, but what other choice do you have?'

Caine's fists balled. 'I can protect them.'

Tanner snorted. 'I doubt that. Let's face it, Billy, you couldn't protect your own son, so how will you protect a family in the backwaters of Ireland?'

Caine's arms hung loose by his sides. 'Well that's it then, innit? I'm done. You know what? Fuck it! Fuck it all. I don't need this shit anymore, anyway. You promise me you'll leave 'em alone and we'll talk. Fair?' The guards all breathed again.

'Yes,' said Tanner. 'Fair, and you have my word I'll not harm your sister and her family. But be under no illusion, Billy, if you try to screw me over, things will not go well for them.'

'What is it you want, specifically?' Caine said.

'Everything.'

Caine's mouth dropped open. 'What? Everything? Don't be a prick! I'm not doin' that. I can't. I have people. People waiting for me to step down. They'll be expecting a share, to take my place. It's what they've waited for, served for. You don't think they'll just stand by and let you come swannin' in and take the lot, do yer? You're not that bleedin' mad, surely to God?'

Tanner reached inside his coat again. Caine went for the gun. The guards raised their weapons. Tanner pulled out a silver cigarette case.

'Christ, Bert! What the fuck is wrong with you?' Caine shouted. Last thing he wanted was to be shot in the back of the head by a panicked gunman.

'Oh.' Tanner looked around at the agitated guards, who were hesitantly lowering their weapons. 'Careless of me. I wasn't thinking.' He removed a cigarette, placed it in his mouth and summoned one of his guards over to light it for him. He took a long draw on the cigarette and blew a series of perfect rings.

'To return to your question, Billy. I am indeed that mad, but rest assured, I'll be able to handle any uprising your disgruntled ex-employees may stage. I will of course keep some of them on and they will be paid generously.

Those I let go will be dealt with accordingly.' He threw the barely touched cigarette to the ground and twisted his foot on it. 'I expect you to provide me with all of your business interests, and I do mean all. I expect you to have papers drawn up transferring any and all of the legal business in which you have a controlling interest, and those of your son, Davey, to my holding companies. Once we have exchanged papers, a contingent of my employees will meet with a contingent of yours. We will both be present at this meeting and you will inform your people, clearly, that I am now in control of the streets and that they now work for me. You will inform them, as will I if necessary, of the consequences should they choose not to comply. You will also electronically transfer all of your cash assets to various bank accounts, the numbers of which I will give you.'

'For God's sake, Bert, you're killin' me. There'll be a bloodbath out there, and you know it.'

Tanner cocked his head. 'I do. But it will be short-lived and once the dust has settled, those left standing will see that it was for the best. But I really don't know why you're concerning yourself. I believe that you're, er, unwell. Am I right?'

Caine looked at him. 'I have a few problems, yes. How'd you find that out?'

'I hear things. And, of course, from simple observation. You're stooping slightly. You haven't shaved, most unusual for you, your speech is very slightly slurred, you look tired and you have given in far, far too easily. Not the man I once knew. May I ask what's wrong with you?'

Caine's eyes darted around the room, his mouth felt dry and the big, cold room suddenly felt hot to him. 'I . . . I have . . . I have Alzheimer's. Docs don't really know how long I've got, but the smart money won't be tied up for the long term.' His voice cracked. 'So . . . what the fuck? You can have it. I've got no one to leave it all to, so not much point fighting. Just leave my sister and her family alone and I'll get the papers drawn up.'

'I'm sorry to hear that, Billy.'

'Are you bollocks! You couldn't give a shit, an' we both know it.'

Tanner spread his hands. 'True. But it's what you say to a dying man, I'm told.' Tanner turned his back and began to walk away. 'I'll wait to hear from you then, Billy.' He gave a quick wave without looking back.

'Hold up, Bert. You're forgettin' something.'

Tanner stopped, stiffened slightly, and turned back round.

'I want something from you in return.'

'You already have it, Billy. No harm to your family.'

Billy Caine looked Albert Tanner dead in his good eye. 'I know. You said. But there's the matter of compensation. You killed my son. You pay. That's how it works, as you well know.'

Tanner stepped forward. 'Really? You want me to pay you?' A small laugh escaped him. 'I don't understand, Billy. You've just lost everything. You've seen that I can get to your sister and now you're standing there demanding money from me. Do you think that's wise?'

Caine didn't flinch. 'Compensation for my boy. That's all. You know how it works — it's tradition. Look, you've got everything now. I'm signing it all over to you but the truth is, I'm asset rich and cash poor. Very cash poor. I've got about two hundred grand in a safe at home and that's it. The rest is all tied up and, if I'm giving it to you, then I'm not getting hold of it, am I?'

Tanner listened carefully. Two hundred grand. Fucking hell, he probably had more than that in his glove compartment.

Caine hung his head. 'Truth is, Albert, I've got a year. Maybe a bit more, but not much. I'd like to spend the two hundred knee deep in fanny and coke, take me mind off things, know what I mean?'

Tanner let out a laugh. 'Ah, Billy boy.' He shook his head. 'What are you looking for?'

Straight faced, Caine said, 'A mill. One million.'

Tanner's eyebrows shot up. 'Are you taking the piss?'

'Nope. Deadly serious. One mill. Straight to me sister's account. Nice little present from the bastard of a brother she never sees. You've said you're not gonna hurt 'em, so she'll get to live a decent life with that money. Come on, Bert. It's not much to ask, is it? The empire's worth, what? Two 'undred million. You won't miss a mill, you'll make it up in a month or two.'

Tanner sighed. He hated Billy Caine with a passion. The man had been a thorn in his side, thwarting his ambitions for years and had slapped down every attempt he'd made to strong-arm his way south of the river. But, at the same time, he couldn't help admiring him. He was a tough opponent, and to be magnanimous in victory was the mark of the better man. He knew that the unwritten rules of the underworld demanded that Tanner make some sort of recompense to the dead man's family.

Tanner gave a wry smile. 'Deal.'

'Good. You know it makes sense. Give me a week or so to put things in order. I'll be in touch,' said Caine.

'Just take the million out of what you'll be giving me.'

Caine shook his head. 'Nope. That's not how this works. You pay me — well, not me, my sister.'

'But it will be your money anyway, what's the point? You give it to her.'

'Principle, Albert. Don't matter if you've nicked it from me. Point is it comes from you. *You* owe *me*! That's how this works.' Tanner sighed. 'And we do it electronically. I'm not takin' a cheque off you, you dodgy bastard.'

Tanner smiled. 'Nor would I,' he said, holding out his hand. The two men shook hands. No going back now.

Caine watched as his nemesis picked up his gun, turned and strutted off back to his car. He hated his swagger, hated his bastard glass eye, his top hat, his poncey little silver-topped walking stick, hated everything about him and trusted him about as far as he could throw him. But he loved his stupidity. So Tanner thought he was getting it all, did he? Tanner wasn't getting a thing.

CHAPTER THIRTEEN

Paterson and Clocks strode down the corridor toward the briefing room. It was time to pay Albert Tanner a visit, and Paterson was under no illusions about how the encounter was going to go. Still lacking the firm evidence he needed to make an arrest, Paterson was more than happy to take Clocks's advice and go over to the man's house and rattle his cage a bit. After all, it was no good just sitting back. Paterson skipped making a call to DCI Alliston. Difficult to know who to trust these days.

'How many did you round up, John?'

'Fifteen, guv. Me, you, seven from the team and six SCO19, all fully kitted and rarin' to go.'

'SCO19? How much trouble are we expecting?'

A uniformed PC flattened himself against the wall as the two detectives swept past. 'DCI Alliston reckons the security might be a problem. Won't want to let us in. So, I figured we might have to coax them, and what better way than having six hairy-arsed coppers with machine guns and attitudes do it for us?'

'Is Lyndsey leading them?' Paterson asked.

'Yeah, why?'

'I just can't imagine her having a hairy arse.'

Clocks pointed at Paterson. 'You better not be imagining her arse, mate, hairy or otherwise.' He grinned.

'Does Alliston know about SCO19?' said Paterson.

'I ain't told him. Should I?'

Paterson shook his head, 'No. No need. Just asking. Just so you know, I've spoken to Commissioner Young and he's given us permission to draw firearms.'

Clocks frowned. 'What?'

Paterson grinned. 'We've both done a basic shots course. I told him it could get tasty over at Tanner's and he said we could carry for personal protection. Risk assessment done. I thought you'd be pleased.'

Clocks's face lit up. 'I am. I really am.'

Paterson reached the door, turned the handle, stopped. 'Me and you go in first, John. The shots can wait out of sight, round the corner. If we need them, we call them. We draw only if we have to. Last resort. Understood?'

Clocks's shoulders fell. *Damn.* 'Understood. Softly, softly first.'

Paterson pushed the door ajar and stopped again. 'Reckon we will need them, though. Remember how you pissed off Caine?' Clocks's shoulders lifted. 'Rinse and repeat.' He opened the door and walked into the briefing room. 'Heads up, everybody. We have an interesting evening ahead of us.'

* * *

Albert Tanner's house was a large gothic mansion set in an acre of woodland. It looked like a leftover from a Hammer Horror movie set, complete with large front porch and swing shutters on all the windows. Paterson and Clocks stood outside, looking through the wrought-iron gates. Behind them, a convoy of cars was parked up on the road. The only sign that they were still in the twenty-first century was a small video security buzzer on the wall.

Clocks held a large wooden wedge in his hand. 'You sure this is the right address, guv? Looks to me like it's owned by a Mr D. Racula and if it ain't, it bleedin' well should be.'

'You'll be fine. Man up.'

'I will be if we can find a pointy stick and a silver cross before we get to the door. Fuck me. First we had to deal with General Kamwelu and his child-killing voodoo murders and now vampires. We're gonna get a reputation.'

'Stop being a knob, John. He's just another scum-bucket piece of shit with an overdeveloped sense of the dramatic. It makes up for his deep seated childhood traumas and insecurities.' Paterson pressed the buzzer under the camera.

''Scuse me? Did they have psychology 101 on the menu in the canteen today? I musta missed that, an' you know I like a good dollop of claptrap.'

'Detective Superintendent Paterson and Detective Inspector Clocks to see Mr Tanner.' Paterson stooped and held up his warrant card to the camera. 'I'm sure he's been expecting us.' A faint buzzing was followed by the gate slowly swinging open. As they went through, Clocks shoved the wedge under one of the gates keeping it open, just in case SCO19 needed to make a swift entrance. Paterson pressed gently on the micro earpiece he was wearing. It was snugly in place. They crunched their way along the gravel path. Ahead of them, the front door opened, and a large black man stepped out, crossing his hands in front of him. Classic pose. Tough guy. From what they could see, this one probably was.

'Did you see that?' said Clocks.

'See what?' said Paterson.

'I swear I just saw a flash of lightning and bats flyin' around.'

'They'll be the ones from your head. Sounds like they've found a way out.'

Clocks smiled. 'Funny fucker.'

The big man, his gruff voice reminiscent of Frank Bruno, politely invited them in and they found themselves standing in a large hallway. It came as quite a surprise. Completely at odds with the exterior, it was tastefully decorated and definitely modern. There was little in the way of furniture, but the two sideboards were made by Boca do Lobo and must have cost more money than some people make in a year. The hallway floor was carpeted in white, and it amused them both to see these tough guy guards all standing in their socks.

'Is this a religious thing?' said Paterson to the big man, grinning.

'A cleanliness thing. Mr Tanner don't like filth in his house.'

Paterson smiled. 'Oh, good one,' he said. 'I see what you did there. Very clever — filth. Could have been a genuine comment or it could have been an insult to us police officers, us being known as the filth an' all.'

The big man gave a faint grin and flashed his eyebrows.

'Well done, big boy,' said Clocks. 'Good start.'

Dotted along the hallway were more security personnel. Paterson counted three, with two outside one particular door. He guessed that was where he'd find Tanner.

'Need to search you,' said the big man.

'What's that now?' Clocks was getting in an early start.

'I need to search you.'

'Yeah,' said Clocks. 'You can take a flyin' fuck, mate. That ain't happenin'. Jog on.'

The big man managed to look both disappointed and slightly pleased. Most people who came to this house understood the need to be searched but there were always one or two who took offence. Those were the ones who went back out of the door faster than they came in. Policemen or not.

'I've shown you my warrant card,' said Paterson. 'That's all you're getting.'

'Then I'm going to have to ask you to leave, gentlemen.' The big man always started out politely. Then he could turn nasty if necessary, but it was difficult to start nasty and then lose face if you had to back down.

Clocks moved toward him. 'Listen, mate,' he eyed the man up and down. 'What's your name?'

'Mark. Mark Edwards. Known as "King."'

Clocks looked at Paterson, then back to the big man. 'Really? King Edwards. You're havin' a laugh!' Mr Edwards wasn't. 'Okay,' said Clocks. 'Thought you might have a sense of humour on yer with a name like that, but . . .' he shook his head. 'Never mind. I can tell you're not too bright. Not your fault. Now, listen. I'm already in enough trouble for pissing off ethnics and fuckwits so just run along and tell your boss that the nice policemen are here. Oh, an' see if you can rustle up two teas and a couple of Jammie Dodgers, will yer? Good lad.' He started to move past King. 'Is he in there?' He pointed toward the guarded door.

A large hand fell onto his shoulder. 'I'm sorry. Not without being sea—'

Clocks batted his hand away and stepped in close. 'Hey, hey! Take your fuckin' hands off me, son, or you'll wind up with a mouthful of slack teeth.'

The other guards started to move toward them. Paterson closed his eyes for a second. *Bollocks.* Could have done without this just yet. Mr Edwards, now suitably riled, made to grab Clocks, who skipped back and squared up to him.

Paterson stepped between them and turned to Edwards. 'That's enough! We just want to talk to Tanner, that's all. But, be clear, we're not being searched and that's the end of it. If we have to, we'll get backup in here and believe me, you're not going to want to see what that looks like.' King stared at Paterson, almost growling. The tension crackled for a few seconds until, behind them, a man threw open the double doors and emerged into the hallway.

'Mr Edwards,' he called. 'That's okay. Mr Tanner will see them. No need for any unpleasantness.' Edwards stepped away. Clocks grinned at him. 'Superintendent,' called the man. 'Please, do come in.'

Paterson and Clocks breezed past the security men on the door and found themselves in a vast living area. The firm that did Graceland for Elvis had obviously had a hand in the decor. The main room was furnished with two white leather chairs and a matching four-seater sofa, a mirror-topped coffee table with painted gold legs, and yellow carpeting which extended through a glass archway with art deco stained-glass peacocks on either side and into the back room. The wallpaper in both rooms was a burnt orange colour. The only thing missing was a guitar hanging on a wall. Clocks entered, did a double-take, poked his head back out into the tastefully decorated hall. Muttering to himself, he went back inside. In the living room stood another two men, arms crossed at their chests, feet apart, eyes following their movements closely.

'This way.' The man who had shown them in stopped short at the archway and held up his finger for them to wait. 'Sir? Superintendent Paterson and,' he looked back over his shoulder, 'another policeman, I presume.' Clocks's eyes narrowed. This was going to be easy. The man stepped aside, and Paterson gave him a lop-sided grin as he walked past.

In the centre of the room, with two more guards either side of him sat Albert Tanner in a large wing-backed white leather chair. His hand rested on a shiny black cane and he wore a large top hat. Back straight, he had one leg crossed over the other.

Paterson stopped dead and stared, causing Clocks to walk into him.

'Shit, Ray.' Clocks bumbled past him. At the sight of Tanner, he let out a small laugh. 'Oh, fuck me! No! I don't believe this.' Taking the piss was going to be just so easy.

'Gentlemen,' said Tanner. 'Please, do come in. I apologise for my man at the door. He sometimes takes his job a little too seriously.' He turned to Clocks. 'Mr . . .?'

'Clocks. Detective Inspector Clocks.' He gave a slight nod.

'Mr Clocks. Thank you. You seemed somewhat startled by my appearance.'

'Yeah. Sorry about that. Caught me off guard. No offence. It's just that . . .'

'Yes?' Tanner asked, smiling.

Paterson stepped in before Clocks could say anything too tactless. Time enough for that. 'Mr Tanner, I'm Detective Superintendent Paterson. We're from the murder investigation team over on the south side of the water. We'd like to have a chat with you, if you wouldn't mind.'

Tanner grinned. 'Of course. Please.' He gestured to a couple of empty chairs. 'Make yourselves comfortable.'

'No thanks,' said Paterson. 'We're not stopping. Just wanted to drop by and make ourselves known.'

Tanner cocked his head. 'Make yourselves known? I don't quite understand, Superintendent.'

Paterson decided to break up the conversation, a tactic used to confuse the person being questioned. He turned his attention to the room. 'Very nice, Mr Tanner. You have expensive, er, taste.' Clocks eyed up the guards, who seemed quite calm. 'Do you listen to the news, or read the papers, Mr Tanner?'

'I do. How does that—?'

'Do you have any family? I don't see any pictures in here.'

Tanner seemed puzzled by the question. 'I have a wife, a son and a daughter. They live abroad. Unfortunately, in my particular line of work, I collect a fair few enemies. It's well known that I'm a rich man, and I'm concerned about kidnappers. You understand, I'm sure. I'd rather my family was out of harm's way. Better to be safe than sorry.'

'So, what you up to then?' said Clocks. 'What sort of business you in that you have to hide your family away?'

Tanner stiffened. Paterson jumped in, taking the conversation in yet another direction. 'You're no doubt aware that two men have been found burned alive. A third man was shot in the head. Executed.'

Tanner slowly uncrossed his legs. The guards stiffened slightly. Clocks watched them for any sign that they were about to make a move. Paterson kept his gaze on Tanner.

'I did hear,' Tanner said. 'Dreadful state of affairs. Far too much of this sort of thing going on nowadays. Must be difficult for you boys.' His gaze met Paterson's.

'Not much of it does go on, Mr T. Not burnings, anyway,' Clocks said. Tanner looked at him with dislike.

'One of the problems I have, among many, is that the first victim, the first one burned, was a David Caine. I believe you know him?' said Paterson.

'I do. Or I did. Yes. He was the son of an associate of mine, Billy Caine. Seemed like a nice young man.'

'Well, he wasn't,' said Clocks. 'He was nasty piece of shit like his ol' man. No one's shedding any tears for either of 'em, least of all you.'

Tanner raised an eyebrow. 'I'm not sure that I understand what you mean.'

Clocks shook his head. When would the day come when someone just held up their hands and said, "Fair cop, guv. You got me." No one had done that since Dixon of Dock Green. 'Let's see if this helps. Not too many people get burned at the stake, Bert — don't mind if I call you Bert, do yer? Stabbings? Ten a penny. Don't even waste our time on 'em. Shootings? Pretty common. Not overly worried. But burnings? At the stake? Now, that's something we don't see too often. In fact, I'll bet there's not been too many since the last witchfinder general back in the sixteen 'undreds.' He paused, watching to see how Tanner reacted. He didn't. 'I know there 'asn't. I checked. And I know about the ones you're down for.' Clocks stared hard at him. *This'll do it.* It did.

Tanner stood up. The guards snapped to attention. 'What did you say to me?' Tanner said.

'I said,' Clocks pointed his finger at him, 'you. This is your little ball game, ain't it? Setting fire to people.' Tanner's face contorted. He brandished the cane, holding onto it with both hands. Clocks had already had it for a sword-stick. It'd be about right for this brand of nutter.

'Albert! Don't talk to those bastards!' The voice came from behind them. They turned to see an elderly man, standing in the doorway, his rheumy eyes afire with hatred for the two policemen.

'Officers,' said Tanner, 'meet my father, Reginald.'

'Don't say anything to them. Filthy, dirty, bastards!' The old man tottered into the room and stared from Paterson to Clocks.

'Father. Thank you for joining us, but please don't concern yourself. The gentlemen were just about to leave.' He smiled at Paterson.

Reginald Tanner turned to Paterson. 'What do you want? You've no right coming here and harassing my boy.'

Paterson weighed up the old man. In his day, he'd have been a handful. Paterson had skimmed through the notes on him just before they headed out to the house. The old boy had certainly had a colourful life. Armed robbery, GBH, fraud, murder, attempted murder, there was little the old man hadn't done in his time. In between his numerous stretches of prison time, he'd built a reputation and an empire that extended into every corner of the East End — the empire that Albert now commanded.

'Ease up, old 'un. No one's harassing anyone,' said Clocks. 'Just popped in for a social, that's all.'

Reginald wheeled around, almost losing his balance. 'Who the fuck you calling old 'un, you piece of shit?' He held up a bony fist and waved it at Clocks.

'Whey hey, you're a lively old sod, ain'tcha? You forget to drink your Horlicks?'

'Mr Clocks,' said Tanner, 'I'd advise you to show some respect.'

'Two-way street, mate,' said Clocks, still watching the old man, who'd no doubt have taken a swing at him if he'd had the strength.

'I've no respect for you or your kind. Filth! All of you. Fuck off out of my house. Now!' Reginald shouted.

'Mr Tanner,' said Paterson, 'I'd be grateful if you would calm your father down. There's no need for unpleasantness, that's not what we came here for.'

'What about you, Mr Paterson? You've caused unpleasantness. Coming into my house, accusing me of murder—'

'No one has accused you of murder,' Paterson said.

'You didn't think that would cause unpleasantness?'

Paterson scratched the side of his head, smoothed his hair back. 'Wasn't my intention.'

'What *was* your intention, sonny?' Reginald said. Paterson chose to ignore him, keeping his eyes on Tanner the younger.

'Oi, filth!' shouted Reginald. 'I'm talking to you!'

Paterson turned. 'You really are a rude, obnoxious old sod, aren't you? Just do us all a favour and shut your trap.'

This was evidently too much for Tanner junior. 'Out, Paterson.' He nodded to his guards, one of whom put his hand inside his coat.

That was good enough for Clocks. He pulled out his gun and pointed it at one of the guards. 'Back the fuck up, boys. Stand down.'

Paterson double-tapped his earpiece, putting it in the transmit position. Their backup could now hear every word. 'Lyndsey,' he said, staring down Tanner. 'Stand by. We have a situation. Prepare for assault. On my word.'

'You better not be carrying any weapons, gents,' said Clocks. 'Open your coats. Do it. Slowly.' The old man snarled at him. 'Don't even think about it, Skeletor. I'm not above putting you out of yer misery.' The old man's eyes widened, burning with pure hatred. 'Coats, boys. Now!' The two guards slowly opened their jackets. Each of them were wearing shoulder holsters.

'Boys, really? That's not good. What are they, Tasers? That's classed as a firearm, fellas.'

The men said nothing.

'Turn around, lift the coats.' They did. Both clean.

'Finger and thumbs, boys. Lift 'em out gently. Put them on the floor. Do it.' Clocks grinned at the guards and touched his earpiece. 'Nineteen. We have weapons on premises. Situation is contained. Request backup. Assume all guards on premises are armed. Approach with extreme caution.'

Tanner waved his cane, agitated.

'Do I have to give the word, Tanner? You want me to ramp this up to a full-on assault?' said Paterson.

It could have gone either way for a few tense seconds. Tanner put down the cane and called to the guards outside. 'Armed police coming. Do not resist.' He turned back to Paterson, and gave him the one-eyed hard stare. 'No. No need, Mr Paterson. But if you don't intend to arrest me, get out of my house, now.'

Paterson smiled. 'Happy to, Mr Tanner, but before I go,' Paterson leaned in to him, 'I'll tell you what I told Caine. This is not a fucking game that you two are going to keep playing. Now, I could have you lifted for keeping firearms on your premises, but that would just be an inconvenience to you, wouldn't it? You'd worm your way out with your fancy lawyer. Not worth the time or the bother. I've got nothing on you right now, nothing that'll stick anyway, so consider this a social call. But, if one more body shows up, we're coming back and next time . . .' He turned to Clocks. 'Okay, John. We're done.'

Clocks turned to the guards. 'SCO19 are on their way in, boys. You'll both be arrested for illegal possession of a firearm and, if you're sensible, you'll not make a move on those Tasers when they get here. Understood?'

Each guard gave Clocks the death stare.

'Tough man with the gun, copper,' said the old man.

'Yep. That's me, pops. Hard as nails. Now shut up and give it a rest. You're gettin' on my ear 'ole.'

He followed Paterson toward the door. In the hallway he could hear Lyndsey's familiar voice, shouting her orders to the guards in the hall. But Clocks couldn't resist one last dig. 'Tanner. What's the deal with the glass eyeball? That supposed to scare people, is it?'

'The black one usually does, Mr Clocks. Pray you never get to see it.'

CHAPTER FOURTEEN

Ray Paterson was an early riser and whenever he could, he liked to get to the Dojo for his martial arts training. The place opened at six, and it was often packed with students, all as serious as him, getting in a couple of hours before starting the day's work. Because of the murders, Paterson hadn't been able to attend, but this morning was important to him, and he had booked the day off months ago. He'd arranged with Clocks that, should anything kick off, he would hold the fort until Paterson got there. He stood in the shower wrestling with himself. The job always came first, but today it could wait, he decided. As soon as he was done, he'd cancel his day's leave and get back in to work. He'd meet his idol, and be at the station by eleven thirty.

* * *

The man standing opposite Ray Paterson was the kind of man that, if you saw him on the street, you'd pass him by without a second glance. Nothing about him stood out. He was getting on a bit now, in his late sixties, but he kept himself in good physical condition and worked out every day, just as he had for the last sixty years. Off the mat he wore small horn-rimmed glasses that enhanced his humble demeanour.

He noted the bruises he had already inflicted upon Paterson and hoped that next time he hit him his opponent would stay down.

Yet again, the two men took up their fighting stances — legs wide, sideways on to each other, the backs of their hands touching at arm's length. They stared at each other, in absolute concentration. The first to move was usually the one to make the hit and win the point. Paterson sprang forward, his hand now a fist as he struck out at his opponent's face. Where he was expecting bone, he felt only air, followed by intense pain. In one smooth movement, the older man stepped to the side, deflected Paterson's fist with one hand and with the other, hit him with a four-finger strike just behind the ear. Paterson yelped. He didn't even feel his leg fold under him from the kick to the back of his knee. He dropped, confused and powerless to resist. The older man stepped around and behind him and pulled his head backward, dragging him to the floor, where he pretended to stamp on his balls, stomach and chest.

The audience gasped at the skill and speed of Wang Wei, a Chinese master of martial arts. Wei was proficient in at least seven of the arts, and held the title of Grand Master. He had retired from competitive fighting more than twenty years ago, and had gone on to establish a number of highly respected schools around the world. There were five of these elite schools in the UK. He was here to give a demonstration, and had asked to meet and spar with those the school considered to be their best and most respected students. Paterson was first up.

'Stay down, Ray!' Whoever it was, they were handing out sound advice. Six times this morning he'd squared up to Mr Wei, and six times he'd wound up on his back while the bruises on his face grew ever more numerous. Mr Wei was certainly a hands-on kind of teacher. Paterson rolled over onto his stomach and pushed himself up. Giving in wasn't an option.

Now standing, he turned to face Mr Wei, who had assumed the position again. Paterson nodded, walked forward, raised his hand to touch Wei's but suddenly lunged forward and threw his weight against Wei. Taken off guard by the change of tack and breach of rules, Wei reacted a fraction too slow. Paterson lifted him off of his feet and dumped him down onto his back. Hard.

Then Paterson was on him, straddling him to keep him down and punching wildly at the smaller man's body. His face had turned puce, and his teeth were bared. All he was aware of was the man beneath him. Pandemonium broke out among the watchers, and two of them ran forward to drag Paterson off. They weren't needed. Wei retaliated with a surgical strike. He swung his hand down, and with a short, hammer-like blow, struck Paterson's penis. He used the same hand to hit Paterson in the solar plexus with a back-hand strike. Paterson doubled up, leaning toward him. As he did so, Wei struck out with a palm strike and hit Paterson on the chin, causing him to jerk backward. As he began to topple backward, Wei brought his hands underneath Paterson's knees and with a strength that belied his size, threw Paterson up and off of him.

The two watchers dodged Paterson and, unnecessarily, helped Wei to his feet.

* * *

'An interesting fight, Mr Paterson.' Wang Wei handed Paterson a towel. They were now in the changing room. Paterson took the towel and gingerly dabbed at the cuts on his face. Terribly ashamed, he couldn't look Wei in the face.

'I . . . I'm . . .'

'Sorry? I expect you are. But you shouldn't be apologising to me. You should be asking why you lost control. You are a skilled man, you've been a martial arts practitioner for many years now, and I hear good things about you. I am told you normally remain focused and calm in combat, but that, of late, you are displaying an increasing loss of control and allowing your temper to get the better of you. People are . . . concerned.'

Paterson fiddled with the towel, his eyes on the floor. 'I have no excuse, Master. I can only say that the last couple of years have been somewhat challenging. I guess my frustrations just got the better of me, and I took them out on you.'

Mr Wei took the bloodied towel away and handed him a clean one. 'The question is, why me?'

Paterson dabbed his face some more. 'Because you're the only one capable of stopping me.'

CHAPTER FIFTEEN

This particular November day was one whose lowering skies warned of imminent rain and death. Kevin O'Connor, rumoured to have once been a commander in the Provisional IRA, and his drinking partner, Mark Folds, were tucked away comfortably at the back of the Crown and Sceptre, just off Bermondsey High Street. The pub was a gloomy little affair, a bit on the rough and ready side, with grey lino floors and walls papered with old-style Fleur de Lys, the kind that was fashionable back in the seventies. The only splash of colour was provided by a forty-two-inch telly that hung, slightly wonky, near the entrance to the toilet. The pub's only saving grace was that it still possessed a market licence. This was a throwback to the days when street markets were thriving, and pubs were granted licences allowing them to serve alcohol to the early morning market workers.

Kevin and Mark were watching the horse racing on Channel Four, busily marking up a battered copy of the *Racing Post* in search of a winner or two.

Behind the bar, Sammy Crags, the owner, was absently drying up a pint glass, with one eye on the racing. His daughter, nineteen-year-old Trudy, was wiping down the bar with a cloth that looked as filthy as the floor. Back in the day, Sammy had been a bit of a tearaway, running with the villains but never quite making it to the top with them. That was down to Trudy. From the moment she was born, Sammy's life had been transformed. Fighting and thievery lost their appeal, and he'd found work in this little rat-hole of a pub. It paid the bills and even for some holidays, and he was grateful to the landlord, Billy Caine, for looking after him.

Lifelong regulars, Kevin and Mark considered this place their own, somewhere to go to get away from the wife and kids, and just be themselves, do the things they liked doing and talk the sort of shit they were good at. The problem with having a place to call your own is that you become a creature of habit. And creatures of habit are easy pickings for someone with a job to do.

Nobody took much notice of the young man, dressed in black motorbike leathers, who stepped into the pub. Sammy glanced up briefly. The man did a quick scan of the room, and found his targets sitting facing toward him with their heads buried in the paper. Sammy Crags looked up again, sensing that something was wrong. Why wasn't this bloke ordering a drink?

The man in black strode across the room toward Kevin and Mark. As he went, he lifted his right hand and Sammy clocked a gun. It didn't look like any he'd seen before. There was a thin plastic tube coming from the bottom of it, running into the backpack slung over his shoulders. The man walked past him toward his targets, and Sammy suddenly spotted the tiny blue flame coming from the barrel of the gun.

'Oi!' shouted the man in black. Kevin and Mark looked up. This sounded like trouble. Their eyes widened at the sight of the gun and at that moment, he pulled the trigger. A huge jet of flame shot out and engulfed them. The man in black held the trigger for a few seconds, ignoring their screams, making sure his victims were well and truly alight before he left. As the two men writhed and screamed in agony, the man let the flame gun drop and pulled a small handgun from his waistband. He put two shots into each man and turned away.

Sammy immediately reverted to his old ways. From under the bar, he swung up an old sawn-off shotgun and collected a bullet full in the face for his trouble. The man in black sauntered out of the pub, followed by the sound of Trudy's hysterical screams.

* * *

Paterson eased himself carefully into his car. For a few seconds he sat, savouring the silence that comes with sitting in a car with all its windows shut as the world rattles by outside. He stole a glance at himself in the mirror, frowned at the cuts and swellings on his face and shook his head. A wave of self-loathing washed over him and he reached into his jacket pocket for his phone to dispel it. Five missed calls and five voicemail messages, all from Johnny Clocks. He dialled the message service.

He listened to the first one, called Clocks and floored the Bentley.

* * *

Paterson walked through the pub doors and stopped dead. All hell had broken loose in here. Over to one side, herded together in a little bar off the main one, a small huddle of people stood crying and whispering in shocked voices. Uniformed police, ambulance and fire officers were milling about. At the back of the pub Paterson could see the charred, smoking remains of a table and two men, pitch black and dripping wet. He moved toward Johnny Clocks, his feet squelching. The place was pretty much soaked from floor to ceiling. The fire brigade were a thorough lot. Not too good at preserving evidence though.

'Jesus! What the fuck 'appened to your face?' said Clocks.

Paterson touched his cheek. 'Fell over. Don't worry about it.'

Clocks didn't. He shrugged and went back to the business at hand. 'Coupla witnesses, Ray, but not reliable. They say a bloke walked in dressed all in black, pulled out a — wait for it — a fuckin' flamethrower and then everybody dived under the tables.'

'What d'you mean, a flamethrower? How'd you "pull out" a flamethrower? I don't understand.'

'Me neither. Not properly. Witness said it was a small thing, like a gun. He had a backpack on, so I guess it was some sort of homemade contraption. I don't know. I've got DC Harper on it. He's checking Google, the military and our own databases to see if any of them can shed any light.' He nodded toward the firemen milling about near the bodies. 'Trumpton turned up and splashed the place with water to put out the fire that had started. The curtains and the chairs had caught, and it was beginning to get a good hold. Lucky the station is literally around the corner, or the whole gaff could have gone up. Ballsed up the evidence though.'

'Why the fuck is everybody still in here, for Chrissakes? Why aren't they all outside?' Paterson nodded toward the group of people in the adjoining bar.

Clocks shrugged. 'Uniform duty officer said to keep them all in one place. Didn't want anyone wandering off, never to be seen again. Seemed sensible to keep everyone in that little bar out of the way. Most of the evidence will have gone though, Ray. Bloody water everywhere. We're gonna have to go old school and, God help us, rely on eyewitness accounts.'

Paterson looked around the bar. No sign of any sort of CCTV, nothing to verify anything the witnesses may or may not have said. 'Who's she?' he said, pointing to where Trudy Crags was sitting on a bench near one of the two entrances. With her was a paramedic, kneeling and holding her hand, and a middle-aged woman with her arm around her shoulder. Both women's eyes were red with crying. The older woman was Mary Bettson. She was a regular who'd wandered in for her daily G and T a couple of minutes after the killer had left, and had found herself smack-bang in the middle of the carnage.

Mary knew Sammy and Trudy well. She'd watched the girl grow up and had always considered herself to be a bit of a mum to Trudy, so she'd always looked out for her. When she walked into the pub, the first thing she saw was "her" girl standing looking down at something, wide-eyed, mouth open and tears streaming down her face. Mary moved closer and saw that Trudy was looking at her father.

Kevin and Mark were long dead by then but still on fire. Mary turned her attention to them. Witnessing such things can do strange things to a person, as Mary well knew. Two men, sitting in a pub with their heads on fire, and the furniture and curtains around them being eaten by flames — it was a surreal scene, of the sort that would leave some onlookers paralysed with fear. Mary was not one of them. After throwing a half-empty pint of lager at the two burning corpses, she quickly realised that more liquid was required, so she took out her mobile phone and called the fire brigade.

Paterson went over to the bar, where a couple of CSIs were busy milling around, one of them taking photos.

'That's the guv'nor, Ray. Bloke called Sammy Crags,' said Clocks behind him. 'Took one right in the face. Hit him smack in the 'ooter.'

Paterson peered over the bar and saw Sammy's body crumpled on the floor. He noted the shotgun lying next to him. 'D'you know the story here?'

'Not much. The young girl said the fella came in, torched the two blokes over by the window and was on his way out. Seems her old dad pulled a shotgun on him and didn't live to regret it.'

'Why would he do that? He's just seen two people get killed. Where's the sense?' Paterson asked.

'I wondered that too, until I found out who the licensee is.' He pointed to a small brass plate screwed into the wall behind the bar. 'There's your answer. Licensee is William Caine. Our Billy.'

Paterson ran his fingers through his hair and rubbed the back of his neck. 'Shit. If there was even the slightest doubt before this — and there wasn't — there's no fucking doubt now that this is down to Tanner. Those two over by the window probably worked for Caine. Sammy here had to do something, I guess.' He shook his head. 'Stupid bastard.'

They sloshed over to the two dead men, both charred beyond recognition from the waist up. 'Any idea who they might be?'

The CSI stopped what he was doing, pulled down his mask and said, 'Both had ID on them. Driving licences. A bit on the charred side, but readable. Luckily, they were in their wallets in their back pockets. They're bagged up and with the evidence officer.'

'Good stuff. That's something, I suppose.'

They walked toward the front door.

'A bloody flamethrower, John. What the hell is going on here?'

Clocks shrugged. 'I know. It's mad. But, if you're gonna set fire to two people sitting in a pub, it's a shitload easier than strolling in with a can of unleaded and splashing it about over them. People tend to get the 'ump about things like that.'

'What the fuck does Tanner think he's playing at? He knows we're going to come for him now. It's just madness.'

'Clearly, he don't give a rat's arse, Ray. He's got away with shit for so long, maybe he thinks he's above the law.'

'Well, he's bloody well mistaken. Make a few calls, John. I want eyes on the house. Round up the troops and get a full contingent of SCO19. Two hours from now we're going back, heavy and hard. I want this bastard banged up before the night's out.'

Clocks grinned. Things were about to get good.

'I want a full search team. We're going to strip the place down, tear it to bloody shreds. And dogs. Get the canines. Nothing like a bunch of Alsatians going mental to quieten people down. And, John,' said Paterson, as Clocks pulled out his mobile phone, 'make sure they all bring fire extinguishers.'

CHAPTER SIXTEEN

Paterson pulled up a few yards shy of Tanner's front gate. Behind him, hidden by the trees, was a long line of police vehicles. He'd got everybody he wanted. Clocks got on the radio. 'All units, standby. On my shout, Trojans to take the gate out, all others wait until DS Paterson and me follow them in.' There was a collective burst of replies, each unit acknowledging they understood.

Clocks dropped the radio into his lap and took out his gun. Paterson patted his coat pocket, comforted by the weight of the Glock he carried.

'Ready?' said Paterson.

'Born ready, guv,' said Clocks, with a broad grin. He picked up the radio again. 'Trojan One, Trojan One. Attack! Attack!' He threw the radio down again and sat back in his seat as the SCO19 Land Rover, fitted out with a metal ram, hurtled past them. He watched in awe as the vehicle slammed into the metal gates, throwing them wide open. Paterson gunned the Aston and followed them in.

Ahead, Paterson could see the guard go into panic mode at the sight of the convoy of police vehicles steaming up the drive toward him. He smiled slightly. The guard was the same big black man they'd tangled with on their last visit. He saw the man hesitate, unsure of what to do next. By the time he'd made his decision — to raise the alarm — Trojan One had skidded to a gravel-spitting halt, decamped from their vehicle and hit him with 1,500 volts from a Taser.

Paterson and Clocks bailed out of their car and ran behind the SCO19 officers, weapons drawn. Earlier, the decision had been made to shotgun the door if necessary, and it turned out to be just that. With an ear-shattering bang, the lock was blown off and the door kicked in. The Trojans poured into the hallway, swinging raised guns from side to side. The two guards inside surrendered at once. The two lead Trojans grabbed them, threw them down onto their stomachs and began to secure them with plasticuffs. Their colleagues, following behind, moved on past them. No further resistance.

'Door on the right!' Paterson barked to them. One of the men kicked open the door and jumped back, flattening himself against the wall. He poked his head around the frame and took in the scene. Three men, two seated — one old, one dressed like a circus performer and one guard. This latter had a gun drawn and pointed at the Trojan.

'You inside! Armed police! Drop your weapon. Do it now!'

Paterson and Clocks stopped dead in their tracks.

'Put the gun down! We are heavily armed.'

After a few seconds, the guard shouted, 'Okay, okay. It's down.'

The Trojan peered around the door. It was. 'Kick it over. Keep your hands up.'

The guard did as he was told and the Trojan, with backup, entered and secured the room. After a few seconds he shouted, 'Safe!'

Paterson and Clocks walked in. The guard was down and cuffed. Sitting in his chair was Albert Tanner, his father next to him. Dad was not in a good mood. 'You fucks!' he spat. 'I hope you fuckin' die.'

'That's not nice, is it, Reg, you old bastard?' said Clocks, beaming from ear to ear. 'If I didn't know better, I'd say you didn't like me much.'

'Clocks!' Tanner shouted. 'Don't you dare talk to my father like that. I've warned you before . . .' He rose up out of his chair, turning toward Clocks. One of the Trojans moved forward.

Paterson put his hand on Tanner's chest. He could feel the man trembling with rage. Tanner turned on Paterson and pushed his face in close, his one good eye ablaze with hatred. Paterson didn't feel much like being threatened right now. He brought his hand up sharply under Tanner's chin and Tanner clattered backward. The old man screamed and launched himself forward. Clocks grabbed him by the arm and swung him back round. As he came around, Reg swung his bony arm wildly in an attempt to punch Clocks in the face. He failed miserably. Clocks easily blocked it and, grabbing the old man by the collar, pushed him backwards into a table, struggling to restrain the furious bag of bones.

'Wind yer neck in, pops,' he said. 'No good will come of it.'

Tanner, looking dazed, stood himself up. Paterson waited, tense, ready for round two. Paterson knew he could destroy him if it came to it. Part of him wanted to.

'What do you want, Paterson?' Tanner spluttered. 'Father! Shut up! Stop it!' The old man, exhausted, slumped against the table.

'You. That's what I want. Murder times four.'

Tanner shrugged. 'Don't know what you're talking about.'

'Oh, fuck off. Two of Billy Caine's boys get themselves torched in a pub, and you don't know what I'm talking about?'

'If you have proof, then arrest me. I assume that's why you and all these other pricks are here.'

'You assume right. Albert Tanner, you're under arrest on suspicion of the murders of—'

'Don't you fuckin' touch him!' Reg had found his second wind and tried to barge past Clocks, who held him back. Reg swivelled around and launched a gob of spit right into Clocks's face.

For a second, Clocks stood stock still. The room went silent as Clocks wiped his face with the back of his hand. He looked at his hand and suddenly back-handed the old man, leaving a streak of mucus. 'You disgustin' dirty old piece of sh—'

'I'll fucking kill you, you bastard. I'll fucking kill you!' Clocks stopped in his tracks and the room came back to life. Clocks whirled around to see both Paterson and the Trojan struggling to restrain Tanner, who screamed and struggled, desperate to get to Clocks. Finally, Paterson swept his legs from under him, rolled him over face down and cuffed him. He dragged him up, manhandling him roughly and bouncing him off the furniture, keeping him off-balance. Tanner kicked out at him, and Paterson threw him down a second time.

'Pack it up, Tanner. You're nicked. Consider yourself cautioned.' Paterson stood over him, half-hoping he would kick out again. He had enough witnesses to justify knocking the shit out of him if he did.

Old man Tanner wasn't finished yet, not by a long chalk. He straightened himself up, flexed his shoulders, balled his skeletal fists and shouted, 'Clocks! C'mon!'

Clocks wheeled around only to bump up against a Trojan, who grabbed the old man by the scruff of his neck, chucked him back over the desk, cuffed him up and marched him outside.

With things now under control, Clocks began to look around the room. Spotting a pretty silver filigree box, he lifted the lid. The eyes stared up at him. Clocks did a double-take, peered closer and pulled out the black onyx.

'Oi, Bert. This the death eye then? The one you wear when you've got the 'ump?' Tanner said nothing. 'Last time we met, you said I'd better pray I never saw you wear it. Sounded like a threat.' He tossed the eye in the air a few times before putting it in his pocket. 'I'll 'ang on to it for a while then, just in case.'

* * *

Four hours later, a dishevelled Albert Tanner sat in a small interview room on the top floor of Tower Bridge police station. Next to him was his brief, Leonard Stickson, a man well known for his impeccable taste in clothes and encyclopedic knowledge of the law. This was not a man you could dance rings around. He opened his briefcase, took out a gold Mont Blanc fountain pen, a small digital recorder and a yellow legal pad and positioned them in perfect alignment on the table. On the opposite side of the desk sat Detective Sergeant Laurence Macksy and Detective Constable Margaret Shannon. As DS Macksy busied himself with the preparations for the interview, DC Shannon flipped through the notes she'd been provided with. Protocol dictated that the interview be conducted by officers with specialist training in the art of interviewing, and that the arresting officers would not be present, thereby being unable to bring their own prejudices to bear on the questioning. In the case of Paterson and Clocks, it was the sensible thing to do.

DS Macksy switched on the recorder, introduced everyone in the room, stated what Albert Tanner had been arrested for and cautioned him.

Mr Stickson had been waiting for that bit. He put down his pen and peered at Macksy over his gold-rimmed glasses. 'Officer, before we begin, my client wishes it to be known that he was never properly cautioned at the time of his arrest. In fact, he has not been cautioned at all until now.'

Here we go, thought Macksy. *Not heard that one before.* 'I'm satisfied that he was, Mr Stickson, so if you don't mind we'll contin—'

'I do mind, Sergeant. What steps have you taken to ensure that my client and his father *were* properly arrested and cautioned?'

Macksy frowned. This didn't bode well. 'I have Detective Superintendent Paterson's arrest notes and they state, quite explicitly, that he informed Mr Tanner of the reason for his arrest and that he gave a full caution.' Tanner gave a sardonic smile.

'May I see them, please, Sergeant?' Stickson sounded extremely smug.

DC Shannon sifted through the paperwork until she came to the arrest notes. She gave a little smile, pulled them out of the folder and handed them to Stickson. 'For the benefit of the recorder,' she said, 'Mr Stickson has just been handed Detective Superintendent Paterson's arrest notes, as requested.'

Tanner leaned across Stickson to read the notes for himself. The wry smile turned into a self-satisfied grin. Stickson found the section that indicated arrest and caution. 'How unfortunate.' DS Macksy eyed him warily. This wasn't going well. 'It would seem that there is a discrepancy in these notes.'

'Discrepancy?' said DS Macksy. 'What discrepancy?'

Stickson took out a small digital recorder from his briefcase and snapped it shut. 'The one between the truth and the lies told by Mr Paterson.' Macksy's brain fizzed a little bit. He hated these sorts of moments. Luckily, they didn't happen often.

Stickson held up the recorder. 'My client has informed me that his house contains a number of recording devices. It is not necessary to go into why this is, as it's irrelevant here. He asked me to stop off at his house, where I would be handed a recording of the police assault on his property.' He looked at Tanner and blinked slowly. 'I've taken the liberty of running it forward to the time of the arrest.' He pressed play. Macksy's heart sank and Shannon dropped her head. They had a bad feeling about this.

'Pack it up! You've lost. You're nicked. Consider yourself cautioned.' Paterson's voice was crystal clear, captured in high-definition digital clarity. Macksy looked up to the ceiling as if hoping for deliverance.

'I've listened to the recording several times now, Inspector, and I cannot find anything indicating that Superintendent Paterson correctly administered the caution, either before or after Mr Tanner's arrest. Nor did he inform him what he was being arrested for. This is a considerable oversight on the part of a senior officer in charge of a murder enquiry, as I'm sure you'll agree.'

Macksy stared at the arrogant bastard and said nothing. He couldn't think of anything to say in reply.

'I will leave you a copy of this tape, Inspector, which I am submitting to you as evidence of assault, perverting the course of justice and the wrongful arrest of Mr Tanner and his father on the part of your two officers. I fully expect you to open an investigation into their behaviour this very evening. Please ensure that the recording is not "lost." On it, you will hear quite clearly Detective Inspector Clocks verbally and then physically assault Mr Reginald Tanner, a frail old gentleman who is well into his eighties and incapable of defending himself. You will also hear Superintendent Paterson assault my client just prior to his non-arrest.'

Stickson stood up, scraping the chair on the tiles. Tanner followed suit. Macksy looked on, helpless. No point trying to bullshit his way out of this one.

'As you know, my client was not arrested and cautioned in accordance with the rules of the Police and Criminal Evidence Act as is his right and as according to the law, and his subsequent detention has been without any legal basis. We'll be on our way now, Sergeant, as will Mr Tanner's father. Before we go, please know that this tape will also be handed over to your Department of Professional Standards. It contains a number of things that they'll be interested to hear, I'm sure. Shall we?' He gestured for Macksy to show them out.

DC Shannon, the last one in the room, switched off the recorder, completed the log and closed the door behind her.

* * *

Not long afterwards, DS Macksy found Paterson and Clocks sitting in the canteen, laughing and joking with a few uniformed PCs. After sending the PCs scuttling off to do some work, Macksy had a two-minute discussion with the two of them that ended with him explaining how he'd had no alternative but to refer the matter to the Department of Professional Standards. Paterson smiled and thanked him and watched him walk away.

'Knew that was coming, Ray. Me, I expected it. Come to think of it, why didn't you caution him? That's not like you, is it? Especially as you knew the gaff was bugged.'

Paterson grinned. He stood up and pushed his chair back under the table. 'He had to be nicked, John. Nothing I could do about that once you'd smacked his dad, but that doesn't mean I wanted him kept in custody, does it? I want the bastard out, but I want him out thinking he's got the better of us. He now thinks he's cock of the hoop and we're a couple of idiots who don't know what they're doing. That, John, should give us an advantage.'

Clocks shrugged. 'Maybe. But now DOPS will be all over us like a rash. We both ballsed this one up a treat, didn't we?'

'Yep. But I ballsed it up deliberately. You, on the other hand . . .' He grinned at his partner. 'Ah, no point sweating it. I'm not worried about DOPS. We've done worse, and no doubt we will again before too long.'

CHAPTER SEVENTEEN

Caine was getting fed up with this. He decided a bit of tough love was needed. His boy had been dead a fortnight now and still, every time he came home, April was flopping about in the house, crying and snivelling. It was beginning to annoy him. Sure, they'd loved each other and, yes, he knew she was upset. So was he, it was understandable, but she needed to pull herself together now and get on with it. Mind you, he wasn't sure how she was supposed to get on, now that David was dead. They'd moved into the mansion with him temporarily while they sorted out a place for themselves. Clearly, that was no longer on the cards, and he didn't want her around. Not his responsibility. He'd have to give her a talking to when he got in.

As he swung into the drive, he was surprised to see April getting into her car. She was dressed in her usual tight jeans and white T-shirt and he noticed, she'd combed her hair and put on a bit of makeup. Must be feeling better.

'Where you off to?' he shouted. 'Anywhere good?'

She turned and gave him a weak smile. 'Hi, Billy. I'm off out to meet a girlfriend. I can't stay in the house, it's too depressing.' She opened the door of her Merc and slid into the driver's seat. 'Thought it might be best if I talked it out with her, y'know? Girlie chat and stuff.'

'Who is she?'

She started the engine. 'You've never met her. Name's Karen. We went to school together. She was going to be my chief bridesmaid.' She shook her head.

Caine got out of his car and walked over to her. He glanced at her legs and could see why David had been attracted to her. She was, as the kids put it, fit as fuck. 'What time will you be back?'

'Don't know yet. Won't be late though. I just can't sit around in the house anymore.' Her eyes welled up. 'It's just . . . a bit much. I'll be home well before dark. It's just nice to get out.'

'You've been out, love,' he said. 'You stayed with your sister. Remember?'

'Course I do,' she said, 'but we're not particularly close. I needed to be with family then, to tell them in person. Now I need a friend.'

He smiled down at her. 'Go on then, girl. Go and have a good chat. Get yourself sorted out. Lucky you've got someone to talk to.'

She gave him a look that said she knew he had no one and, even if he did, he wouldn't open up to them. He was a man, wasn't he? Men didn't do stuff like that.

'Keep yer phone on. I worry about you, you know.' This was a lie, but he figured he owed it to David to keep an eye on her until he got her to fuck off out of his life.

'I will. Honestly.' She blew him a little air-kiss and drove away. Hands in his pockets, Billy Caine stood and, lost in thought, watched her go. He turned and headed back inside. Something was troubling him, but he didn't know what it was.

He pulled out his mobile phone. 'Ronnie. It's me. You busy?' he nodded. 'Good. Need you to do a follow for me. April's going out to meet someone. I wanna know where she goes and who she meets. Whack the tracker on, will yer, and find the Merc. Let me know what you find.'

* * *

Ronnie Batch, a long-time friend as well as an enforcer and a lieutenant in Caine's little army, managed to pick up the Merc as it drove north across Tower Bridge. He had no reason to suspect that April was surveillance conscious, so he felt more confident than he normally would about staying close. The area she was heading for was always busy with traffic and he had no wish to run a red light, he certainly couldn't afford to draw the police's attention. Fortunately, April drove sensibly, and he was able to stay with her until she parked up. He slowed right down as he passed her, pretending to look for a street sign.

He watched her get out of the car and lock it, feed the meter and head toward a parade of shops. He made a note of what she was wearing, a bright white T-shirt. Easy to spot. *Thank you very much.* He drove on another hundred yards or so and parked on double yellow lines — not ideal, but needs must. There were always cabs if he got towed away.

He walked back to where he'd lost sight of April and saw a dress shop, a charity shop and, in the middle of the two, a small café. He strolled past, hoping to spot her inside one of the shops. April was in the café, sitting with her back to the window. She turned to hang her bag on the back of her seat just as he drew level with her, and Ronnie held his breath. Did their eyes meet? She turned away.

The place looked packed out, but he couldn't see anyone at the table with her. She must have been the first to arrive. He looked for somewhere to watch the café door and saw an old-fashioned red telephone box that had been "repurposed" as a miniature, standing only, coffee kiosk. It

141

had a couple of tables outside. Ronnie, a tea drinker, was pissed off to find it was coffee only. The things he did for Billy Caine.

* * *

He was tearing open one of the little packets of sugar when he noticed a large Range Rover with blacked-out windows glide to a halt outside the café. From where he stood, it was bit tricky to get a clear view of the passenger who got out but he could see it was a man and he watched his back as he walked toward the café. Through the reflections on the large window pane, he saw April look up and give the man a quick wave.

Ronnie wondered if he should take a walk past and see if he could recognise April's companion. He'd be running the risk of being noticed, of course . . . and decided to stay put.

After his third cup of coffee and a helping of stares from the skinny, crop-haired bird who was serving, he saw the Range Rover come back and pull up again. It sat there for a while, oblivious to the frantic hooting of the motorists stuck behind it. Ronnie had a little grin to himself.

April emerged into the daylight, all smiles and hair tossing, looking pleased with herself. The man was behind her. Ronnie still couldn't get a good look at him, but there was something familiar about the way he walked. He bent down. Ronnie couldn't be sure but he thought he'd kissed April on the cheek. As the man sauntered around to the passenger side of the car, Ronnie got his first good look at him. His stomach lurched.

He fumbled for his phone. The man got into the car. Ronnie kept his eyes on it as it pulled away. He turned his back as it passed him, just as Billy Caine answered the phone.

'Bill. Fuck me blind, Bill. You'll never guess what. She's just met up with Albert Tanner.'

CHAPTER EIGHTEEN

Paterson and Clocks were taking advantage of an unexpected break in the normal November drizzle and had grabbed the opportunity to slope off for a quick cuppa in Rosie's burger bar. Paterson was sitting nursing his tea, lost in thought. Clocks was carefully examining the burger he'd just bought.

'Tell me again why we come here, Ray? I've just parted with four pound fifty for what should be a delicious cheeseburger with onions, and what have I got? Four pound fifty's worth of shitty, greasy, floppy cardboard. Fuckin' liberty that is.' He sniffed it. 'An' it smells a bit off. I think it's on the turn.'

Paterson looked at him. 'Take it back then. Not difficult, is it?'

'I can't do that.'

'What? Why?'

'She's tryin' her best, ain't she? Probably don't make much profit. Don't wanna make a fuss.'

'Don't want to make a fuss? What are you doing now? You haven't stopped moaning since you bought it.'

Clocks was still eyeing it warily. 'I'm not moanin', I'm just sayin'.'

'Well go and say it to Rosie then. Tell her you're not happy because your burger looks a damn sight different to the picture stuck up on the menu board. She won't mind.'

'Nah. I'll leave it.'

Paterson shrugged. His phone beeped.

'Who's that?'

'Mind your own business.'

'Alright. Don't get stroppy. Just askin'. Wondered if it was important.'

'It is. Let me read it.'

'Probably some bird. Is it Carrie? What's she saying? Have you knocked her up? That's not good if you have.'

'John, shut the fuck up a minute and let me think. It's from Young.'

Clocks lobbed the burger into a nearby bin. It went straight in without touching the sides and he punched the air. 'Back of the net!'

'Oi!' shouted Rosie from the counter. 'What was the matter with that?'

Clocks spun around. *Caught*. Time to front it out. 'Gotta be honest, love. It's shit.'

Rosie's grin split her face almost in two. 'I know it is. You don't think I'm gonna waste the good stuff on you, do yer?'

Clocks looked at her. He'd known her for years now and always had a good bit of banter with her, but just then he wasn't sure if she was joking or not.

'All the shit you've eaten over the years, I'm surprised you even noticed,' she said.

'Fair point, Rose. I normally do eat shit whenever I come in here but, you know what? That's because you buy cheap crap food and you're a crappy cook and I only come here 'cause I feel sorry for you.' He smiled to take the edge off of it. As they say, many a truth's spoken in banter.

144

'Crappy food for a crappy copper.' Rosie turned back to the griddle and Clocks spun back to Paterson.

'She's talkin' about you, Ray.'

'Fuck off.' Paterson was still reading his phone, scrolling up and down and pinch zooming every so often. His face wore a pained expression.

'Well, come ter think of it, Clocksy, you can always piss off somewhere else if you're not happy.' Rosie had finished whatever she was doing and turned back, ready to resume their little spat.

'I'm 'appy, Rosie. Where else can I get crap food cooked by a shit cook followed by piss-poor banter, all for under a fiver?'

'Home?'

Clocks raised his middle finger.

She chuckled. 'Just the one, Clocksy? You'll need more than that for me.' He shook his head. No words. She'd won. For today, anyway.

'What's he want, Ray?'

Paterson put the phone back in his jacket pocket. 'He's done some digging for us, as he said he would. He can't find any hands-off policy on Tanner or on Caine. He's confirmed there is twenty-four-hour surveillance on them both and there are UCs working deep in both places, but there's no one from on high dictating what we can or can't do. Obviously, we have to be a bit sensible about how we go forward, but if we have to, we have to and if it comes to the crunch, the UCs will have to be pulled but, as he said, there's no reason for us to even consider that as yet.'

Clocks was frowning. 'So Alliston's shittin' us?'

'I don't know, John. Seems like it. I'm still thinking.'

'Fuck me, we'll be here all day. I don't think it's too complicated, Ray. He's been in charge of this operation since day one. He's lived it, breathed it and got two boys in deep an' he's worried about them. Don't want us throwin' bottles of piss everywhere and ruinin' everything for him.'

'"Bottles of piss?" What are you banging on about now?'

Clocks blinked. 'It's an expression. It means he don't want us to, how'd you say it, compromise the integrity of the operation and therefore endanger the lives of his wonderfully dedicated undercover officers.'

Paterson grunted. 'You're a total dick. There's no such expression.'

'Yes, I am and no, there isn't. But there should be. We'll use it from now on.'

'I won't. If anything, it means behaving like a bull in a china shop.'

Clocks shrugged.

'Either that, or he's being precious,' said Paterson. 'Protecting his investigation. You do something like that for long enough, it becomes difficult to extricate yourself from it.'

'Or,' said Clocks, 'he's protecting them for some reason.'

'Who? His UCs, or Tanner and Caine?'

'Tanner and Caine.'

'For what reason?'

'Dunno. Maybe he's as bent as a nine-bob note,' said Clocks. 'You never know.'

Paterson shook his head. 'It's not that. I just don't think he wants us, as you said, throwing our piss around. He doesn't want us to screw up his operation. I get that. Not happy he lied to us though.'

He looked around for a bin and spotted the one Clocks had used. 'Come on,' he said, 'Time to go.' He waved to Rosie, who waved back.

'Ta ta, Ray,' she called. 'See ya later, Clocksy.' She gave him the finger.

He returned the gesture with the middle fingers of both hands. 'You love me really, Rosie. You know you do.'

'I would love you, Clocksy, but I've heard it's not worth the bother. Someone said you've got a tiny organ.'

146

He couldn't let that one slide. 'Economies of scale, Rosie. It's gonna look tiny if it's playing inside the Albert Hall!' She burst out laughing.

Clocks started to open the car door and stopped. 'Plan?'

'We carry on. Nothing to worry about,' said Paterson with a shrug.

CHAPTER NINETEEN

After Ronnie's bombshell phone call, Billy Caine thought about things and began to put the pieces together. He'd spent a good half hour berating himself for his stupidity after it slowly dawned on him that he'd actually let this girl into his house, let her get close to him, without having carried out any background checks on her. That was unforgivably stupid. He tried to justify it to himself by saying that if David trusted her, that was good enough for him. In truth, he knew it was his Alzheimer's clouding his thinking. This led to him spending another half hour cursing whoever the bastard was that had decided to give him Alzheimer's.

Now Caine and Ronnie were sitting in the safe room, away from prying ears and kicking the arse out of a bottle of Smirnoff. Caine was in a foul mood. 'And you're sure? You're positive? She met *Albert Tanner*?'

Ronnie was busy slugging away at a big tumbler of vodka. 'Positive, Bill. 'Undred percent. Albert Tanner himself. She's got to be his daughter, Ruby. No question.'

Billy Caine looked haggard. He kept asking himself how much he actually knew about the girl and was forced

148

to conclude: it was only what she'd told him. Which wasn't much, and certainly not enough to warrant letting her live in his home. Her name was April Ratenn. Mum and Dad put her into care when she was young, she found herself a job when she was eighteen and moved in with a girl who turned out to be a crack whore. She'd walked out on that and moved in with another girl until she hooked up with his David.

'Oh fuck me, Ron! It's just dawned on me.'

'What has?'

'Her name. Ratenn. It's a bleedin' anagram for Tanner. Stupid fuckin', stupid motherfuc—' He hurled the glass against the wall, slightly satisfied when the crystal tumbler shattered into pieces with a loud pop. 'Right in front of me. How the fuck didn't I see it? Little bitch must have been pissing herself with laughter.'

'You weren't to know, Bill. How could you?' Ronnie hung on to his vodka.

Caine ran his hand over his bald head and sighed loudly. 'It all makes sense now. Tanner sent her over here to get around Davey, get herself in his bed and into the firm. That explains it — why Tanner's making his move now. He knew I was ill, knew I was fucked. That's how he knew about my Alzheimer's before I told him. She fuckin' told 'im.'

Ronnie nearly choked on his drink. 'Hey? What? Alzheimer's? You've got Alzheimer's? When'd you get that? You never said anything.'

Billy Caine looked at him, his face rigid with anger. 'You didn't need to know. Nobody did. Davey was the only one who knew. Must have told her, and she told her old man.'

'Why would Davey do that?'

'Dunno. Pillow talk? But the bitch knew and . . . of course she knew. That's how Tanner knew I was screwed and it was a good time to make his move. Killed Davey to get him out of the way. There was no one else, so I'd have little option but to give everything over to him.' Caine stormed over to his bookcase, pulled out a bundle of false books and opened the safe behind. He pulled out a gun and a clip of bullets. 'Dirty little slag's gonna pay when she gets in!'

Ronnie was up on his feet at once. 'Bill. No! That's not the way. Plods'll be all over you.'

'Fuck 'em. Bitch had my son killed.'

Ronnie laid a hand on his arm. 'Think, Bill. There must be a better way. You can turn this around, you must be able to. Think about it.'

Caine stared at Ronnie. They'd been friends for years. They'd first met in a pub one summer's night, when Billy got himself into some bother. It was one of the rare occasions when he'd gone out on his own, and he'd chosen to go to a local pub where he'd be among his own kind. He'd got a bit pissed, tried it on with some girl and found himself the recipient of a right-hander from Micky Shaw, the local head-banger and wannabe hard man. Having caught Billy off guard, he bravely set about kicking him when he was down. A couple of other wannabes saw their opportunity and joined in the kicking. All was going well for them until Ronnie, who'd been drinking with some friends and generally minding his own business, decided he couldn't let this cowardly attack go unpunished.

He launched himself into the fray, armed only with a barstool he'd picked up on the way. He managed to smash two heads with it before the third man cottoned on and ran. Micky Shaw was one of the two who'd received a chair across the head. He froze, shocked. A mistake that had allowed Ronnie to snatch up a pint glass and ram it into Micky's face, taking out one eye and leaving a scar that destroyed his hopes of ever being somebody. Fight over, Ronnie bent down and hauled up a beaten but unbowed Billy Caine, and they became friends for life.

Ronnie was right. Caine put the gun down on the desk and flopped into a chair.

'You know what? Tanner thinks I'm going to sign everything over to him, just like that. Well, I won't, never even considered it. I was gonna fuck him over somehow, but I've had a proper idea now. A better one.'

* * *

Billy was in the kitchen chopping up some vegetables when April returned. He heard the key in the lock and his hackles rose. He pushed his anger down. He had to play it cool with her.

'You 'ave a good day then, babe?' He watched her slip off her jacket. She was such a pretty girl too. Shame, really. She draped her jacket over the back of a kitchen chair and strolled over to him, smiling.

'I did, yes. It was really good to catch up with her.' She pecked him on the cheek, with one eye on the kitchen knife he held. She began to wash her hands. 'She was so supportive. I should have talked to her earlier. Got a lot of stuff off of my chest.' Her eyes brimmed. 'Oh, Billy. It's so hard. I'll never get over Davey. He was a diamond, so good to me . . .' Her voice trailed off. It was all Billy could do to stop himself from jamming the knife into her throat and cutting the lying whore's tongue right out of her head. For a moment, he almost lost control. He turned away and closed his eyes, willing himself to calm down.

He turned back to her, a painful half smile on his face. 'Yeah, I know. It's not easy for me either, but I'm dealing with it. You will too. Takes time. You'll meet someone else. Not yet, but you will. You'll be happy again.' She looked doubtful. 'Just don't get hiked up with a bunch of lowlifes like us next time, and hopefully your old man won't get killed.' He picked up a bottle of wine, poured two big glasses and handed her one. 'To Davey,' he said, holding his glass high.

'To Davey.' They chinked glasses and smiled at each other.

'Listen,' he said, 'I've got to go away for a while. I've decided to call it a day. I'm off to live out the rest of me time in the sun. As you know, I haven't got too much of it left, so I thought I'd make the most of it. I'm going to sell off all the businesses and I need to sort a few things out for me and for you.'

April sipped at her wine. 'Me? Oh?'

'Davey loved you, and you were gonna be my daughter-in-law. If you'd got married, you wouldn't have wanted for anything, so I think it's only proper I do the right thing by him and by you. I've got a few bob stashed away over in Switzerland and I thought I'd give it to you. It's about five mill.'

Her eyes widened. 'What?'

'That should set you up nicely, get yer a decent house and leave you a few quid in the bank. If you're sensible, it should last. Don't blow the lot on booze though!' He smiled at her.

'I . . . I don't know what to say.'

'Nothing to say. It's fine.'

'Who you selling the business to?'

He cocked his head, shook it. 'No one you know. Some bloke called Albert Tanner.' She didn't react. 'Works the East End. Nasty, ugly, bat-shit crazy piece of shit. Thinks he's gonna get it all but, hey, there's five mill he'll never see, right?' Still no reaction.

He knew she'd go running to Daddy, but he also knew there was nothing either of them could say or do without her compromising herself. If Tanner queried the "missing" five million, it would be obvious where the info had come from. No, Tanner would stay quiet. He still wanted his little girl on the inside. Besides, he'd reckon on getting the five mill one way or the other.

'Come on, gel,' he said after a few seconds. 'I've got three bottles of this so let's get off our nuts.'

* * *

Billy Caine checked his watch. 11:30 p.m. He looked across at April sprawled on the sofa, empty bottle on her stomach and empty glass lying on the floor at her side. She was out for the count and the addition of three dissolved Rohypnol tablets would make sure she stayed that way. Caine pulled himself up out of the chair he had been dozing in and wobbled across the room toward her. He'd drunk a bit more than intended but he had to look convincing. She was lying on her back, head to one side, mouth open and drooling slightly. He bent down and snapped his fingers a few times next to her ear. When she didn't move, he knew he was safe.

From the small table by the side of the sofa, he picked up her iPhone and peered at it, trying to get it in focus. He flipped it over and found the fingerprint pad. Gently picking up her hand, he straightened out the index finger. She didn't resist. He pressed it on the pad and gave a little grin when the phone unlocked. He made his way back to his chair and fell back heavily into it. He looked across at April. Not a flicker. He went through her contacts but found nothing of note. Certainly, Daddy's phone number wasn't in there. He went through a few apps until he found an accounts program. He needed her fingerprint again. Back he went and repeated the procedure. It took him a few minutes of vacant staring and a couple of head scratches, but finally he realised that he was looking at all of Albert Tanner's business documents.

He walked out of the room and went to his office where he fired up his laptop. While he was waiting for it to boot, he opened and closed a few drawers, looking for a USB lead that would fit her phone and his laptop. He found one, and while all the files copied across, he sat wondering how to use this to screw everybody. Billy Caine wasn't a man to waste an opportunity. If he played his cards right, he could shaft that prick Paterson as well. And his gobby mate.

CHAPTER TWENTY

'What'd you reckon then, love?' said Johnny Clocks. He was standing in front of his bedroom mirror admiring himself in his new suit. Clocks wasn't a suit man, but he'd been getting a bit more used to wearing them now he was a DI. It was kind of expected that you didn't dress like a bag of shit held together with sellotape, which was Clocks's own preferred look. His other half, Lyndsey Mullins, along with Paterson had been nagging him for ages to open his wallet and buy a decent suit. He'd almost passed out when Paterson told him he'd have to pay at least a grand for a real good one. He'd bought cars that cost less than that.

'Hang on,' Lyndsey said. 'I've just got out of the shower.' Everybody that knew them was amazed that they were still together. Lyndsey, an inspector with SCO19, was a girl who didn't suffer fools gladly, and it was widely accepted that Johnny Clocks could be an absolute knob when he wasn't fast asleep. Lyndsey padded into the bedroom in a pair of knickers and a loose T-shirt, towelling her hair dry. Clocks was disappointed. He knew that look. *Not today, big boy*.

'Well?' he said, smoothing the fabric. 'Tasty, or what?'

'Well, in case you forgot, I was with you when you bought it but, yeah, it's much better in the daylight. You look gorgeous!'

'I know. If I was you, I'd do me right now.'

'Luckily, you're not me. You do look lovely though, John.' She straightened his tie and gave him a kiss, the sort that made him wonder if his luck was back in. It wasn't. She pulled away from him and headed for the door. 'Any idea what time you'll be home tonight?'

'Nope,' he said. 'We'll have to play it by ear as usual.' With one last quick look in the mirror, he followed her down the stairs.

'You taking your car?' she said.

'No, love. Ray's picking me up at the corner. Sent me a text, said the traffic's a bitch and he's running a bit late. Might as well go now, in case you suddenly realise how gorgeous I am and lose control of yerself.'

He kissed her on the cheek and headed out the door. Lyndsey wandered into the living room and watched him though the net curtains as he ambled off down the road, plugging in his ear buds and looking at his phone. She thought about how far they had come, and gave a little smile. Despite all his talk, Johnny Clocks was a good man and she knew he loved her deeply. After some of the men she'd had in her life, Lyndsey was thankful to have found him.

Lyndsey moved away from the window and went through her to-do list for the day — take the team through a room clearance training session, attend a meeting with the Specialist Crime and Operations Assistant Commissioner in the afternoon, plus a half-dozen other things she would need to do in her role as a SCO19 team leader.

Just as her foot landed on the bottom stair, she was gripped by a sudden feeling of unease. She stopped dead, turned and hurried back to the living room window. At the top of the road, a white van was moving slowly in John's direction. She knew at once it was coming for him. She had, at best, thirty seconds before the van got to him. No point shouting, he'd never hear. Moving fast, she ran into the hall, wrenched open the under-the-stairs cupboard door and punched in the security code for the gun safe. She snatched up her Glock, rammed in a clip and headed for the street.

The van was picking up speed. Lyndsey ran barefoot across the path, oblivious to the gravel. She could see Clocks crossing the road. She screamed his name as she raised the gun, two-handed, and pointed it at the van. The man in the passenger seat looked directly at her and turned sharply toward the driver. As she reached the gate at the end of the drive, the van accelerated away, leaving her standing. She screamed again.

Clocks, in his own little world, had been happily bouncing along to Sting and Shaggy's "Don't Make Me Wait." It was now coming to the end. As the music faded, he was about to hit repeat when he half heard someone shouting his name. He turned and his eyes widened. Van. Coming at him fast, too fast. Lyndsey running behind it. Gun. Fuck! The van skidded to a halt a few feet from where he stood, frozen to the spot. Three men piled out. Lyndsey was still coming. He heard her scream, 'Armed police! Armed police! John! Run! Run!' But there was no time to run. He planted himself low and held his hands up. He'd started to draw back his right hand when two of the men piled into him like a couple of runaway trains. They smashed him off his feet, sending him backwards into a parked car. The air punched its way out of his lungs. He would offer no resistance now.

The third man drew a gun and fired at Lyndsey. She crouched low, veered sideways and took cover on the far side of another parked car. She stood upright behind it and brought her arms out straight, looking for her target. She caught a glimpse of Clocks being bundled into the van through the side door. She considered taking aim at his captors, but it was an impossible shot from here. The windscreen of the car she was crouching behind exploded, blown out by a bullet. She heard the van roar off and knew she'd lost him. She watched helplessly as the back end of the van skewed wildly across the road leaving a trail of smoke, tyres screaming. It turned into the main road and disappeared.

Lyndsey stood still, panting. Paterson was nearby. She had to call him. She was running back toward the house when she saw a girl pointing a phone at her. It took Lyndsey a moment to realise what she was doing — the girl was filming her.

'Give me the phone,' she said.

The girl, who looked like she was in her early twenties, thrust it behind her back. 'No way! This is going straight on YouTube.'

'Is it fuck. That's evidence. Hand it over.' Lyndsey made a lunge for it.

'You can have it when I've posted,' the girl said.

Lyndsey raised the gun and pointed it straight at the girl. 'Or I can shoot you in the face and tell everyone I thought you were pointing a gun at me.' She shrugged. 'Stress. They'll believe me. As you can see, bitch, I'm having a fucking bad start to my day.'

* * *

'What the hell happened?' Paterson was inside the living room with a distraught Lyndsey. Shaking from head to toe, she recounted the story, trying to keep calm and remember everything. The smallest detail might just be the one to save Clocks.

Before he screeched to a halt outside their house, Paterson had already put the shout out over the radio, stressing the need for extreme urgent assistance. India 99, the police helicopter, was en route and fast proceeding in the last known direction of the van. Paterson held out little hope of them finding it. Less than two minutes' drive from Clocks's house was a set of railway arches that local businesses used as garages, workshops and storage spaces. They could have hidden the van away and swapped vehicles by now, and there was no way the police could block off enough streets in time. He glanced at his watch. Already ten minutes since Lyndsey had called him. Johnny Clocks was long gone.

Paterson walked out into the front garden and studied the road outside, in the futile hope of spotting something that might help them. All he could see were nosey neighbours milling around. He pulled out his phone and called the officer who was next in line to command his team, Detective Sergeant Alan Grayson. He spent a couple of minutes filling him in and instructed him to get the team together immediately. He wanted them briefed, every single snout squeezed and re-squeezed until their eyeballs popped. Even as he issued his orders, he knew who was responsible. *God help us*. In the distance, the wail of sirens signalled that the local police had begun the hunt for their missing colleague.

As he ended the call, he heard a sound behind him and turned to see Lyndsey, now in her uniform, marching off towards her car. Her tactical bag swung from her shoulder.

'Lyndsey! Wait! What are you doing?'

'I'm going to work, Ray. Have to find these bastards.' She began to open the car door.

Paterson got to her as she bent to slide in. He put his hands on her shoulders. 'Lyns, listen. You can't. We don't know where he is. Don't, please.'

She shrugged him off, got in the car and started the engine. 'When they find him, I want in.'

'I know. I know you do, but you can't. You know that. You're not thinking straight, Lyns.'

She glared at him for a moment and then she lost it. Tears running down her face, she threw herself back in her seat and punched the roof. 'Christ, Ray. I'm so scared. They're gonna kill him.'

'No, they're not. They wouldn't dare. He's a policeman.'

She shook her head. Like that mattered in this day and age. They both knew no one gave a toss.

She turned the engine off. 'So what do we do?'

He knew she wouldn't like the answer. He felt exactly the same way. 'We have to wait. The world and his oyster are out looking for him now. They'll find him.'

Would they? In truth, Paterson wasn't so sure.

CHAPTER TWENTY-ONE

Detective Chief Inspector Lambert took his last look of the day at the murder board. He was no nearer to catching the killer operating on his ground. It had been a bad day for the Met all round. The news had been full of the kidnap of Johnny Clocks and he, like all policemen, was deeply concerned for his brother's safety. Everyone knew that it might just as easily have been them. They knew too, that policemen don't just get snatched off the street in broad daylight for no reason — Clocks must have been involved in something far bigger than most of them would ever have to deal with. *Thank goodness.*

He switched off the office lights and stood for a moment or two enjoying the darkness, lit only by the faint blue glow of the odd computer screensaver. The room was silent. He glanced at his watch — 10:29 p.m.

What to do now? There was nothing left really. Just go home, kiss the kids goodnight and try not to wake them. Kiss the wife on the forehead because that was the stage they'd reached in their relationship. Eat a warmed-up microwave dinner, knock back a bottle of white, tumble into bed, fail to switch his mind off properly and lie there for a few hours hoping that the nightmares wouldn't disturb his sleep — for once. Much like any other night. Except it wasn't.

For the third consecutive night, rain was falling. Not hard, but enough for the wipers to begin swishing intermittently. The neon lights of the shops painted smeary, abstract patterns on his windscreen. His Met radio burst into life, making him jump.

'All units, all units.' It was the Scotland Yard control room. Someone with an emergency to report had hit nine three times. The control room was dishing it out for action. 'Reports of a female being carried onto some wasteland off of Lordship Lane, Dulwich. Units to respond?' The voice was calm and matter-of-fact.

'Papa-Mike One. Five minutes,' a voice crackled over the radio.

'Papa-Mike One, thank you.'

'Papa-Echo Five,' came another voice. This was night duty CID.

'Thank you, Papa-Echo Five. Anyone else?'

Lambert picked up his radio. He knew exactly where this wasteland was. 'DCI Lambert. I'm less than two minutes away. Request other units make a silent approach.' He dropped the radio into his lap, flipped on his blue lights and pushed the accelerator.

'Thank you, DCI Lambert. Mike-Mike One, Mike-Echo Five. Silent approach. Repeat. Silent approach. Confirm.'

Both units confirmed.

'All units, be aware that there is a small, disused alleyway at the back of this wasteland,' said Lambert. 'My guess is, he'll go there.' The efficient lady operator repeated the information for the benefit of the attending units.

Two minutes later, Lambert pulled up just shy of the entrance to the wasteland. He jumped out and made his way, as silently as he could, across the wasteland and up to the mouth of the alley. Not for the first time, he wished that they were allowed to wear trainers to work. They'd have afforded him a much better grip than these boots. He stopped, listening for a sound, anything that might tell him how far into the alley he would have to go. He looked along its length. Maybe three hundred yards long. Residential properties on either side. Overgrown bushes and bracken. No lights. A few dozen industrial wheelie bins dotted about, the odd damaged and discarded pushchair and the obligatory stolen moped. As his eyes adjusted to the dark, he counted about six bins. The victim would most likely have been taken just beyond those. What should he do? Run hollering into the alley and hope that he disturbed the suspect before he did anything nasty? Or move slowly through and hope to catch him in the act.

Time to start the game of Russian roulette.

Mentally pointing a gun to his head, he took a step into the alley and cracked a branch that went off like a real gunshot. No point creeping about now. 'Police!' he shouted. 'Come out now. Hands up! I am an armed officer!' The bluff brought no response.

Lambert knew he should wait for backup. It was only sensible, but a girl could be badly injured in that dark alley and needing his help.

His heart punching at his chest, he gingerly made his way up to the first bin. He grabbed the smooth cold plastic handle, and cocked the other fist. He wrenched the bin backwards, away from him. Nothing. He moved on. Behind this one? No. This one? No. This one? As he reached the last bin, a dark shape shot up and barrelled into him, punching him backward and knocking him off of his feet. Instinctively, he grabbed hold of the man's body. Lambert felt the air explode out of his chest as his back slammed into the brick wall behind him but he held on. His attacker was powerfully built, strong and fast. He felt something hit him in the stomach rapidly, two or three times. A knife? Lambert tried to shout for help but no sound came out. He had no breath left.

All he could think of was that he might just be able to hang onto the man long enough for the uniforms of Papas One and Five to show up. If they didn't, then he was at least going to smother himself in as much of his attacker's DNA as possible. He put his head down and rubbed it against his assailant's, hoping for a hair transfer. He couldn't get it. The man was wearing some sort of nylon hood.

Lambert was faltering. He was still winded and his grip was loosening. The man managed to push him off and began to scramble to his feet. With his last ounce of strength, Lambert swung a wild right-hander. He felt a satisfying crack as his hand connected with the man's face, and then he slumped back, all out of strength. As he lay on the ground, desperately trying to breathe, he could make out the sound of running feet. He heard shouts. One pair of feet stopped in front of him and someone bent down. Other feet pounded straight past and he could hear voices shouting into radios as they went.

'Sir! Sir! Are you okay? Talk to me!' Lambert, still unable to speak, struggled to sit up. The PC got to his feet and barked into his radio, shouting something that Lambert never quite heard. He wasn't listening. The PC absently looked back down at him and, frowning, turned to see what Lambert was pointing at.

Next to a bin opposite him and struggling to get up, was a young girl. Her dress was torn and one of her shoes was missing, but she was alive. Lambert fell back, slowly regaining his breath. She was alive. He was alive.

Beat you this time, you bastard.

CHAPTER TWENTY-TWO

10:30 p.m. and Johnny Clocks was still missing. A countrywide alert was in place and every copper on duty was on the lookout for something, anything that might lead to his release from capture. Within an hour of his being snatched, a warrant had been obtained to search Caine's house. Nothing was found. There was no evidence against him, no chatter, nothing.

Tanner was not at home. Nobody was, apart from a handful of guards. Some "persuasive" questioning revealed that Tanner and his father had gone to Scotland earlier that morning to visit some "business acquaintances." No evidence to link him to Clocks's disappearance.

* * *

10:31 p.m. A distraught Johnny Clocks was dumped out of a van, face down in the dirt.

'Get the fuck up, you piece of shit!' barked one of his captors.

Clocks stayed where he was for a few seconds and then struggled to pull himself upright. The plastic ties that bound his hands behind his back bit deeply into his flesh and made it difficult for him to regain his balance. He made it to his knees. He was badly bruised and dishevelled but still had his wits about him. He had no idea where, but he was deep in a woodland, and he hadn't been brought here to look for nocturnal wildlife.

'Might as well stay like that,' said the man by the van. 'No point getting all the way up. They'll be pleased to know you died on your knees.' The other two men spread out around him. All of them pulled out guns.

The hard man of the group, the one that had given him a beating in the van, laughed. 'This is it then, fella. End of days.'

Clocks lifted his head and looked at him through a painfully swollen, purple eye. Hard Man pointed his gun at Clocks's head. If he was going to die, he wasn't going out begging, that was for sure. 'Crack on then, son. Enjoy yerself. Not every day three cowards get to shoot an unarmed man, is it? One to tell the grandkids, if you manage to make old bones.'

'We're gonna make older bones than you, mate,' Hard Man said.

'Seems that way. Come on then, wanker. Get on with it.' Clocks brought his head closer to the barrel of the gun. 'There you go. Just in case you're as useless a shot as you are a man. Oh, and when you see that fuckin' abomination, Tanner, tell him I said he's a cowardly, fucked-up, no-good prick! *And* his half-dead bastard of a father. Should have finished off that bucket of bones when I had the chance.'

Hard Man grunted. 'Before you go, Albert wants to know what you've done with his eye. He'd like it back.'

Clocks laughed and spat blood into the dirt. He grinned, revealing teeth stained red. 'Tell him I chucked it in the bog, shat on it and then flushed it away.'

The man stood poised, finger on the trigger, his face black with anger. Clocks pushed his head right against the gun barrel and the gun began to waver. The other two men stood stock still, watching. Hard Man dropped his arm. 'This is too easy,' he muttered. He turned and walked off toward the van, returning with a five-litre petrol can. The one still standing by the van pulled out his mobile phone and began filming.

Clocks's heart hit the floor. One in the nut would have been a blessing compared with this. He lowered his head, utterly defeated and terribly afraid.

'A little going-away present from Mr Tanner and his dad.' Hard Man unscrewed the cap. 'What was that old film line — "I love the smell of petrol in the morning."'

'Napalm, you dumb fuck. I love the smell of *napalm*.' You had to hand it to Johnny Clocks — wisecracking and defiant even in the face of an inevitable and agonising death.

Hard Man splashed the petrol over him until he'd emptied the can and Johnny Clocks was saturated from head to toe. He coughed, bent double and spat out petrol. Hard Man grinned, glanced around at his audience, turned back to Clocks. He pulled out a lighter, looked at his friend with the camera and said, 'Any last words for Mr Tanner?'

Clocks raised his head and looked directly at the camera. 'Yeah. Tanner, you and that fuckin' stick insect you try to pass off as a father — you're dead men walking, you one-eyed piece of cowardly shit. Go fuck yerselves.'

'That'll do,' said Hard Man. Grinning, he looked down at Clocks. 'Oi, copper. Joke for you. How'd you make a pig go "woof?"' He flicked open the top of the lighter.

'Woah, woah, *woah*!' It was one of the other men, the youngest. All eyes turned to him. 'What'd you mean, "copper?" He's a policeman?'

Hard Man stopped and turned toward him. 'Yeah, he's filth. This here,' he waved towards Clocks, 'is the infamous Detective Inspector John Clocks. The one involved in shooting that serial killer and all them blacks.'

'What? Why the fuck didn't you tell me? You never said he was a cop.'

Hard Man sighed. 'Tanner didn't want you to know. This is your first outing with us. He thought you might . . . bottle it. Wasn't sure if you'd have the balls.' He smirked at the young man.

'Why? Why would he think I'd bottle it? I've been loyal, haven't I?'

'Yeah, you have. No one's arguing that, but you haven't killed, have you? And killing pigs, cooking bacon,' he grinned at his own joke, 'that takes a bit more. Albert wanted you to be a part of this so there'd be no chance of you ever backing out or grassing us all up.'

The young man wavered, lowered his gun slightly. 'I have killed.'

Hard Man spun the little wheel on his lighter. A spark flashed. He clicked it again and a flame wavered in the breeze. 'What? When? Who've you ever kill—?'

As he spoke, a bullet blew out his face. The man by the van froze for as long as it took the young man to put four shots into him. He slammed back against the van and slid down, leaving a bloody snail trail behind him.

'You two pricks for a start.'

Johnny Clocks kept his eyes fixed on the lighter. He watched in horror as it bounced on hitting the ground. He squeezed his eyes shut. Nothing happened. He let out a deep breath.

'Woah, that was tight,' said the young man. 'Always liked the sound of his own voice, that one.' He pulled Clocks to his feet. He could feel him shaking. 'It's okay, sir,' he said. 'It's over. You're safe.'

Clocks turned towards him and mumbled, 'Thank you.' Then, 'Who the fuck are yer?'

The man pulled out a knife, stepped behind Clocks and cut the plastic ties binding his wrists. Clocks rubbed at them. If this kept on, he might start believing in God. 'I'm Detective Sergeant Kenny Rogers,' the man said. 'And before you say anything, I've heard all the jokes.' He turned Clocks back around and looked into his face.

'You'll be okay. A few lumps and bumps, but you'll survive. Probably be throwing up for a coupla days until the petrol's out of your system, but overall, you're good. Come on.' He pulled Clocks toward the van, scrambled around under the seats and pulled out a litre bottle of water. 'Shut your eyes.' He slowly emptied the bottle over Clocks's face. 'Keep your mouth shut, too.'

As the water poured over him, Clocks started to shake uncontrollably. 'Shock's hitting you. Take it easy, sir.' Sergeant Rogers found an old blanket in the back of the van and wrapped it around Clocks's shoulders. He sat him in the front passenger seat and reached into the glove compartment, removing a mobile phone and a small plastic packet. He tore it open and unfolded an aluminium blanket. 'Put this on under the blanket. It's only a shitty Poundland one, but it might help. I'm calling an ambulance. Bear with me.' He walked away, checking for a signal.

Clocks felt the tears begin to slip out and he couldn't hold them in. He'd done some shit in his time, even stared down both barrels of a sawn-off, but this . . . this was way too much. He took a deep breath full of petrol fumes, and coughed. The water hadn't been a great deal of help. He sniffled and rubbed his eyes as DS Rogers came back.

'All done,' he said, looking at Clocks. 'You alright?'

'Yeah, all good. Bastard petrol's stinging my eyes, 's all.'

Rogers gave a small smile. 'Yeah, course. It must be. Ambulance and police are on their way. Be about twenty minutes or so. We're tucked away here.' He got in beside Clocks.

'I'm sorry, mate, who are you again? I wasn't taking too much in just then,' Clocks said.

'Sergeant Rogers. I'm part of DCI Alliston's team. Took me the best part of five years to work my way up in this lot. Finally got myself into a position where Tanner trusted me. At least, I thought he did.'

'To do what?' For some reason, Clocks took off his jacket and began shaking it out.

'To come out with the team assigned to kill you. You see, you disrespected him, and his dad too. I'm told you also clumped the old man. Shouldn't have done that. That was a bad move. He loves his old dad.'

Clocks stared at him in disbelief. 'He did this because I clipped his old man? The old bastard gobbed in my face. Lucky I didn't snap his scrawny little neck, but I bloody well will when I see him. And that bastard one-eyed mental case. He's done for too.'

'Let's get you home first, guv. You've had the mother and father of all shitty days.'

Clocks said nothing, mulling something over in his mind. After a while, he said, 'Listen, skip. I'm not thinking too straight at the moment, but help me out here. If you're a cop, what the fuck were you doing coming out in the woods to kill me?'

Rogers said nothing.

'You never knew I was police, right?' said Clocks. He didn't wait for an answer. 'I can understand you shooting those two pricks when you found out about me, but still . . .'

'I know. I know what you're saying. You're right. Listen,' he bowed his head, 'I'm in far too deep, sir. I've lived among these animals for five years. Five long years, morning, noon and night. I've seen so much, so much violence, and been part of it too . . .' He leaned his head back, looking up at the roof. 'I've had to do bad shit to keep my cover, to stay alive. I wanted out, but I couldn't. I couldn't get out. He wouldn't let me. Bastard wouldn't let me . . .'

Clocks knew the answer but had to ask. 'Who? Who wouldn't let you out?'

Sergeant Rogers turned to face him, his eyes empty. Gone was the confident man who had just shot to death two criminals and helped him to safety. Here was a man whose world had suddenly caved in around him. A man who knew his time was up. 'Alliston. Something's not right with him. I don't know what he's up to, but he won't let me out.'

'Is he on a bung?'

'I dunno. Maybe. Yeah, maybe he is. I don't know.'

'Sounds like he wants to keep you in so you can report back if things start getting hairy for him. Pricks like Tanner can turn on a sixpence. He might decide one day that Alliston's no more use to him, decide to dob him in to the higher-ups at the Yard. Might decide to set fire to him. And how'd he even know it was coming? Best to keep you in for as long as possible, keep your ear to the ground for him.' Rogers grunted.

'Just out of interest,' said Clocks, 'did he know that Tanner had ordered me dead? Did he know I was tonight's target?'

Sergeant Rogers snapped his head back, looked up at the stars and sucked in a lungful of cold, country air. 'Tanner called me into his room. Those two were already there.' He nodded toward the dead men. 'He told me I was going out on a job. Someone needed to be dealt with. I knew what that meant, of course. Some bloke called Johnny Clocks had been stirring up shit. That's all I knew. He never said you were police. Well, I couldn't really say no, could I? He'd have had me killed there and then. It's all about trust, see? Anyway, when it was safe to do so, I called Alliston, and told him what was going to happen. He said I had no choice but to go through with it. I didn't want to kill anyone. Christ! He said he'd get it cleared upstairs, that I wouldn't be prosecuted, that it was a necessary part of bringing down a major player. Said if I didn't, then five years of hard work, five years of my life were going down the shitter. I wanted him to find me a way out, to bring me in quickly, get me out of there, but he put it all on me. No way out.'

'So, you told him my name? You told Alliston that you'd been given the nod to take out a bloke called Johnny Clocks?'

Rogers shook his head, not in denial but despair. 'Yes. Yes, I did.'

Clocks punched the dashboard and jumped out of the van. He stomped up and down, muttering, 'Bastard! Fuckin' no-good, dirty bastard! Why? Why would he do that?'

Rogers shrugged. 'Dunno, sir. If he is bent, then maybe he was worried that you were about to take out Tanner and put an end to his paydays. He lives well, I know that.'

Clocks stopped ranting. 'What good is that? He'd have had every copper in the Met going after Tanner.'

'For what? Who'd have known it was down to Tanner? What evidence would there have been? Once you'd been . . . taken care of, we had orders to bury you. Deep. No one would have found you, and with no body and no evidence, life would have gone on. Tanner wasn't going to get banged up, was he? Alliston would have stayed in charge for the Met and on the payroll of Tanner. Win-win all round.'

In the distance, the wailing of sirens cut through the still night. Clocks looked at DS Rogers. 'You know you're in the shit, son, don't you?'

A few minutes ago, this man had taken the initiative and confidently whacked out two men without a moment's hesitation but now, faced with reality, he looked utterly defeated. He gave a small nod. 'I know. I'm . . . sorry. I lost my way.'

'So why didn't you kill me, then?' said Clocks. 'You could have gone along with it and you'd have been in the clear.'

Detective Sergeant Kenny Rogers lifted his head, pulled his shoulders back and faced Clocks. 'I told you. I never wanted to kill anybody. But Alliston wouldn't get me out. I'd have had to kill a scumbag at some point anyway, to ensure I lived and to keep my cover intact. I would have had to find a way to live with that. But killing a policeman, one of my own, was a step too far. I wasn't prepared to do that, even if it cost me my life. I said that I'd lost my way, sir. Not my soul.'

'Hmm,' said Clocks. 'Lucky for me they happened to mention I was a copper. So, what happens now?' He brushed his hair away from his face, squeezing out petrol.

'Now? Now I come in, put my hands up and take Alliston down. I have to put this right. I didn't know . . . I'm so sorry. I really am.'

'Yeah, I know,' Clocks said. 'I get it, mate. Listen, thanks for saving me life, son. I mean it. I appreciate it. I thought I was a goner, I really did.'

'Jesus, no! You don't have to thank me for anythi—'

Clocks head-butted him in the face, dropping him to the floor. 'But next time, don't leave it so late. Me suit's completely fucked.'

CHAPTER TWENTY-THREE

Johnny Clocks's first stop had been the hospital, where they cleaned him up, took away his clothes for examination, let him shower after the forensic boys had done their work and gave him an ill-fitting pair of jeans and a jumper to go home in. No one was allowed to speak with him — other than the senior police officers debriefing him — but they did inform Paterson and Lyndsey that he was safe, if not in the best of shape. His second stop was home.

As soon as the police car pulled up, Lyndsey came bursting out of the front door, followed closely by Paterson. Clocks was tired, shaken and depressed — it showed in the way he stood. He managed a smile, a beamer, but pleased and thankful as he was to see Lyns, his mind was back in the woodland. Lyndsey threw herself at him, smothered him in kisses, and held him tight, very tight. Paterson came up behind them and stood around, feeling a bit like a spare prick at a wedding. Clocks caught his eye and gave him a knowing nod. It was the first time in their lives that either of them had wanted to cuddle another man tightly. The cold November air bit into them and they walked back into the warmth of the house. Clocks lifted his face to the gentle rain that was beginning to fall.

'Come on,' Lyndsey said, her arm around his waist. 'Inside.'

'I'll get the kettle on.' Paterson moved ahead.

In the hallway, Clocks caught sight of himself in the mirror. Blank face, a lot paler than normal, bruised, cut and swollen. His lips were almost white, his eyes red from the petrol. 'I'm sorry, love. I still stink. Petrol. I had a shower at the hospital, a change of clothes before the debrief, but it won't wash away. Not properly.'

'It's okay, John. Have some tea and then, if you want, have another shower. It'll go. We'll get you some new clothes too.' It was not Lyndsey's style to fuss, but tonight her mother would have been proud of her. Sometimes it takes a massive shake-up for two people to really understand what they mean to each other.

Paterson came out of the kitchen with a tray of teas. 'Come on. Tea's up.'

He carried on straight to the living room. Lyndsey and Clocks trailed behind.

'Tanner's gonna pay for this,' Clocks said.

Paterson glanced at him, then at Lyndsey. He set the teas down and started sugaring them. 'We'll worry about that in the morning.'

'Have you spoken to that cowson, DCI Alliston? Anyone know what's happening with him?' Clocks asked Paterson, picking up a mug.

Paterson settled himself into one of the armchairs and shook his head. 'No. But I've heard bits. His supervising officer called me to tell me the situation. I'm a bit confused by it all. DS Rogers has been arrested, right?' Clocks nodded. 'And he's being kept incommunicado, to stop word getting back to Alliston that's he's in custody whilst they interrogate him? Alliston's been a naughty boy, then?'

'Naughty boy? Fuckin' naughty boy? He knew I was gonna get swagged off the streets. He knew I was sentenced to die, and the scrote was gonna let it happen. Let me get burned to death. It was only 'cause Rogers couldn't bring himself to kill a copper. Otherwise . . .' His voice trailed off.

'Did Rogers say why Alliston wanted you out of the way?' Paterson asked.

'Nope. Not really. The only thing we can think of is he's bent — well, clearly he is — but we're not sure in what way. I can only think he's on Tanner's payroll and he's protecting himself. If Tanner gets nicked for anything, good chance Alliston will be too. Might just be that Tanner wanted me whacked out and he thought it wasn't necessarily a bad idea. The smart money's on both of those.'

'Alliston was due to come into the office later today for a routine update. The chief at the Office of Professional Standards says that by the time he comes in, they'll have enough from Rogers and they'll be ready for him. Plan might change, of course, but at the moment, it stands. It seems Rogers was to call it in to Tanner when you'd been, er, rested, and then his next call would have been to Alliston. He's called them both and told them the same thing to avoid arousing suspicion. For all intents and purposes, you're dead, Johnny boy.'

Clocks sipped his tea, burnt his lip and smiled. A little burn like that he could live with. 'I want to be there when he comes in. Piece of crap nearly got me killed.'

Lyndsey hadn't taken her eyes off of him since they'd all sat down. 'Hun,' she said, 'I know you're angry. We all are, but I don't want you going in. There's no point.'

Clocks flashed her a hard stare. 'There's every point, Lyns. Tanner ordered me burned alive and Alliston was up for it. Burned. Fuckin' snot-gobblin' scumbag. Bent coppers are one thing but this . . . Gloves are off, Lyns.

I'm gonna fuckin' iron him out good an' proper.' He shook his head, adamant. Nothing left to say.

Except Paterson couldn't let it drop. 'It's not a good idea, John. The last thing you want is to get yourself nicked for assault.'

Clocks shrugged. 'I'm sure we can say he just fell over. Can't we?'

'Maybe,' said Paterson, 'but I guess that depends on how many times he falls over, eh?'

Clocks glanced sideways at his partner and gave a wry smile.

'Listen up, John. Tanner's gone on the trot.'

Clocks looked up to the heavens.

'No, *listen*. We're not sure where he is, but we know he's coming back. He has to. He thinks you're dead. Rogers said that after he'd made the call, the plan was for all three of the killers to go into hiding for the next few months until things died down. No communication allowed. They wouldn't call him, he wouldn't call them. No calls, texts, messages, nothing traceable. Standard protocol for these sorts of things, apparently. Tanner made sure he wasn't anywhere near the crime scene when it went down. What is it you say?' he smiled. '"Nothing to do with me, guv. I was upstairs collecting fares."' Clocks didn't smile back. 'So, he'll come back home thinking it's safe to do so and *then* we take him. We'll work it out, John, I promise you.'

Clocks rubbed his eyes. *Christ*, they stung. And now they'd started watering again. He sniffed. 'Okay. He's mine though, Ray. When we go for him. Mine. Fair?'

Paterson pulled himself out of the chair. 'Yep. All yours. Now,' he glanced at his watch — 6:47 a.m. That meant nearly twenty-five hours without sleep. 'I'm going home to catch a few zeds. You two get some rest as well, if you can. I'll see myself out.'

'Hang on, Ray.' Clocks got up and turned to Lyndsey. 'Can you put the shower on for me, hun?'

'Of course,' she said. 'Don't be long.' She gave Paterson a peck on the cheek and headed up the stairs. The two men went into the hallway.

'What's up, John?'

Clocks opened the door, and a blast of cold night air swept in. 'Just so we understand each other. When I say, "he's mine," you do know what I mean, don't you?'

Paterson stared into his partner's eyes. They were bloodshot, watery — and resolute. He flashed him a smile. 'Yep. Course I do.' The rain was now falling steadily and Paterson pulled his collar up. 'You know what? Sod it. Alliston's due in at two, if you fancy it.' He walked off, head down.

Clocks closed the door and went upstairs to the bathroom. Lyndsey was already in the shower, waiting for him. He opened the door, stepped inside, and pulled her to him, holding her as if he'd never let her go. Then, slowly, like a balloon that's losing air, his legs crumpled under him and he sat on the floor. Lyndsey put her hand on his shoulder and wept for him, as the man she loved drew his knees up into his chin, put his head down, and began to sob.

CHAPTER TWENTY-FOUR

Ray Paterson glanced at the clock on the dashboard. He'd managed a couple of hours' sleep on and off, but was up, showered and dressed within forty minutes of his alarm going off. It was only eleven o'clock. He ran a quick mental check over the myriad things that fought for his attention, trying to prioritise. He always tried to stay organised as best he could, but invariably everything went to rat-shit. Still, some things had to be attended to, his meeting with DCI Alliston for one. He wasn't looking forward to it. He would ring in soon to see if anything had changed in the couple of hours he'd been out of it.

His phone rang, showing an unknown number and for a moment, he thought about rejecting it. Something told him not to. He swiped answer.

'Mr Paterson? It's me, Billy Caine.' The previous day's events had wiped Caine from his mind. *What the hell does he want?*

'You there, Paterson?'

'Yes, I'm here, Mr Caine. What can I do for you?'

'Other way around, really.'

Paterson said nothing for a second or two. 'What does that mean?'

'It means I have something of interest for you.'

A motorcycle courier cut across in front of him before roaring off along the road. He blasted his horn. One finger salute delivered right on cue. 'And what would that be?'

'Not on the phone. You know Stone Cross industrial estate?'

'Yep.'

'There's an abandoned warehouse, Direct Packing it's called. It's mine. One hour. Oh, and do me a favour. On yer own. Don't bring that bleedin' headcase of a mate of yours.' Paterson was silent again, quickly running through the possibilities. *Why on my own? A trap, perhaps? Is he looking to square up the hiding I gave him?*

'You comin' then?'

'Depends why, Bill. You've not given me any reason to want to meet you. Gotta be a good one for me to trip up to an abandoned warehouse in the middle of nowhere on my own. Would you?'

Caine was silent. Possibly he was nodding. 'Fair point. I understand you're looking for a certain someone. I can give him to you plus a whole lot more. Up to you.'

Paterson pulled up at a red light and glanced down at his phone. The call was being recorded. Thank God for automatic recording phone apps. 'A certain someone?'

'You know who I mean.'

'Albert Tanner?'

'Good gawd, Paterson. Who else? Albert Tanner. You want him or not?'

'And why would you do that? Thought there was a code with you boys.'

'Code? You've been watching too much telly. Ain't no code, Mr Paterson. If I'm getting fucked, he's getting fucked harder. Now, you comin', or do I give this to someone else? Makes no odds to me.'

'See you in an hour.' Paterson turned the phone off, pulled away from the traffic lights and stopped on the forecourt of the nearest petrol station. He played back the conversation and uploaded it to his personal email with a copy to Johnny Clocks.

He called him. 'John, how you feeling?'

'Like shit. And I coulda done without a phone call.'

'Yeah. Sorry. But listen, I've just had an interesting conversation. Billy Caine called. Wants me to meet him.'

'What? What for?'

'No idea, mate. Your guess is as good as mine. Said something about being able to give me Albert Tanner and more. No idea what it's all about.'

'Talk to me, Ray. Where you meeting him?' said Clocks. Paterson gave him the gist of the conversation and explained that there was a copy of the call in his inbox, to be used as evidence should something happen to him.

'Gimme twenty minutes. I'll be there.'

'Nope, not this time. I have to go alone. I don't think he's too fond of you.'

'Christ! You piss on one slag's bathroom floor . . . Look, I'm not 'appy about this, Ray. I'll back you up, from a distance.'

'No, John. I'll be fine. Caine's no fool, he knows I'll ring it in, give you the heads-up.'

'Still not 'appy.'

Paterson gave a little laugh. 'I know, mate. Tell you what. I'm meeting him at midday. If I don't ring in at a quarter to one, then you and the boys can come get me. How's that sound?'

'I'm a bit 'appier. Be careful, guv. These people are scum,' Clocks said, with feeling.

Paterson hung up and pulled back out into the traffic. He had roughly half an hour to kill before he had to be there, so he took his time, on the lookout for a decent coffee shop.

* * *

'Good to see you again, Mr Paterson. Looking sharp as ever.' He was, always did. 'Never got the chance to mention it before, but nice car you've got there. Always loved an Aston when I was younger. Prefer a Bentley these days. Bit more room in them.'

Paterson took the chair that was offered. 'I can see the appeal,' he said. 'The Aston can be a bit tricky to get out of in a hurry.'

The office they were in was typical for this type of industry. It had a certain smell to it, a tang, like oil. Oil and dirt, tobacco, sweat, years of it ground into the filthy carpet. That undefinable but unmistakable smell that said "workshop." There were a couple of grimy old filing cabinets stuck in the corner behind the desk where he sat. Dangling on the wall from a thumb tack was a copy of an old *Sun* newspaper glamour girl calendar. He couldn't see the year, but he vaguely recognised Samantha Fox. Clearly this place hadn't been used for a very long time. He wondered why . . . and then it dawned on him that Caine was probably waiting for the price of the land to skyrocket. Crossrail was well on its way to completion, and some dopey developer with too much money would no doubt pay him top dollar to build on the site.

'So, why are we here? Not looking for round two, I take it?'

Caine gave him a rueful grin. 'No, I'm not. Clearly my best years are behind me.'

'Good,' said Paterson. 'Pleased to hear it. So . . .?'

'Wanna drink?' Caine pulled a bottle of vodka and two glasses from one of the desk drawers.

Paterson thought about it for a nanosecond. 'Go on then.'

Caine poured until Paterson put his hand over the glass.

'You're looking for Tanner, right?' Caine said, sliding the glass over to him.

'How'd you know that?' Paterson took a sip, grimaced. He needed that.

'What? Who doesn't know that? Word is out all over that Tanner had a copper 'oiked off the streets. Your mate, Clocks. Dirty little bastard's no friend of mine, son, but swagging coppers, any coppers, is really bad for business. You found Clocks yet?'

Paterson made some rapid calculations in his head. If Tanner knew Rogers had been nicked and Clocks was alive, he might never come back, and Paterson didn't trust Caine not to tell him. The expression "thick as thieves" came to mind. 'Not yet. We'll find him though. Just a matter of time.'

'I hope so, son. I really do.' Caine nodded, slugged his vodka back and coughed. 'Bastard stuff. Shouldn't really mix it with me meds, but . . . I take it you know?'

Paterson shook his head. 'Know what?'

'That I'm dying.'

Paterson took another sip of his drink. 'Oh, that. Yeah, heard the word.' He kept up a show of indifference. 'From what I understand, Billy, you won't be missed by too many.'

Caine shrugged. 'What can you do, eh? Another?' Paterson shook his head. 'When you do get Tanner,' said Caine, 'will you be able to make anything stick?'

Paterson shifted slightly, enough for Caine to know he couldn't. 'I can,' he lied out loud. True, he could arrest Tanner for kidnap and the attempted murder of a police officer, but in reality their case would depend on the word of a single undercover copper — a copper buried so deep inside a criminal organisation that Tanner's lawyer would make mincemeat of anything he said. It wasn't enough.

'Do you know where he is yet?'

Paterson shook his head. 'We're working on it. Won't be long.'

Caine knew he was lying. 'Well, save you all chasing yer tails hunting for him, I can give him to you. I *will* give him to you.'

Paterson sat up straight. Took another sip of his drink. 'And why would you do that?'

'Good old-fashioned revenge, mate. We both know he killed my Davey, and I owe him one for that. Ever hear about my sister?'

Paterson cocked his head. 'Sister? No. I didn't know you had a sister.'

Caine sat back in his chair and put his feet up on the table. 'Good. You weren't supposed to. No one was. She grew up different to me. We wanted different things from life. I respected that, didn't want her involved in all this . . . shit of mine. She went her way, I went mine, and to be honest, I can't remember the last time we spoke. I just bung a few grand in the bank account every Christmas, so she and the family can have a good time.'

'Decent of you.' Paterson couldn't quite hide the sarcasm.

Caine ignored it. 'Anyway, as I said, no one was supposed to know about her, but somehow Tanner found out, and he's threatening to kill her and her family if I don't sign over.'

'Just to be clear, sign what over?'

'Everything. My businesses, my rackets, my buildings, the lot.'

'Money too?'

'Yep. He wants it, but he ain't getting it.'

'I hear you're going to do what he wants.'

A pained look crossed Caine's face. He dropped his feet to the floor and sat up. 'Looks that way, don't it? But let me tell you something. From where he's sitting, I don't have a lot of choice in the matter. He knows I'm on me way out, knows I can't protect me sister after I've gone, and he'll kill 'em all if I don't give him what he wants. He knows there's no one else to leave it to, so it's not like I'm gonna benefit in the long run. But . . . that doesn't mean he's going to benefit either.' He threw Paterson a wink.

Paterson glanced around the room. What a dive it was. 'You don't strike me as the sort to roll over. Bit surprised, really.'

'Oh, no, no, don't get me wrong, son, I'm not rolling over. He thinks I am, but in my opinion Albert Tanner deserves a good fuckin' and I'm the man for the job.' He took from his pocket the USB containing the copied files. 'I'm going to need your help to hold him down while I'm administering it.'

Paterson looked at the USB. 'What's on that?'

'Enough to bury Tanner so deep he'll come up arse-first in Australia. There's all sorts of records on here, the names of his drug partners, bank account numbers — mostly off-shore — lists of people who, if you dig about, I think you'll find match the names of a ton of corpses. A few bent coppers too. One of 'em's gonna be of interest to you.'

Paterson raised an eyebrow.

'Your mate, DCI Alliston. He's a cheeky bleeder, ain't he? For the last coupla years I've been giving the greedy little bastard five 'undred a week to give me the nod if your lot were up to anything with my name on it. Seems he's been doing the same with Tanner for three times that amount. Guess he's been playin' favourites.'

Paterson's face grew dark. 'Where'd you get the key from, Bill?'

Caine smiled. 'Good question. Believe it or not, I got it from my Davey's missus, April. I had her followed. Turns out she's not really called April. Her real name's, wait for it . . . Ruby Tanner.' He stopped to let his words sink in. 'Albert must 'ave put her up to it, to pretend she was in love with Davey just so she could keep an eye on what I was up to. Clever, really. Gotta be 'onest, I never saw that one coming.'

Paterson carefully considered what he was being told. 'So, what d'you want for it?'

Caine leaned back again and swung his legs up on the table. 'Just for you to do your job, that's all. I want the bastard nicked and banged away. I want him to rot away the rest of his miserable life in an eight-by-six box with a postage-stamp window in it. From him, though, I want money.'

Paterson frowned. 'Money? You're not telling me you're broke, are you? You just said you were holding some back.'

'I've got a few quid stashed away but I need that to disappear with. I have a plan, yer see. You're gonna have to hear it 'cause you're gonna help me with it.'

'Is that so?'

'Yep. You are. Listen. I've arranged a meeting with Tanner here, in a couple of days. He thinks I'm going to turn up with a briefcase full of signed documents giving everything to him. What he doesn't know is that I've offloaded it all.'

Paterson knew he wasn't going to like the next bit. He had to ask though. 'To . . . ?'

Caine threw his hand up and out, like he'd scored a goal at the World Cup final. 'The Albanians. But here's the good bit. You know I said I wanted money? I do — a million — but it's not for me, it's for my sister. I've told Tanner he can have the lot but I wanted compo for Davey. He's agreed.'

'Why would he give you any money when he's taking everythi— sorry, thinks he's taking everything from you anyway? Doesn't make sense.'

'Course it does. I told him I'm cash poor, asset rich. Look, his biggest weakness is his ego. You've seen what he's like — swanning around with his wanky little top hat and swagger stick. He's gone in the nut, mate,' Caine tapped at his temple, 'and it gives him a big gloat to think he's giving pathetic, dying, thoroughly beaten me a pissy

185

little million quid while he's robbing me of everything else. Something he can boast about.'

Paterson could see the appeal. 'So, how do you get the million? Cash?'

'Nope. Secure transfer. Telephones. When we meet, I'll hand over the briefcase with all the documents in it. His brief will check them over and verify. He's a happy bunny. I give him a bank account number that he doesn't know is me sister's, thinks it's mine, and transfers the money over. She's up a million and he gets fucked up the arse by the Albies. Don't forget, there'll be three lots of the buggers by this time, and they'll squeeze him like a zit. Beauty is, he'll also be piss poor because — and this is why I need you — your boys can get into his accounts and freeze everything. He gets screwed from arsehole to breakfast time and has to watch the lot being taken from 'im. Beautiful.'

Paterson drained his glass. 'Christ! You're a slippery sod, aren't you? But, hang on. His brief, Stickson, is going to see the signatures on the paperwork, isn't he?' Then it dawned on him. Silly thing to say. False documents. 'Scrub that. I've worked it out.'

'Good lad. Knew you would. Like I said, I'm giving you this key, an' you'll pass it up to your fraud and banking boys. They're gonna examine it and no doubt freeze his accounts. That's fine, exactly what I want, but you 'ave to promise me you'll let the million go through first. That's all I want. Let my sister have that million and you and your boys can have the rest.'

'Why the hell don't you just give her a million?'

'I could, yeah, but this is *my* gloat, Mr Paterson — knowing that I've screwed him *and* he's paid me a million for the privilege. C'mon. You can see that, can'tcha?'

Paterson shook his head. 'Sounds like a plan but problem is, Bill, once I hand the key over, we're looking at letting a million run out of an account stuffed with illegal money. Pretty sure I can't sit back and watch that happen.'

Caine got to his feet. 'Yeah, ya can. Look, I knew you'd pick up on that so, as a sweetener, I'll wear a wire at the meeting. I promise you, Tanner will admit to my Davey's murder, and the others too. I'll also get him to talk about your mate, Clocks. See what's going on with 'im. So you'll have him bang to rights on just about everything. How's that?'

Paterson stood up too. 'When you meeting up with him?'

'Friday. Two days from now. Midnight. Gives you time to get your house in order.' He stretched out his hand. 'Deal, Mr Paterson?'

Paterson looked at the hand and his stomach tightened. He shook.

'Deal, Mr Caine. God help me.'

CHAPTER TWENTY-FIVE

Paterson was sitting in his office checking through the daily record book, catching up with his team's ongoing enquiries. Despite Tanner being the best and only suspect for the killing of Davey Caine and the two men in the pub, there was the matter of the murder of one of Tanner's men. He'd failed to bring this up with Caine at their meeting and it was weighing on his mind. Tanner was fast becoming an obsession with him and he couldn't afford to let it cloud his thoughts.

He'd have to figure out a way to use Caine and then double-cross him later. He was aware that he was running out of time.

A gentle tap on his door brought him back to the present. DC Karen Johnson's blonde head poked around the door. 'Sir,' she said, 'DCI Alliston is here to see you.' *Show time.* Paterson's plan was to find out from Alliston how much he knew about Clocks's kidnap and Tanner's involvement therein. As soon as he had what he wanted, he would call the main office, where officers from Professional Standards were waiting to make the arrest.

'Send him in, Karen.'

'Sir.' She pulled the door to and then opened it again. 'Do you want tea, sir?' Paterson declined. She showed DCI Alliston in.

'Mr Paterson,' said Alliston with a brief nod.

'Don't sit down, Mr Alliston. You won't be staying long today. I've got a lot to do.'

Alliston put his case on a chair and his hands in his pockets. 'Yes, sir, I heard. Inspector Clocks, kidnapped. Jesus!' With his eyes on Paterson, he shook his head slowly. 'Do you have any leads as to his whereabouts yet?'

Paterson stood up slowly. His face was set, hard as stone. 'I do.'

Alliston's eyes opened wider. 'Is he safe, sir? Do you have him? Do you know who took him?'

'Tanner,' Paterson said. 'Not him personally, he doesn't have the guts for it, but my money's on him ordering it.'

'Oh dear. That's not good at all.'

'I know. So, tell me — you have his house bugged from floor to ceiling, what do you know?' Paterson stared at him, impassive.

Alliston looked slightly rattled at this. 'Nothing. We haven't heard a word. I'm sorry—'

'What about your UC? He reported anything back?'

Alliston shuffled his feet. Looked down, then up, meeting Paterson's stare. 'No. Nothing from him. I'm sure he'd have said if he knew anything.'

'Would he? You sure about that?'

Alliston stiffened. 'Of course I'm sure. I know my man.'

Paterson intensified the stare, his eyes boring into Alliston's. 'Who the fuck do you think you're talking to, Alliston?' Paterson jabbed a finger at him. 'Knock the attitude now, or me and you are gonna fall out even further.' It suddenly dawned on him that he sounded just like Johnny Clocks. It surprised him a bit.

'Sorry.' Alliston coughed. 'Sir, if my UC knew anything at all about Inspector Clocks's whereabouts, he would have told me.'

'And if he did report back, what would you be expecting to hear?'

Alliston visibly froze. 'I . . . I . . . sir?'

'Would you be expecting him to tell you that it was done? That Johnny Clocks was dead? That he'd been executed by your UC and the other two that snatched him away?' Paterson was struggling to keep his voice from shaking with the rage rising up in him.

Alliston turned white. He said nothing.

Paterson came around the desk, grabbed the terrified Alliston by the jaw and held his face close to his. 'We got your man, Rogers, and we got Clocks, safe and sound. Rogers told us everything. *Everything*, you dirty, no good, conniving bastard. You were gonna let Clocks die to protect Tanner and your fucking backhanders.' He shoved Alliston, who staggered backwards. He forced himself to turn away.

With a loud bang, the door flew in, smashing against the wall. Johnny Clocks hurtled towards Alliston, grabbed him by the throat and pushed him back over the desk.

Paterson spun around. 'John!'

Clocks never heard him. 'You piece of shit!' he snarled and drove his fist into Alliston's face. He began punching him wildly, furiously, until Paterson put his hands on him and tried to drag him off. Professional Standards would be here any second and he didn't want them arresting Clocks too. A struggle ensued between the three of them.

'You prick!' Clocks yelled. 'You were gonna let 'em burn me to death, you dirty piece of shit!'

On hearing the commotion, some officers from the main office piled into the room. Paterson turned on them. 'Out!' he shouted. 'And shut the door.'

As the bemused officers began to back out of the room, three others, suited and booted, pushed their way in. 'Allo, allo, allo,' said one of them. 'What have we got 'ere?' Commissioner Young and two officers from Professional Standards stood looking at them, Young grinning at Clocks.

'Put it down, John. Go on. Put it down now.' After a couple of seconds, Clocks thrust Alliston from him disgustedly.

'I see that Mr Alliston here has unfortunately tripped over the carpet a couple of times. Oh dear.' Young strode up to Alliston, who kept his eyes down.

'Look at me,' Young commanded. Alliston kept his eyes on the floor. 'I said look at me, you piece of filth. Do as you're told!' Slowly, Alliston lifted his head. His gaze wavered, until it finally settled on Young. 'Detective Chief Inspector Martin Alliston, these men are from the Department of Professional Standards. They're here to arrest you, and be in no doubt that we're going to make sure you go away for a very long time. It takes a lot to bring me out from behind my desk these days, but today was special. I wanted to see what kind of filth would send one of his own to his death for money. Now I've seen it, and I can go back to my comfortable desk and make my calls to the Director of Public Prosecutions and the head of the CPS safe in the knowledge that there's been no mistake, no chance that Rogers was lying to save his own arse.' Young shook his head slowly, looking disgusted. He turned away. 'Over to you, gents.'

'Detective Chief Inspector Martin Alliston, my name is Superintendent Heston and this is Sergeant Wish. As Mr Young said, we're from DOPS. I'm placing you under arrest for conspiracy to murder, conspiracy to commit acts of violence and for receiving payments from a known criminal for the purpose of perverting the course of justice. You do not have to say anything, but it may harm your defence if you do not mention, when questioned, something which you later rely on in court. Do you understand?' Alliston stared blankly in the direction of the voice, apparently unable to comprehend what had been said. He was spun around and roughly handcuffed. 'Two ten p.m.,' Heston added. 'Alliston makes no reply. Take him downstairs.'

As Alliston was led out of the office, Superintendent Heston turned to Paterson. 'See?' he said. Paterson looked perplexed. 'That's a proper caution. That's all you have to do. It saves us all a boat-load of trouble.' He rolled his eyes at Young.

Young turned to Clocks, who stood panting. 'John, I don't blame you for clumping him — I'd have done the same — but you knew DOPS were outside. You make my life so bloody difficult, son.'

Clocks nodded. 'I know, I know. I'm sorry, guv, I really am, but . . . come on, you said it yourself . . .'

Young held up his hand. 'It's over. Let it be.'

Lambert turned to Paterson. 'You two must have been shagging the Blarney Stone, let alone kissing it. That USB you gave us, I got the boys to check it over quickly and they found some dodgy stuff on it about Tanner's brief, Stickson. His office has been turned over and a bus-load of paperwork has been seized. He wasn't there. His secretary said he seemed panicked about something and had gone off somewhere — she didn't know where. Just wild speculation here, boys, but I'd say he's on the run. We don't know where he is at the moment but we'll find him. He'll be getting his collar felt at some point.' He stared at Paterson. 'And, oddly, it would seem that the searching officers couldn't find Stickson's file or any record of Tanner's arrest. Seems to have gone missing somehow. Perhaps he took them with him. Who knows? Doesn't really matter, but it seems you both got bloody lucky. Again.'

Paterson and Clocks smiled. 'But don't allow yourselves to think that'll always be the case,' said Young. 'That would be a mistake.'

CHAPTER TWENTY-SIX

Paterson and Clocks were sitting opposite DCI Lambert and DI Butler in a small café in the middle of Greenwich, round about half way between their respective divisions. Lambert had called the meeting, telling Paterson that they may have had a breakthrough and he wanted to talk a few things over with him.

Today was a half decent day weather-wise and they'd all opted to sit outside in the sunlight. Pale and insipid as it was, it was still a welcome change from the continual November grey. They sipped at their coffee, faces turned to the sun, until Paterson decided it was time to get the conversation started. 'How can we help?'

'Before we start, good to see you safe and well, DI Clocks, er, John. From what I hear, you had a rough old time of it.' Lambert looked at Clocks's swollen and battered face.

'You could say that, sir. Things got a bit rowdy, but all sorted now. 'Preciate the concern.'

He turned to Paterson. 'On the subject of rowdy, what the hell happened to you, Ray? You look like you've gone ten rounds with Anthony Joshua and lost. What a pair you two are.'

Paterson touched his face. The bruises and swelling were going down a bit but still noticeable. 'Like I would have won that fight! No, my man was a lot smaller and faster. Martial arts bloke. Very good at what he does.'

DI Butler frowned. Lambert tore open his packet of sugar and emptied it into his cup. 'Hmmm. Glad it all turned out okay. Grapevine says one of ours got nicked for it. That right?'

'Sadly, yes. As you say, one of ours. Not going to go too well for him. Serious prison time,' Paterson said.

'Good riddance to him. Hope they leave him to rot in there.' Lambert lifted his cup to his lips and put it down again. 'I was attacked last night.' Paterson and Clocks both stared at him. 'Got a call about someone carrying a girl into an alley. Went there, disturbed him, got jumped.'

'Are you alright?' said Paterson, looking at his unblemished face.

'Yeah. Caught me by surprise and I got the wind knocked out of me. Pride damaged, but that's all. Thought I'd been stabbed but turns out it was just a few punches. Scared me shitless though, I can tell you. And then the bastard got away. Uniforms arrived to back me up but this bloke was well on his toes. Fit and fast, he was. Plods couldn't get near him with all the shit they have to carry dragging them down. He's away.'

'That's a bitch,' offered Clocks by way of insight. 'Did you get a look at 'im?'

'It is, Mr Clocks, a real bitch. No, I didn't get a look at him, but the good thing is I got a shitload of his DNA on me — made sure of it. Forensics boys are having a collective wank they're so thrilled. Can't believe their luck.'

'I take it this is the breakthrough you mentioned?' said Paterson.

'Yep. I know Dulwich can be a bit rough in places but even for there, carrying a girl off into an alley is a bit different. Uniforms said he was all in black, like he was wearing a one-piece suit of some kind. Looking back, I guess he did feel a bit . . . slippery, but maybe that's me remembering details that fit with what they told me after.'

'You got a hit on him yet? Is he in the system?' Clocks said.

Lambert shook his head. 'Not yet. Hopefully he'll be in there somewhere. Matter of time. Just thought I'd let you know.'

'What's the story with the girl, then?' Clocks said. 'She alright?'

'She's fine. Scared out of her skin and I'm guessing she'll not be walking around alone at night for a while but physically, she's okay — no injuries other than a few scratches and bruises.'

'That's good to know,' Clocks said, 'but let me get this straight — didn't your man clobber his victims to death with a hammer? That's what you said, right? That's what he does. So, how come this girl has no injuries and yet gets herself dragged off? That doesn't sound like the same bloke to me.'

DCI Lambert took a deep breath. DI Butler watched his senior officer expectantly. 'It was him.'

'But how do you know for sure? The method was completely different.'

'It was definitely him.'

Clocks shook his head. 'Sir, with respect — how? You've got two dead girls, both taken out the same way, and now a third, completely unharmed. Serial killers rarely become more humane. It's the other way round in my experience.'

'He has a point, Mr Lambert,' said Paterson. 'Are you sure you're not so desperate to catch him that you're grabbing at straws? No offence or anything, but it does seem odd. Maybe — and I don't mean to sound unfeeling

— maybe he was a rapist or something. Perhaps he drugged this girl in a club. Do you have the toxicology reports back?'

Lambert cocked his head, evidently still convinced that he had prevented a murder. 'No, not yet. Still waiting on the lab results. Shouldn't be long.'

'What did the girl have to say?' Paterson asked.

'Not much,' said Butler. Clocks and Paterson both looked slightly startled. He hadn't said a word so far. 'Doesn't remember too much about it. Has vague recollections of being out for a drink with her friends and heading outside for a smoke. Then she says she hazily remembers the sensation of being carried away. Wasn't scared. That's about it.'

'Sounds like a Rohypnol job to me,' said Clocks, still looking at Butler.

Paterson drained his coffee. It was served in tiny quantities, not that hot and definitely not worth three pound seventy-five of anyone's money. He ate the little biscuit that had come with it. 'Well, I hope it was your man and I hope that the DNA comes back with a match, I really do.' He glanced at his watch. 'I'm sorry, but is there anything else? It's just that we're up to our eyeballs.'

'No worries,' said Lambert. 'I appreciate you taking the time out.'

'Just wondering why we couldn't have done this over the phone. We're all busy men.' Paterson smiled at Lambert, then swung around to face Butler, who gave a weak grin in return.

'No reason. We thought we'd take the opportunity to get out in the fresh air, see what's what and just generally catch up, you know? Bring you up to speed in person.' He drained his coffee and stood up. Four metal chairs scraped the pavement. 'Thanks for coming though, Ray,' Lambert said. 'I'll keep you posted when I have something more.' Paterson smiled. 'One other thing though, I did manage to get a dig in. Smacked the bastard right in the face. He didn't half holler. Felt good, I can tell you.'

'Good on yer,' said Paterson. 'Pity you didn't knock the shit out of him.' Clocks took a breath. Butler watched Paterson. Nothing else was said.

As they walked back to their car, Paterson said, 'What the hell was that all about? How can a DCI in a murder squad ignore the differences between those girls?'

Clocks looked at his boss. 'That Lambert's a slippery ol' bastard. He's up to something.'

'Oh? What d'you mean?'

Clocks opened the door and got in. 'Dunno. But I've got me a feeling that something's not right, and it's most probably coming our way.'

* * *

'Well, sir, I must say this is some serious shit you've brought us.' Larry Bannon, a senior investigator with the Met's serious fraud squad, was in a happy place. When he, Paterson and Clocks had sat down for this meeting just under an hour and a half ago, his hopes hadn't been particularly high. Paterson explained what he had been given and by whom and why, and that while he hoped Caine was on the level, part of him suspected he was being mugged off. It seemed he wasn't.

They were sitting in a small, meticulously organised office on the ninth floor of an office block just off the Lambeth Road in Kennington. The building itself was nothing special. Built in the late sixties, its minimalist exterior — horrendous yellow panel cladding alternating with orange brick every six feet or so all the way up to the top — was typical of its age. Inside, though, it was seriously high-tech and housed some very smart people doing some very smart work. Not only was it a centre for fraud investigation, it also contained departments working twenty-four seven to scour the dark web in search of terrorists, paedophiles grooming kiddies, arms and drug dealers. Cyber criminals like to hack into banking systems and government departments, and all these groups met and plotted on the dark web, in what they thought was complete anonymity.

'So, what have we got?' said Paterson. 'Anything any good?'

Bannon leaned forward. 'Oh yes. We have, among other things, a complete record of all of Tanner's financial activities. The boys are going over it in more detail, but I can tell you right now that we've found accounts stuffed with millions upon millions, originating from places like Columbia, Russia, Mexico, the US and, surprisingly, Australia. We've started to cross-check names and we've already had one hit — a link to a known Aussie drug smuggler. Big player too.'

Clocks and Paterson sat up, pleased with what they were hearing, Paterson especially so, seeing as how he'd taken a chance on Caine. 'Anything else?'

'Yes. As I said, plenty. We have records of all his contacts, past and present, plus a few names he was lining up to deal with in future. Bloody fool kept an appointments diary! The people in it are quite significant players, many are known arms dealers. Chances are he's looking to flood the streets with cheapish guns.'

'Is anything on there actually legal?'

'Technically, probably. But that'll most likely be shell companies he's set up to launder money through. Usual stuff, but this is on a grand scale. We'll figure it out in time.'

'So, what happens now?' said Clocks.

'Well, a number of things, Inspector. We have enough here to have all of his accounts frozen while we dig into it, but we'll have to consider very carefully before we take that step.'

'Why?' both men said in unison.

'We don't yet know if this is all of it. There may be more. We'll have to see where the trail leads us, but if we do freeze and he has more, he could use what he has to get away, and we don't want that, do we?' Both shook their heads. 'But, if we don't freeze them, we run the risk of allowing him to move the money around and then we end up with nothing substantive. We might get him but we won't be able to recover his assets. That said, my gut says cut him off now, at the knees, once he's arrested. I take it you're in the process of arresting him?'

Paterson shook his head. 'He's done a runner. Sorting out an alibi for the attempted murder of Mr Clocks here, but I'm expecting a call from the person who gave me the USB. He has a meeting set up with him.'

'I see,' said Bannon. 'Interesting. May I ask how he came by this?'

Paterson shrugged. No point bullshitting him. He explained how Caine had gained access to April's phone and saw how the man winced. No way Caine's approach had been legal but then neither were any of the individuals implicated in all of this, so six of one . . .

'What I'm curious about,' said Paterson, 'is who leaves all their important stuff on a phone?'

Bannon shook his head. 'Wasn't on the phone itself. It was actually in the cloud. You know, internet storage. Comes standard with most phones. Tanner, or whoever looks after his paperwork, would seem to have backed everything up to the cloud. It's probably all on his computer, protected by a military-grade encryption program and he probably thinks he's safe, but once you choose to upload content like that to the cloud . . . well, security can sometimes get a bit, shall we say, looser.'

Bannon noticed Clocks's frown. 'Do you do internet banking?' he said. Clocks and Paterson both nodded. 'And do you do it on your phone?' Again, both nodded. 'Take your phone out, Inspector.' Clocks did. 'Now open the app.' Clocks touched the fingerprint ID on the back of his phone, tapped his screen a few times and touched the ID again. 'Done. I'm in.'

'Excellent,' said Bannon with a smile. 'Same principle as your man and his accounts. You now have access to all of your money and all of your accounts. Your fingerprint went straight past all of that military-grade encryption that banks use to keep your money safe. So, if you fell asleep and I put your finger on the pad, *I'm* into your accounts.' Clocks looked a little bit uneasy.

'So, if this dozy girl goes and puts an app on her phone that accesses their cloud account with all their business on it, then — what can I say? She's a very, very careless first-class fuckwit.'

'Ha! Dozy cow,' said Clocks. That cheered him up. He licked his lips. 'You ain't got a cuppa floatin' about by any chance, 'ave you? I've got a mouth like a camel's flip-flop.'

Bannon smiled. 'I'm sure we can rustle something up.' He turned to Paterson. 'Your difficulty will be getting it admitted as evidence, considering how it was obtained.'

'Not going to be difficult at all. It just turned up in an envelope addressed to me. Anonymous. That's all I know.' The two men exchanged glances. No more needed to be said.

'Fair enough,' said Bannon.

'One other thing, please.' He wasn't sure how to phrase this, or if it could be done but he'd made a deal with Caine and, having come through with the USB, Paterson believed he would also wear a wire if it meant getting his million.

'The man who gave us this, the one who's meeting Tanner, has agreed to wear a wire and get him to confess to his part in a number of murders. That will be the moment we move in and arrest him. But — and this is a big but —' Clocks grinned, Paterson ignored him, 'he wants a million out of Tanner's money and he wants it transferred into a particular account at the meeting. Tanner's already agreed to it. If our source doesn't get the money, we don't get Tanner for murder and I really, *really* want Tanner for murder.' Bannon said nothing. He watched Paterson closely. There was more coming.

'So, I have a few questions for you, please.'

'Go on,' said Bannon.

'Can you freeze all of these accounts instantly?'

Bannon considered it. 'Probably not instantly, instantly. With the right people, we could maybe do it within about twenty minutes or so.'

Paterson nodded. This was good. 'Obviously we don't know which account Tanner will use to make the transfer, but can you monitor them all and see when the transfer is made?'

'Again, yes. I don't see why not.'

'Okay, excellent news. Thank you.'

'I'll need proper authorisation. I take it you do have that?'

'Not yet, no.'

'It would help.'

'Who? Me or you?'

'Both of us.'

Paterson could feel it all slipping away from him. He wasn't about to let it. 'Well, I'm giving you my authorisation, and I'll get mine as soon as I'm away from here — how's that sound?'

'If I'm being honest, a tad suspect, sir.' Bannon looked him dead in the eye. Paterson feigned a hurt expression.

'When is the meeting?' said Bannon, shaking his head.

'Tomorrow. Midnight.'

Bannon pushed himself back in his chair and rubbed his face before letting out a big sigh. 'Then there's not much else to talk about, is there? You go away and get your authorisation, write out your instructions and make the arrangements to pick us up. We'll be ready.'

CHAPTER TWENTY-SEVEN

In his hidden office, Billy Caine downed his fourth and final glass of vodka before pulling himself up and out of the Chesterfield seat. Ronnie Batch, finishing up his third, noted the gun tucked in his waistband.

'This is it then, Ron. All over and done with,' Caine said. The TV on the back wall was hiding a retina ID control panel. Caine swung the TV back, looked at the panel and stepped away as the wall sank slowly into the floor, TV included. Ronnie's jaw fell as the slowly descending wall revealed a large vault and more cash than he had ever seen in his life.

'Jesus, Bill! How much you got here?' Ronnie was up on his feet, not quite sure if what he was seeing was real.

'Should be three mill. Give or take.'

'Christ! Why've you got so much? Surely that oughta be in a bank. Gotta be safer.'

Caine smiled, shook his head. 'What, safer than here? Don't think so, Ron. I've got CCTV hidden in every room, a top-level digital laser dog's-bollocks of an alarm system and, to cap it off, the bleedin' Old Bill have got the place under twenty-four-hour surveillance and they've bugged it up everywhere. No sod gettin' in here without the law knowing about it, and they can't just sit around and let someone break in if they know about it, can they? They'd be shittin' themselves that someone might be trying to do me in. Nah, they'd be through those doors so bleedin' fast you'd get knocked over in the draught.' Ronnie saw his point. 'This 'ere is rainy-day money, my son, and today it's bleedin' pissing down.'

Ronnie stepped into the vault and stared in wonder at the bricks of fifty-pound notes, all sealed in cellophane and bundled in large blocks of £100,000. One pack was open. 'Can I?'

Caine gave him an amused look. 'Be my guest.'

Ronnie picked up a small bundle, brought it up to his nose and sniffed. Nothing quite like the smell of newly printed money.

'Here's what we're gonna do,' Caine said. 'Out back is two vans. One for you and one for Tommy Bell. He'll be here soon. Me and you, we're gonna box this lot up and Tommy is gonna make a delivery for me.'

'Where to?'

'I've got a sister.'

'You what? A sister? Bloody hell, Bill. Something else I never knew.'

Billy took the bundle of notes off of him and put it back. 'You weren't supposed to. But what you do need to know is one million of this is yours.'

Ronnie stood stock still, struck dumb, mouth open. 'What?'

'One mill, Ron. Yours. As a thank you. Company's folded, new management. Figured you wouldn't wanna work for a new boss and besides, you're an old fucker like me, so this is your pension. I know you're not short of a bob or two anyway, so use this as a top up. Go enjoy yourself.'

'Jesus Christ, Bill. I don't know what to—'

'Nothing to say, me old mate. You've been a good friend to me down the years, watched my back. God knows, you're the only one that hasn't tried to shaft me, so I figured, why not? You're a good man.' Caine pulled out the handgun from his waistband and pointed it at Ronnie. 'And, while I do trust you, don't be gettin' any ideas about trying to jump me and nick the other two million. Clear?'

Ronnie nodded his head furiously. 'Leave off, Bill. I'm not doing that. Never even thought about it. I'm bleedin' well happy enough with what you've given me.'

Caine smiled. 'Good man. Just making a point.' He tucked the gun away.

'I saw. Point well made.'

'Grab a few boxes then. Tommy'll be here soon.'

Ronnie picked up a couple of FedEx boxes, put them on the table and started to lift out bundles of cash from the vault. 'I know it's none of my business, Bill, but you trust Tommy with this much dough?'

'Nope. Don't trust him or anyone. Tommy won't know what's in the boxes unless he looks in them. I'll tell him not to, just to deliver. If he does as he's told, he's in for a nice little thirty large, but if he does decide to take a peek, he'll have a choice to make. Pretend he never saw anything and carry on with the delivery, or he can nick it, and weigh it up against his entire family, including his little twins, getting slaughtered. Girls, ain't they? There's a note in there for my sister to call my brief to acknowledge safe delivery. If he don't get the call within twenty-four hours, well,' he shrugged, 'a certain someone will have a bigger payday than thirty grand.'

Ronnie knew what that meant.

'Tough old game we're in, Ron. Eh?' Billy Caine sealed up the first box.

'So, what happens now, Bill? Where are you going to go?'

Caine stopped what he was doing and looked at his old friend. Part of him wanted to tell him everything —

205

that he'd thrown his lot in with the police and was about to deal with his problem and get his revenge for Davey. All he said was, 'I'm gonna go fuck Albert Tanner.'

* * *

By 10 p.m., the briefing room was full. Paterson's entire team had turned up. Though tired and dishevelled from a long day at the coal face, not one of them would have dreamt of missing this raid. SCO19 were present, fully loaded and led by Lyndsey Mullins. Both Paterson and Clocks had expressed their concern about this. Should Lyndsey be leading a team of heavily armed officers on a raid to capture the man who'd ordered her boyfriend to be burned alive? Lyndsey was adamant. She was also a consummate professional. She wouldn't shoot him if she wasn't forced to, but Paterson and Clocks were well aware that they wouldn't be able to stop her giving him a good old-fashioned kicking if she got the chance. They didn't consider that a particular issue.

Sitting apart from the rest at one of the tables, Larry Bannon and two of his computer boys were running some last-minute checks on their laptops. They were none too happy to have been handed Kevlar vests to wear, but Paterson swore it was just a health and safety precaution.

Paterson and Clocks were standing in Paterson's office watching a technician taping a minute microphone into the armpit of a very hairy Billy Caine. It used to be that people had them taped to their chests, but the flaw in this positioning soon became obvious: if the person's shirt was ripped open for inspection, the wire was there for all to see. That could lead to a bad day for the wearer. Nowadays, the armpit was considered a better option, with the head of the mike just poking out. It was very rare for anyone to insist on a strip down and, having dramatically ripped open a shirt, nobody bothered to pull it open wide enough to expose the shoulders. Ergo, Paterson reckoned Caine should be safe.

'I wouldn't worry about it too much,' said Caine, grinning at the technician. 'No way he's getting a look at my tits.'

'You sure about this?' said Clocks. 'You can get him to put 'is hands up and admit to murder?'

'You transfer my money and I'll get him to admit to killing my Davey. He did it before, so he'll do it again, and anything else he might come up with is just gravy.'

'Just make sure you keep things as natural as possible. Be careful how you say things. If he smells a rat . . .'

Caine began buttoning his shirt back up. 'Don't stress it. I've got this. You just make sure that once I've got my money and you've got your confession, you don't balls it up and let him get away. If you do, you'll never find him again.'

'Thing is, Bill,' said Clocks, 'we'll have it all. What can he do if he hasn't got a pot to piss in?'

Caine slipped on his jacket. 'You won't have it all, mate. He's a slippery little shit. He'll have money stashed away that *nobody* knows about. Rainy-day money. I know I have.' He gave Clocks a wink.

CHAPTER TWENTY-EIGHT

Tanner's gothic house was the scene of a number of different activities. Outside, and in silence, officers from the covert surveillance squad had taken up strategic positions a safe distance from the building. One was hidden in the upper branches of a tree — not unlike a sniper, except that this officer was armed with a night-vision monoscope and an encrypted two-way radio. If this should fail, he was also carrying a sat-phone. From where he was positioned, the monoscope gave him a clear view of the front door. The back and sides of the house were also covered, but all involved knew that the front entrance was the most likely place for Tanner to emerge. Commissioner Young had taken the decision to leave Tanner in play instead of just storming in and arresting him for the attempted murder of Johnny Clocks. If events worked out as planned, they would have him on tape admitting to the murder of Davey Caine, the attempted murder of a police officer and hopefully a few other victims besides. That, along with the other evidence they had amassed, would be enough to put him away for the rest of his natural life.

The man in the tree had been sitting there since the previous day — nearly eighteen hours now, without a break. His muscles ached, and his bladder was so full he would have done just about anything for a leak. He couldn't use his bottle in case the movement gave away his position. He'd just have to piss himself. That's what the SAS had taught him. He guessed that made it alright.

There had been quite a few comings and goings at the house throughout the day, but as darkness fell, there were even more. Tree man counted at least five vehicles, carrying in total the entire top level of Tanner's team. He, like everybody else on the raid, was unaware that Tanner was about to be double-crossed.

At eleven thirty precisely, Tanner emerged from the house and climbed into his Roller. To tree man's surprise, there was only one other occupant in the vehicle. In the driver's seat was a smartly dressed man who'd gotten in carrying a suitcase. He passed the information along to Paterson and, satisfied that nothing would likely happen now for an hour or so, wriggled himself up into a standing position, put his back against the trunk and almost cried with relief as he pissed.

While tree man was enjoying his comfort break, another equally patient man had been skilful enough to slip past the Met's finest observers. He took up position in a thick clump of shrubs. He, too, had watched Tanner get in the car and leave. Now he had a job to do. Caine had paid him extremely well to kill whoever was inside.

He stood in the shadows, camouflaged in his all black clothing, switched on his night-vision headset and looked up at the tree where the police officer was hiding. *Bloody amateur. I saw you as soon as I arrived.* To distract the officer's attention, the assassin had simply thrown a stone at a car some fifty feet away from the tree. When the alarm went off, tree man had instinctively turned toward the sound and had been blinded by the flashing lights. By the time he'd got his vision back, the assassin had scaled the wall and found a hiding place. So easy.

Next he needed to take out the security light in case the sensor lit up the lawn like a football stadium and showed him up. Pistol silenced and resting on his arm, he took careful aim. It took him just two shots to pop the light. The pieces landed on the grass without a sound. Assured of darkness, he crossed the lawn and flattened himself against the wall of the house, edging along until he came to a door. Locked, but not against his pistol.

The room he found himself in was in darkness. The assassin stopped to listen, allowing his eyes a moment to adjust. He could make out the muffled sound of voices coming from somewhere ahead of him. Couldn't tell how many exactly, but there were a few in there. He froze. Footsteps, moving away. He crept toward the door, which was ajar. Through the gap, he saw a man walking away from him toward a further room. The man threw open two enormous wooden doors and entered Tanner's kingdom.

Thank you, mouthed the assassin. He counted four men, including the one who'd just walked in. Kneeling in front of the sofa, a naked woman was busying herself with two of them. Both men had their trousers round their ankles and were in no position to offer any form of resistance. In the scheme of things, it wasn't a bad way to die.

The third man in the room was swigging from a bottle of brandy and cheering on the happy threesome. So, four men and at least one woman. That tallied with those he'd counted arriving. There might possibly be a few more somewhere, but he fancied he'd got it about right. He opened the door and stepped through, swinging the gun from side to side. The cheering man saw him coming, panicked and fumbled inside his coat. The assassin's shot hit him high in the chest and punched him backward over the sofa.

For a second, the girl looked puzzled. Why had the two men suddenly pulled away from her? She frowned as a warm liquid splashed over her that wasn't what she had been expecting, nor where she had been expecting it from. She just had time to scream before a bullet hit her in the face.

The man who had preceded the assassin into the room turned and took two in the chest, one in the face. He dropped where he stood. The assassin heard a sound behind him and spun around to confront a terrified, naked brunette. She was holding two glasses of wine that spilled over her trembling hands.

He put his finger to his lips and smiled the smile of a man who was pleased with his night's work. He took one of the glasses from her, raised it and drank with relish. He'd have to take the glass with him — his DNA would be all over it — but he was enjoying himself. He took another sip. 'Not bad,' he said. 'Not Tesco's finest, I suspect.' She didn't answer. 'Don't suppose you've got any crisps?'

'I'll get some,' she said, her voice shaky. 'Please . . . please don't shoot me.'

'Shoot you? Why would I do that?'

She looked over his shoulder at the carnage in the room.

'Oh, I see your point. Got any cheese and onion?'

She shook her head.

'Salt 'n' vinegar then. How about that?'

She shook her head.

'Shit balls! What *have* you got?'

'B . . . b . . . bacon. Mr Tanner only likes bacon.'

'Bacon? I can't stand bacon!' He shot her in the head.

CHAPTER TWENTY-NINE

You'd never give the observation van a second glance. Looking the best part of twenty years old and pretty battered, it was covered in scratch marks, with various dents on the wings and sides. The odd mark of splashed paint completed the picture.

Inside sat Paterson, Clocks, Mr Bannon, a surveillance engineer who was monitoring Caine's transmissions and Lyndsey Mullins, all tooled up and ready to roll. Lyndsey was the designated "locksmith" for the operation, equipped with a Benelli M4 semi-automatic shotgun and eight frangible rounds whose cartridges were designed to decimate deadlocks, bolts and hinges without danger of ricochet or onward travel. Outside, tucked away in the shadows at the back of the estate, were a couple of equally nondescript observation vans. One held Lyndsey's team of fully kitted SCO19 officers and the other contained three of Bannon's tech boys running last-minute checks on their laptops. Each man would monitor six of Tanner's accounts. The second they saw a million pounds leave one of them, they were to radio through to Bannon. After that, it was a case of waiting for him to confess to Davey's murder and then they would move in.

Paterson sat hunched up next to Lyndsey, lost in thought. He'd pushed for this operation and was all too aware that it could go badly wrong. Nicking Tanner was a given, no problems there, but what to do with Caine? Caine couldn't be trusted. He was a suspect in the murder of Graham Stokes, the villain who'd been shot in the head, but Paterson knew there'd be no evidence to link him to it. If he nicked Caine and questioned him, Caine would simply tell the investigating officers that he'd obtained the information illegally, that he'd done a deal with Paterson for the USB — thus ruining any hope of a conviction. Reluctantly, Paterson came to the conclusion that he'd have to allow Caine to escape in the confusion following Tanner's arrest. Caine would easily bypass any checks at ports of exit and make his way out of the country.

For that, Paterson needed his colleagues' collusion. As he'd guessed, Clocks didn't give a rat's arse. All he wanted was Tanner. Paterson turned to Lyndsey and was more than a little relieved when she simply said, 'Whatever John wants.'

'Final check,' said Clocks. All made sure that their earpieces were settled nicely and working. Bannon whispered into his radio and confirmed that his boys were up and running, with full radio signal strength, and the same with Lyndsey. 'All units,' Clocks whispered, 'we're about to go dark. Full radio silence. Stand by. On my word.'

Paterson checked his watch — 11:45 p.m.

They waited.

A hushed voice broke the radio silence. 'All units, target vehicle approaching entrance. Stand by . . . Target confirmed.' They were now blind and relying on Caine to do his bit. Show time.

It bothered Lyndsey that they were working blind, stuck inside the van with no idea of what was going on outside. All they had to rely on was Caine's microphone and, hopefully, disguised commentary. Of all of them, she knew how badly this could go.

As if to prove her right, three men wearing trainers made their way carefully and quietly across to where the vans were parked. Each man was carrying a piece of 4x4 timber, which they gently wedged against the doors before backing away and disappearing into the shadows. Inside, Lyndsey cocked her head, turned her ear to the door and raised her shotgun slightly.

* * *

Tanner and his lawyer, Stickson, stepped out of the car and into the crisp night air. His breath visible, he looked around and saw nothing in the vicinity to bother him. Caine wouldn't try anything, not now he knew his sister could be got at. Assured of that, Tanner had come to the meeting with just his lawyer. Even if Caine had brought some of his boys, he wouldn't deploy them against Tanner. No. He was safe.

Inside, Tanner strolled through the warehouse like an eighteenth-century dandy, complete with frock coat, tails and top hat, tapping his walking stick on the floor to add to the effect. Caine watched him strut toward him in disgust.

"Allo, Bert.' Caine was once more behind the packing crate. 'Playing dress-up again?'

As Tanner and his brief came closer, Caine saw his eye tonight was onyx. He knew what it meant. 'What's with the eye? Is that meant for me?'

'Good evening, Bill.' Tanner stopped just short of the crate and made a show of removing his gloves, one finger at a time. He took a few seconds to survey the scene. On the packing crate was a gun, like a statement. Standing next to Caine was, presumably, his lawyer, holding a black attaché case which he swung up onto the crate before taking a step backward. Behind them, a wall with nowhere for anyone to hide. They were alone. 'The eye? I suppose you could say it is for you, yes. I feel that I have killed you in a perhaps more . . . satisfying way than plain old murder.' He stared at Caine. 'Would you not agree?'

Caine could feel his temper rising and took a breath. 'I take your point.' He grinned. 'Gun,' he said, pointing to the crate. Tanner reached inside the frock coat and pulled out a Magnum .365. As he put it down, he aimed it at Caine. Caine never flinched.

'Must be feeling pretty good about yourself, Bert,' Caine said.

Tanner gave a small, condescending smile.

'Not sure how smug I'd be feeling if the only way I could take over another man's firm was to wait until he was dying of Alzheimer's, kill his only son and then threaten to wipe out his sister and her family.' The grin disappeared from Tanner's face. 'But — fair play to you — you've got what you always wanted. I'll be out of your hair. To tell you the truth, you're welcome to it. I've had enough. This is a young man's game, and I can't be doin' with it all any more. Besides, the fuckin' Albanians will be knocking on your door soon enough, and you'll have them to deal with.'

Tanner's eye narrowed. 'Soon?'

Caine shrugged. 'Yep. Come on, we both know they're all over the country, and moving in. They'll come for you eventually, and you and I are a pair of sweet'earts compared to those mad bastards. All I can say is good luck. Glad I'm off out of it.'

'I don't anticipate they'll be too much trouble, William. I will now have half of London. That should be sufficient, I imagine.'

'If you say so.' Caine opened the attaché case. The sound of the catches echoed around the warehouse. Caine spun the case around to reveal four bundles of paper, all neatly tied with purple ribbons and bows. Underneath were another four bundles.

'That's everything, Bert. The lot. All we have to do is sign them, the briefs will countersign, and we're done.'

Tanner's one good eye almost lit up the night sky. Tanner's lawyer picked up one of the bundles and pulled on the ribbon. He spent a moment or two flicking through the papers, pausing every so often before giving a minute nod of the head and moving on. He went through the remaining seven bundles in the same fashion. He stepped back, saying he was satisfied that all appeared to be in order. All that was left was for the signatures to be appended.

'Here's how it's gonna work, Bert. I'll sign four bundles, you then transfer my million. When I see it in the bank, I'll sign the other four.'

Tanner squinted, thinking quickly. *No, Caine wouldn't risk his sister.* He was just trying to ensure that his money went in. Not unreasonable.

'Agreed,' said Tanner. Both men set about signing the papers under the watchful eyes of their respective legal advisers.

Tanner put down his pen. 'This is quite the historic moment, William. Quite historic.'

'Depends how you look at it, Bert. To me, it's just another Friday night. No biggie. You just get yer phone out and transfer me my million quid, the compensation for my Davey, and I'm off into the sunset. Booze and whores and then over a cliff before I forget me own name.'

'Indeed, William. I realise you're keen to get on. Having so little time left must be weighing heavily on you.'

'Nah, just gotta accept it. Besides, none of us know how much time we've got left, do we?' He winked.

'When you're ready, Mr Tanner,' said Caine's lawyer, Mr Trimble. 'We can begin.' Trimble was holding a heavily encrypted phone that was currently monitoring Billy Caine's nominated bank account. He handed a slip of paper to Tanner's lawyer and took a step back. Stickson, on his own encrypted phone, began punching in numbers

— Caine's account and the amount. One million pounds sterling.

'Sir,' he said, handing the phone to Tanner, 'you just need to push the button and the money will transfer to Mr Caine's account.' Caine looked on, anxious. He was keen to move on to the next bit. The good bit. Tanner held the phone up and peered at it. He pressed the button, a cruel grin on his thin lips.

After a few moments, Trimble declared, 'Transaction complete. One million pounds. I believe we're done, sir.'

In the van, a technician radioed through to Bannon. Transaction was indeed complete. Paterson, Clocks and Lyndsey stood half crouched, ready to burst out of the back doors and begin their assault.

Mr Trimble made to pick up his pen when Caine held up his hand. ''Ang on, Bert. Changed me mind.' Tanner froze. The lawyers froze. 'I've decided to give everything to the cat's 'ome instead.'

At first Tanner thought this was a poor attempt at a joke. He stared at Caine, who wasn't smiling. 'What? Have you lost your mind? We had a deal. You just signed.'

Caine moved out from behind the packing case. 'We did have a deal. Now we don't, and I ain't signed shit. Those papers ain't worth a carrot.' He looked at Stickson and gave him a grin. 'See him, Bert?' He nodded toward Stickson, whose legs had suddenly turned to jelly. 'He's done a deal with the Old Bill, mate. Proper grassed you up.' Tanner's head snapped around and he fixed Stickson with a death stare. Stickson froze, a rabbit caught in the headlights. 'Well, he ain't yet, but he's gonna, the shit they found in his office. Paterson told me. Listen, did you really think I'd turn my business over to a two-bob little twat like you? In what world do you imagine you're fit to wipe my arse? So, you can take yer fuckin' dodgy eye and your silly carnival costumes and get the fuck out of my sandbox and thank your lucky stars I've decided to let you live.'

217

Tanner's cruel smile curled into a snarl of rage and his face was puce. 'You bastard! You realise you've just signed your sister's death warrant, don't you?'

'Yeah, dream on Bert. Christ, you're such a thick bastard. The only fuckin' hold you had over me was my family and instead of keeping yer powder dry, you had to go and tell me about it a bit too early in the game, didn't you? Couldn't keep yer trap shut like a good villain should. Bad enough you killed my Davey, there was no way I was going to let you ever, ever go after the rest of my family. So, I had me a little brainwave.'

Listening to all of this, Paterson was desperately willing Caine to goad Tanner into holding his hands up to killing Davey Caine. Somehow, he knew this wasn't going to happen. He could feel it in his gut. Caine was pulling a stroke, and the whole thing was going south, fast. Decision time. Paterson listened on.

Tanner, too, waited to hear what Caine was going to say.

'I managed to figure it all out, Bert. Let me tell you what I know, shall I?' Tanner waved a hand. 'Well, I sure as shit know about April.' Tanner stiffened slightly. 'She's your daughter, Ruby, and she used my Davey to get inside and feed back to you. That's how you knew I was dying. Only way you could have done. That day she met up with you, she was being followed.' Tanner winced. 'Then I had a word with my sister, who gave me a copy of her CCTV. It records twenty-four seven. Living in the sticks like that, makes sense for them to have one. Looks like your boy, whassis his name . . .?' he clicked his fingers. 'Oh, what's his bloody name? Jeremy! Yeah that's it, Jeremy. Looks like he went along with young Ruby for the ride.' Tanner was looking increasingly uncomfortable. 'Anyways, knowing that you'd had my boy killed and would most likely have the rest of my family done in at some point, despite your promises, I thought it best to make a few provisions of my own, to protect them and also even the score for my Davey.'

Tanner's face went dark. 'What did you do, Bill?' he almost whispered.

'Something I'm not particularly proud of — well, a few things actually. The first is, I drugged up your Ruby and got hold of her phone. I got it open, and there were all of your dodgy goings-on. You've been a busy boy, Bert. Impressive. Of course, I didn't know what to do with it and so, and here's the second bit, I gave it to the law — Paterson and his mate, Cocks. I think that's what he's called — should be anyway.'

Tanner's mouth dropped open. 'What? You grassed? What the fu—?'

'I know, I know. I said I'm not proud of myself but fuck me, Bert, this was different. You stepped over the line, mate. Couldn't let that go, could I? Anyway, I made a deal with Paterson that he would let you transfer a million over to me and then they'd freeze all your accounts. They'll have done that by now. Your lawyer will confirm it, so you don't have to take my word on it. And the businesses? They were never gonna be yours. When Ruby told you I'd gone to Switzerland, I had, just to put you and the coppers off the scent. Once I got there, it was a coupla hours on a light plane over to Albania. I've already signed it all over to them.'

Tanner was dumbstruck. Ten minutes ago, he was poised to own the biggest criminal empire in London, and now he was sucking shit through a straw. He had to think, and fast.

'Why so surprised, Bert? You knew I have businesses over there. Surely it must have crossed your mind that I might actually have gotten to know them, done a bit of business with them? Bloke I dealt with is a Mr Gashi. Fuck me, Bert, he's a piece of work alright.'

Tanner shook his head, confused. 'I'll still have your sister killed. You'll fucking pay!' It was the best he could think of.

'I'm not that bothered, mate. Y'see, part of the deal with the Albanians was that they'd look after them. Keep an eye on them when I'm gone. I think they will. Honour is a big thing to them. And there'll always be people keeping their ear to the ground. I told Gashi that if anything 'appened to me sister, I'd already put someone on a two 'undred and fifty grand retainer to deal with him for failing to keep up his end of the deal. He'll keep his eye on her.'

Tanner's roar startled Caine for a second. Tanner went for his gun but ran straight into a right-hander that knocked him back, sending him to the floor. Caine flexed his fingers. *That hurt.* After a few seconds, with the aid of his stick, Tanner struggled to his feet. He pulled on the stick and began to unsheathe the sword inside.

But Caine was faster. He snatched up his gun and pointed it straight at his enemy's head. 'Uh, uh, Bert. Behave yerself now. Chuck that away like a good boy.' Reluctantly, Tanner did as he was told. Caine ordered the lawyers to leave. Neither man had any further use for them.

'So, what now?' said Tanner, rubbing at his busted lip. 'Is this where the police raid the place and take me away?'

'Nope. Don't worry about them. They're not coming. Not yet anyway.'

Inside the van, the three police officers looked at one another, puzzled. Lyndsey had one hand on the door handle and the other on the transmit button of her radio.

Tanner spat out a wad of blood. 'So what the fuck was this farce all about? Why'd you really want a million quid off of me?'

Caine's face lit up. Now they were getting somewhere. 'Glad you asked, Bert. This is the third thing I'm not particularly proud of.' He took out his mobile phone and

220

opened up Facetime. 'I'll show you in a minute. Oh, just so you know, your top guys have just been wiped out. I sent in someone to take care of it for me.' Tanner said nothing. 'By the way, Bert, just so I know, was it you or Ruby that had Davey killed?'

Tanner's last little victory. His grin turned into a derisory chuckle. 'My orders, Bill. But my little girl killed him. *She* torched him for me.'

Caine paled slightly. He knew she was her father's daughter, but he'd never had her down as a killer.

'The old story, Bill. She got him into bed, shagged him senseless, plied him with drink and drugs and waited till he was out of it. She'd never killed anyone like that before. Wanted to know what it was like. Turned out she thoroughly enjoyed herself, said she couldn't believe how much he screamed. Wasn't too keen on the smell though.'

Caine's eyes filled, and he swayed a little.

Now was the time to drop the hammer, and drop it hard.

CHAPTER THIRTY

Paterson had what he wanted. He gave the order — 'Go!' Lyndsey yanked down on the door handle and got it open an inch or so. Paterson and Clocks piled in behind her and they all came to an abrupt halt. The door wouldn't budge. She tried again.

Paterson freaked. 'What's the fucking matter? Get out! Go, go, go!' Lyndsey tried again. They were going nowhere. A voice crackled in her ear. 'Trojan One! Cannot decamp. Doors are secured, repeat, doors are secured!'

Cool as always, Lyndsey raised the shotgun and shouted, 'Turn away!' She fired a breaching round at the doors. Her team, hearing the shot, did the same.

The lock disintegrated under the impact of the round and the doors flew open. All three leapt out, hit the pavement and came under a hail of gunfire that sent them to the floor. They scrambled for cover.

'What the fuck!' screamed Clocks. He pulled out his gun. 'Stay down! Everybody down!'

For a second, Lyndsey's brain scrabbled to make sense of the situation. She ducked low and pointed herself in the direction of the gunfire, scanning the scene. There was nowhere for the shooter to hide — except maybe a low wall. That was the only place he or she could be. Crouched down, she fired a shot toward the wall.

Paterson and Clocks scrambled to the front of the van and fired wildly in that same direction, giving Lyndsey time to find cover. She made for the van, rolled underneath it and crawled back the way she came. 'Get to cover!' she shouted. They backed against the van and gave each other a "what-the-hell?" look.

Lyndsey could hear the distant sound of gunfire and knew her team had been ambushed and were fighting back. 'Fire again, John!' she called. Clocks spun around and fired off several shots before ducking back under cover.

In response came a sudden burst of bright light from an AK-47. Exactly what she wanted, a position. She put the shotgun down beside her and drew out her pistol. From under the van, she fired off a burst toward the shooter and waited. A beat. He fired again. She returned the fire.

In the midst of the hail of bullets, Paterson emerged and sprinted toward the shooter.

'Ray!' Clocks screamed.

Lyndsey saw his feet go past her, let out a whispered, 'Oh, Jesus Christ,' and kept pulling the trigger. Clocks joined in. Both Lyndsey and Clocks's guns clicked empty at the same time. They scrabbled for more ammo. She knew the shooter would pop his head up now. *Christ! Ray!* He was about five feet from the wall, gun in his two outstretched hands and pointing forwards. As Lyndsey had predicted, the shooter raised his head and brought the AK up and over the wall, ready to fire again. Paterson kept running. The gunman swung the gun toward him, and — *click*. Empty. Paterson fired on the run, until his foot hit the wall and he was up and over. He dropped down, crouching and turning toward the shooter as he hit the ground.

The shooter was doubled over, frantically trying to reload. Paterson sprang forward and drove his knee full into the man's face, knocking him backwards. The shooter's head bounced once and he lay, spark out. Paterson kicked the AK-47 away, stood over the unconscious man and pointed his gun at him.

Johnny Clocks froze. He closed his eyes.

'Ray! No!' Lyndsey screamed at him. 'Don't!'

Paterson pulled the trigger.

'Oh, Jesus!' Lyndsey cried, her arms at her side.

Paterson looked over towards them and shrugged. 'What? Shot him in the leg. Bastard won't be coming after us now, will he?'

Clocks opened his eyes. Lyndsey wriggled out from underneath the van and ran to where Paterson stood. 'Fuck me, Ray. What's wrong with you? He was out of ammo. No threat. Why didn't you just cuff him up?'

He gave her a grin. 'Everyone's a threat, Lyndsey.' He jammed another clip into his gun. 'Until they're not.'

She shook her head at him. 'You're losing it, Ray.'

Paterson ignored this, and they turned toward the building. Lyndsey radioed her team. They had one dead shooter and one in custody.

Outside the warehouse, Lyndsey told Clocks and Paterson to wait.

Paterson nodded. 'You deploy your team however you want. Me and Clocks will stick together.'

Lyndsey wasn't happy, but the look on Paterson's face told her not to pursue it. Paterson had his own agenda.

He tried the door, opened it a couple of inches and peered through the gap. It was fastened with a bicycle lock. 'What the hell is Caine doing?' he said.

* * *

The live video feed on the phone screen displayed the face of a man Caine had come to know well. He smiled and handed the phone to Tanner.

'Someone wants a word with you.' Tanner's eyes narrowed as he took it. 'This is Mr Tahir Gashi. He's going to show you something you really won't want to see.'

Tanner squinted at the screen. The signal was a bit scrappy, and Gashi was calling from a dark room. Muffled voices could be heard in the background and Tanner thought he could see something move behind the man's head.

'Mr Tanner. Is pleasure to meet you. Mr Caine, he tells me you are to be my new enemy. He says that you will not be happy that I am now boss. Is pity you feel like this. I think you and me, we could be friends.'

Tanner leered at him. 'I don't know you and I have no wish to. Just don't make the mistake of crossing me.'

Gashi's face lit up with a big beamer of a smile. He laughed. 'Mr Tanner. Please. It do you no good to be, how you say, tough man. You have nothing left now. Mr Caine, he take it all from you, no?'

Tanner glared at Caine.

'Mr Caine also tell me you like burn things, yes?' said Gashi. Tanner said nothing. 'You like burn people, no? I too enjoy this. Is good fun, yes?' Gashi turned around and zoomed in on three figures, bound to chairs and wearing hoods. 'You see these peoples? Have a look at them.' Gashi pulled the hood off of the first one. Tanner froze. His jaw dropped progressively lower as Gashi lifted the hoods, one by one. Tanner felt his legs go as he looked at his father, wife and son. 'No!' He screamed at the phone. 'Don't! Let them go. Please. I'll do anything!'

All three had gags across their mouths. All of them looked as though they'd been beaten. Their eyes were wide and terrified. Caine glanced at Tanner and smirked.

* * *

Lyndsey, whose team had now joined her, shot the door out. Paterson barked out orders. 'Lyndsey, deploy

225

your team wide. We're going straight up the middle — twelve o'clock.'

They went in, guns swinging from side to side, peering into the gloom. SCO19 fanned out along the sides of the building. At the far end of the warehouse, Paterson could see a door with a sliver of light beneath it. He nudged Clocks and pointed. They moved forward.

'See, Mr Tanner. We have saying — live by sword, die by sword. But you live by petrol, so your family die by petrol.' On the screen, two men appeared on either side of Tanner's captive relatives, each carrying a metal can of petrol which they proceeded to pour over them.

'Jesus, no! Don't! Don't!' Tanner fell to his knees, his eyes fastened on the screen. 'Please,' he choked, overcome by sobs.

He turned to Caine, put his hands together and begged. 'Bill . . . please.'

'Oh, really? You want my help? You want me to stop this?' Caine's face wore a mixture of anger and disdain, but there was no pity on it. 'You can jog on, arsehole. Not a snowball's. You brought this on yerself when you had Davey burned.' Caine smiled faintly. 'Expect you're wondering how we got all of them together, eh? Wasn't hard. I've had people watching you, same as you've got 'em watching me. Old people, well, they like their routines. Your old dad, for example. Every other week he liked to see the grandkids for a couple of G and Ts and a plate of fish 'n' chips in the King George pub, and then stay over at Ruby's. No trouble for Gashi's boys to take the lot of 'em.'

Tanner heard the two men click their pocket lighters, followed by his family's muffled screams. 'Gashi! Wait!' called Caine.

Tanner's head snapped around. 'Mercy! Please, Bill. Have some mercy. I'll give you everything. All of it.'

Caine looked at him and spat on the ground. 'What good is any of that to me? I'm a dead man. Give it to him.'

Tanner turned back to the screen. 'Please, Mr Gashi. I'll give it all to you. Please.'

Mr Gashi threw him another big smile. 'This is generous offer, Mr Tanner. I would consider it but,' he paused, 'I will be taking it all anyway.' Tanner dropped his head.

'This is payback, Bert,' said Caine. 'And here's the kicker. Bert, look at me.' Tanner slowly lifted his head. 'Y'know that million I kept banging on about, for compensation?' Caine had been waiting for this moment. 'When you transferred that money over, it never went to me sister. When I found out about your Ruby, I had me a little brainwave. It suddenly occurred to me that I could put it to better use.' He smiled. 'Don't you be worrying about me sister though, Bert. I've seen her right. She'll be okay for a few quid and her old man's a clever sod, he'll turn it into a few more. Turns out you actually sent it to Gashi.' He paused, watching Tanner's face.

'I promised him a little extra if he'd take care of a few things for me. Obviously he don't need it, but we thought it'd be fun if you payed to have your own family burned alive. How does that feel, *prick*!' Tanner retched violently while Caine gave the go-ahead for the execution of the only people in the world he cared about.

A small tear escaped the eye of this man who had never before cried or felt pity. Tanner shook his head from side to side, desperately trying to block out the muffled, agonised screams of his family as the fire took hold. Caine looked away from the screen. If it hadn't been Tanner, he would have felt some pity. 'You shouldn't have fucked with me, Bert. You should have known you could only lose.'

Paterson and Clocks reached the outside door and stood either side of it. Clocks tried the handle. Locked. It would have to be a forced entry. He touched his earpiece. 'DI Clocks to Trojan One. We've housed the suspects.

Forced entry imminent. Keep your team on standby and wait for my call.'

Lyndsey's voice shouted into his earpiece. 'DI Clocks, DI Clocks! Hold your position. Do not, I repeat, do *not* force entry. Stand by until we arrive.'

Clocks looked over at Paterson. *Not a chance.*

'Mr Tanner.' Gashi's voice could just about be heard over the screams and the crackling of the fire. 'Come. I have something else for you.'

Gashi walked him into another filthy room, lit by a single bare overhead bulb.

'Look!' said Gashi, gleefully. 'Is Ruby. Is your baby girl.'

Tanner looked. He felt like a man who'd just had the life kicked out of him, got pulled up by the scruff of his neck and had the shit kicked out of him all over again. 'No . . .' She was tied to a chair, blindfolded, stripped naked and badly beaten. A big bearded brute of a man stood guard over her. Tears streamed down Tanner's face as he looked at his daughter.

'Is good news, Mr Tanner. She alive. Hurrah! We keep her alive. She is, how you British say, a fittie. Good tits. We will make much from her. Your wife, no good. Baktash would not fuck her and he is not, how you say, the fussy. He did fuck Ruby though. Say she good. So good we all fuck her. Together. She not bad at all.'

Tanner willed himself to stand. His sole focus now was on Caine. He neither saw nor heard anything, other than the face of the man who had destroyed him. Caine knew what was coming. He dropped the phone and raised his gun.

* * *

Two loud bangs announced Paterson and Clocks's entrance. The first was Clocks shooting off the lock, the second was Paterson kicking the door open. They burst into the room and fanned out, one high, one low. Textbook entry.

There wasn't much to see. Caine pointing a gun at Tanner. A packing crate in the middle of the room with a gun on it. A couple of filing cabinets standing either side of the door they'd come through.

'Drop your weapon!' Paterson screamed at Caine. Nothing changed. 'Caine, put it down. Put it down.' Still nothing changed.

''Ello, Mr Paterson. Good to see you.'

'Put the fucking gun down, Billy, or I swear I'll drop you where you stand.'

Billy Caine smiled, pulled open his shirt and ripped out the wire. He stamped on the microphone. 'Fed up with people listenin' to me all the time.'

Clocks pushed the door closed behind him and pulled one of the filing cabinets across it. The loud clatter made Paterson jump, but he didn't look back. Clocks pulled the other one over too, and lifted it on top of the first one. They wouldn't keep SCO19 out for long, but hopefully long enough. Clocks walked to the other side of the room and stood at an angle behind Tanner.

'You bastard. You screwed me over,' Paterson spat.

Caine kept his eye and his gun on Tanner 'What can I tell ya? I'm a shonky bastard. But, in fairness, I gave you everything I said I would. You've got Albert here, bang to rights. He put his hands up to killing Davey. You've got his entire life history on that key, so you've got everything you need to cage him up for the rest of his natural. That's what I said I'd do, and that's what I did.'

'Yeah, you did. But you forgot to mention that you were going to wipe out his entire fucking family at the same time, didn't you?'

Caine grinned. 'Well, yeah. I glossed over that bit, but only because I knew you wouldn't approve.'

Paterson stared. 'Wouldn't approve? Wouldn't . . . are you off of your fucking head? You just had his whole family murdered and sold his daughter into prostitution! Jesus Christ!'

'Well, it's not like they're any loss, is it? I did what I had to do. Now, you gonna sort out this piece of shit, or what?'

Clocks raised his gun and pointed it at the back of Tanner's head.

Caine shifted his focus. 'Mr Clocks?' he said. 'I'm guessing that you've put those cabinets there because you intend to kill Albert and you don't want anyone coming in to try and stop you. Maybe you're gonna do me too, I dunno. That's a plan of sorts, I suppose. I can understand that you're royally pissed at Albert here and I can see why you'd want to kill him. Wouldn't blame you either, but think about it. Shootin' him's far too easy. I've done him now. He's got nothing. Let the bastard suffer, live with what's happened, with what he's seen, torture 'imself day an' night right up to the point he tops himself in prison. Your way, he gets off light.' Clocks gave it a few seconds and found he had to agree with Caine. He lowered the gun. A voice crackled in his ear.

Clocks touched his earpiece. 'Trojan. Stand by. Do not enter. Repeat. Do not enter. Entrance is blocked. Fluid situation. Stand by.'

'Y'know, Bill,' said Paterson, 'I'd figured out a way for you to get on your toes, but not now. I can't let you go after what you've done.'

Caine lowered his gun, but raised it again when Tanner made a move toward him. 'Oh no, you don't! Back off, Bert, there's a good boy.' Tanner stopped. 'Truth is, Mr Paterson, I ain't going nowhere. Never was.'

Paterson and Clocks twigged it. He wasn't coming out alive. This made Clocks a happy man. One less piece of shit to worry about flushing away.

'Bill . . .' said Paterson.

Caine held his hand up. 'Let me finish. I've put me house in order, sister's taken care of. Couple of friends will team up with the Albies and they'll take over the whole of London. Me and Bert here, we've had our day. It's a new world, Mr Paterson, so listen to me when I tell you to watch yer back out there. This is a different war you got comin' now. As for me — you honestly think I'm gonna end my days in a home, lookin' at meself in a mirror and wondering who the bloody 'ell's lookin' back? I'm not cut out for dribblin' in me cornflakes. Not happenin', son. So, I got to thinkin'. As I said, you two are a pair of coffin magnets. Lucky for me.'

'Bill,' said Paterson, 'Don't do anyth—'

Caine swung the gun round toward Clocks. Paterson squeezed the trigger twice, hitting him in the chest and killing him instantly. Tanner smiled. There was a loud bang on the door. The filing cabinets scraped on the floor as SCO19 tried to push their way in. 'Stand down!' Clocks shouted. 'Stand *down*! One target down. One still armed. Do not enter!'

Paterson lowered his gun. He watched the blood seeping out from under Caine's body. 'Jesus, God almighty. This is getting to be a habit.'

'Oh, for fuck's sake, Ray. Why'd he point the bastard gun at me? Why's everyone trying to kill me? Jesus!'

Slowly, Tanner turned his head toward Clocks. 'Armed, Inspector? How am I armed?' His voice was flat, deliberate.

Clocks walked across to Tanner, his face tense, every little muscle twitching. 'See you, you sick bastard. We've got unfinished business.'

Tanner sneered. 'Then finish it.'

'You wanted me dead.' Clocks moved in close, nose to nose with the object of his anger. They looked like two hooligans squaring off to each other.

Paterson realised Tanner had nothing to lose. 'John, leave it.' No response. 'Don't, John. You don't wanna be where I am.'

Again, Clocks ignored him. 'What the fuck did I ever do to you that would make you have me burned alive? What kind of crazy fuck does that? What kind of sick, demented bastard are you?'

Tanner pushed his head further forward. 'You were rude, Mr Clocks. I can't abide bad manners. And you hit my father. That was your big mistake.'

Clocks stepped back. He stopped and turned. 'And you know what your big mistake was?' Clocks turned and kicked Albert Tanner in the balls.

'Fucking up my suit!'

CHAPTER THIRTY-ONE

Wallace Young excused himself from the people he was talking to and wove his way through the assembled guests. 'Ray! John! Good to see you both. Thank you so much for coming.' He greeted them with a warm smile and a handshake. Young had decided to forego the full dress uniform he was entitled to wear for this occasion. His civilian suit projected the image that he had cultivated throughout his long and brilliant career — that of a bit of an outsider. He had won the genuine respect of the man on the ground, having gone through the ranks and got out from behind his desk as often as he could. Many a time, even quite recently, he had shown up in civvies for night duty, and had gone on a ride-about with the crews of area cars and vans. The Met would be all the poorer for his departure.

Suddenly overcome with emotion, Paterson was reluctant to let the hand go. 'Sir. This is it then — retirement. Who'd have thought it?'

'Certainly not me, that's for sure.' Young swagged a glass of champagne from a passing waiter and took a sip.

He cast his eye around the packed room and shook his head. 'Goes so fast. I can't quite believe it.'

'You've had a good crack at it though, Wol, mate,' said Clocks. 'I thought they'd cart you out of here in a box.'

Young smiled at him. 'Ah, scarecrow,' he said fondly. 'I think I'll miss you most of all.'

Clocks frowned. Where had he heard that before?

'And don't call me Wol, son. My name is Wallace. But you can call me boss.'

'Sorry, boss.' Clocks grinned and shook his head. 'Look, I know it's hard for you but you'll get over me. In time.'

'He's telling the truth, sir,' said Paterson. 'I'm over him already and I still have to work with him.'

'For your sins,' said Young, and raised his glass. Paterson followed suit.

'For *our* sins,' said Clocks, raising his own glass higher.

'Boys, excuse me a moment,' said Young. Over Paterson's shoulder he'd spotted a worried-looking Commander Susan Mayes. She was holding a small piece of paper and her expression told Young that some manner of shit had hit the fan.

Paterson and Clocks turned to look at the crowd. Clocks had his eye on a tray full of egg pork pie and one of the nearby waitresses. These days a quick side-eye glance had to suffice. Lyndsey's wrath was too much for him. After a minute or so, Young headed back towards them with a face like thunder. Commander Mayes followed close on his heels.

'Oh, shit!' said Clocks. 'He's not a happy bunny, is he? I bet some twat forgot to bring his gold watch.'

'Either that or the jellied eels.'

'With me, gents. Now!' Young walked straight past them, heading toward the exit. They turned and followed him out along the corridor and into his office. By the time they got there, Young was standing at the window, looking out across the streets of London. In two days' time, he would no longer be responsible for keeping them safe. But until then . . .

'What's the matter, sir?' said Paterson.

'Shut the door, John,' Young said, without turning. He rubbed his face. 'Sit down, both of you. You're not going to like this. Not one bit.'

Both men sat down.

Paterson perched himself on the edge of his seat. 'Sir?'

Wallace Young turned to them. 'Commander Mayes has just informed me that earlier today, a transport van taking a remand prisoner to hospital was attacked. The patient inside has escaped.' Paterson felt a knot tighten in his stomach. 'The escape, it would seem, was meticulously planned. The van was happily bumbling along the road when it was ambushed by two vehicles that brought it to a halt. Three armed men jumped out and waved shotguns at the crew. No urgent assistance call was made, which was strange. The crew were apparently forced to follow one of the cars to a field not far from where the ambush took place. There, they blew the bloody doors open and grabbed the prisoner. Both guards sustained some minor injuries, and both are now in custody pending questioning regarding their possible involvement.'

Clocks frowned. 'Never mind all the bollocks, Wol. Who's had it away, then? As if I didn't know.'

Young handed over the piece of paper. He sighed. 'My name is Wallace. Don't call me Wol. I've told you that. And yes, it's Albert Tanner.'

There was silence for a second or two, then Clocks stood up and marched over toward Young. 'There you go. Dot on the card. Fuck. Me. Blind. That mad cowson was supposed to be in a high-security nuthouse pending trial. Round-the-clock watch. How'd he pull this off?'

'As I said, John, he was on his way to hospital. He'd showed signs of a heart attack. The hospital holding him felt he needed more care than they could give him.'

'Care? Shoulda let the snot-gobblin' fucker die in agony. I woulda done.' Clocks turned to face Paterson. 'There you go. I knew we'd ballsed up by nicking him. Shoulda dealt with him the old-fashioned way.' Paterson glowered at Clocks and swiped a finger across his throat. *Shut up!* Susan Mayes, Police Commander and unknown quantity, was looking distinctly uncomfortable.

'How *would* you have dealt with him then, John?' said Young.

Clocks turned and shrugged. 'Tell you the truth, sir, I was planning on shooting him in the face at close range, but Ray here talked me out of it.' Paterson put his head against the back of his chair and turned his eyes to the ceiling. Commander Hayes frowned.

Young said nothing for a moment. He sat down behind his desk. 'In hindsight, it might not have been a bad idea, but here we are. Hindsight's a wonderful thing.'

'What time was the van jacked?' said Clocks.

Paterson checked the piece of paper. 'Says four o'clock this afternoon. Christ! It's now,' he checked his watch, 'ten twenty-seven, so he's been in the wind for about six hours. Why are we only finding out now?'

Young shrugged.

'What else do we know? Do we have any idea where he's gone to?' Paterson looked across at Commander Hayes.

'Not a hundred percent,' she said, 'but the intel we have so far is that the ambush took place less than five miles from Biggin Hill airport. We've been informed that a light aircraft was scheduled to take off about thirty-odd minutes after the van was jacked. It took off, but we can't be certain if Tanner was on board, and if he was, where they've gone to.'

Clocks was looking down at his shoes, thinking. He looked up. 'Can't be certain? Christ, it's not like Tanner's inconspicuous, is he? Surely someone would have noticed him getting on board.'

'They most likely did, but it wouldn't have mattered. It's not illegal to get on a plane and the airport staff wouldn't have any reason to suspect anything. They wouldn't have known Tanner's on his toes.'

'Okay, I can see that, but they must have a record of where it was going to, surely?'

Paterson smiled. *Here we go.* 'You know I've got a pilot's licence, right?'

Clocks sighed. He did.

'This is where it all gets interesting. If he's going out of the country there's two places he's likely to make the jump to — Ireland or France. Ireland's a bit tricky because of the restricted zones over the Irish Sea, so my money's on France. Now, the key to getting out of the country and not getting caught is by making sure everything looks normal beforehand. So, the pilot would file a VFR—'

'A what?' Young and Hayes both said.

'VFR. A visual flight rules. Flight plan. It says something like, "I am call sign Golf Dash Bravo, Echo-five or whatever, flying from wherever to La Touche in France and I will be crossing the FIR boundary at a particular position."'

Clocks looked at him, awaiting an explanation of this other acronym.

Paterson caught on. 'FIR, John? It means "flight information region." Basically, it's a division of airspace that has flight information service and alerts set up. Been in use since the forties.'

Clocks gave him a blank look. 'Don't know what you're talking about, Ray. Don't care much either. Go on.'

'So, who's this flight plan filed with?' Young asked.

'The ATC, sir. Air traffic control.'

'And what is the purpose of this . . . VFR?'

'It tells the ATC what I intend to do, where I intend to go. But — and this is the odd bit — I don't have to go there. I can veer off somewhere else and I won't be tracked.'

'Seriously?' said Young. 'Wouldn't the plane have some kind of tracker fitted? What's it called again?' He clicked his fingers.

'A transponder.'

'That's it. Doesn't that mean it can be tracked easily?'

'Pilot can switch it off.'

'What'd you mean "switch it off?" That can't be right,' said Clocks.

'It is what it is, John. Look, it works like this. If I was him, this is what I'd do. I'd file my VFR plan. Jump in a light aircraft — say, a Cessna 172 — tell control that I'm flying out from Biggin Hill and off to France for a spot of sightseeing and I'll be landing at La Touche airport, flying at a height of about two to three thousand feet. Going to that airport, I can plan my route to avoid the restricted danger zones, keep out of major airspace, and since I'm not a danger to commercial air traffic, I won't be drawing attention to myself. The ATC will acknowledge me, I'll take off, stick to the plan until I'm over the Channel and then I'll turn off the transponder. After that, I can pretty much detour off anywhere I want. Bring it down in some farmer's field if I want. Providing I take off and land where I was originally going to, there's no issue. That's probably what he's done.'

'Hold on. Won't the air traffic people wonder what you're up to? Won't they be concerned that the transponder has been turned off?' Clocks said.

'Nope. They don't care. As long as I'm not in commercial airspace and not a danger, then I'm not a problem.'

'What about the Frenchies then?' said Clocks.

'Mate, they wouldn't even know I was coming in the first place.'

'Can't we arrest the pilot, Ray? When he comes back?' said Young.

'For what, sir? For all intents and purposes, he's done nothing wrong. He might have been weighed off by

Tanner for flying him out and that's another story, but I'll bet this is a pilot who's on the wrong side of the fence anyway. All he'll have done is what he's supposed to do — file his plan, take off and land wherever. Nothing wrong in that and nothing to say that it was Tanner got in the plane with him. He's gone, sir, plain and simple.'

Clocks's face was a picture of bewilderment. 'So that's it, then? Christ, if it's that easy there must be shitloads of drugs and guns and people and all sorts of stuff going in and out on a daily basis.'

'Yep. There is. Customs are aware of it, but they just don't have the manpower to deal with it. The only reason they'd get involved is if the plane kept landing and taking off at a particular airfield on an almost daily basis and someone from Joe Public reported it. Other than that . . .'

'Jesus! I never knew that. So, who gives a shit if we both get the sack? We can fly drugs in and out all day, every day. Wish you'd told me earlier, Ray.'

Paterson gave him a wry grin. 'Where would you go, John? Say you've skipped out of the country and are on the trot. You're not gonna stay in France or Ireland — too conspicuous, too close. If it was you and you're a double ugly bastard with money, and you're going to stick out like a sore thumb, where would you go, where would you fit in?'

Clocks thought about it for less than a second. 'America.'

'Why?'

'Far easier to lose yerself there. We know from the papers that Caine gave us that Tanner had connections there, businesses, so it makes sense to me. He can get some cosmetic surgery done if he wants. Right money, right doctor. That's it. My money's on the States.'

'Hold on,' said Young. 'The intel we have on him also said he was doing business in Australia, and from what our boys tell us, he was in the middle of it when everything came down around him. Supposing he's gone there? America's always the obvious choice, isn't it?'

Paterson nodded. 'Yeah. It is. Okay, we'll alert the Aussies too. I'll drop a call to the Australian Federal Police and the Border Force, see if they can keep a look out for him.'

'I have a good contact in the FBI,' said Young. 'An old friend. He owes me.' He glanced at his watch. 'Let me put in a call to him. They can put out APB's or whatever it is they call them, just in case he turns up there.' He checked his watch again, calculating the time difference, nodded to himself and reached for his phone.

Paterson and Clocks began talking, their voices low. Young frowned at them. He explained to the person who answered that he wanted to be put through to the Director of Operations at the FBI. He said that yes, he would hold.

Then he turned to Paterson and Clocks. 'What are you two whispering about? What are you up to?'

'Nothing, sir,' said Paterson. 'Just killing time until you finish your call.'

'Don't bullshit me, Ray. You're up to something . . . Oh, hello, yes, it's Commissioner Young of the Metropolitan Police in London . . . Yes, the UK. I'm looking for some . . .'

'He won't go for it,' said Clocks. He watched Young, now deep in conversation with the FBI Director.

'Maybe, maybe not. We can only ask.'

Clocks shrugged. 'I don't know how Lyndsey will feel about it.'

'She won't mind. It's all in a good cause. Change is as good as a rest and all that.'

'You say that . . .'

While they talked, they overheard their names as Young continued to outline the situation to the FBI man. After a few minutes, Young hung up. 'Susan,' he said, 'Thank you for coming. Stay in contact and update me hourly.' He walked her to the door and showed her out.

Then he turned back to Paterson and Clocks. 'Okay, they're on it. But there's a million ways Tanner could get into the country and not one of them will be legal. Now, I'll ask you again, what are you two up to?'

Clocks smiled. 'We want to go over the pond and hunt the fucker down ourselves.'

Commissioner Young sat back in his chair and sighed. 'I thought you would. I was just telling the director that I'm looking to send you both over, tasked to run down Tanner. He sees no problem and is making the arrangements now. The Yanks will put their ears to the ground and see what comes back. They'll have their protocols, of course. We'll get a list of dos and don'ts by email tomorrow I would think, and those protocols will have to be followed. To the letter, and, yes, that means you, John. None of your TV coppers — what's his name, Gene Hunt — nonsense out there, y'hear me? They won't put up with it.'

Clocks's face told him all he needed to know. Gene Hunt it was.

'No point going out for a few days though,' said Young, getting to his feet and smoothing out his jacket.

'Why's that?' said Clocks. 'The sooner we get going, the better.'

'Couple of reasons. We still have to check in with the Australians. No point running out to America and then having to go over to Oz, is there?'

'S'pose not.' Clocks shrugged.

'Plus — and here's the best bit, gents — I don't officially retire for another two days but once I've finished up here, I figured I'd come out there with you.' Both men stared at him.

'What's that now?' said Clocks. 'Coming with us, did you say?'

Young smiled. 'Yes, I did. Problem with that?' Both men shook their heads.

'What? Did you think I was just going to sit at home watching telly all day or fanny around in the garden wearing beige Crocs and one of those beige fishing vests, the one with a million pockets? Did you?'

Clocks said, 'Well . . . Don't you have any job offers, sir? Directorships? Security consultant or something?'

'Plenty. But that's bloody well boring. Besides, you two cowboys need someone to keep you out of the shit and on the straight and narrow — make sure you do something right for a change.' He walked to the door. 'Come on then. We've got stuff to do.'

Paterson and Clocks followed Young into the corridor. He switched off the light.

THE END

Thank you for reading this book. If you enjoyed it please leave feedback on Amazon, and if there is anything we missed or you have a question about then please get in touch. The author and publishing team appreciate your feedback and time reading this book.

Our email is office@joffebooks.com

www.joffebooks.com

36047235R00149